He ...nd kissed ... ...ed away, p  He had never been complimented on the way he kissed before.

"You don't know how long I've wanted to do that. Kiss you and not have you run in fear." He kissed the palm of her hand. "You're amazing, Tess Grayson."

A slow smile spread across her face. He had seen the look before, and it melted him every time he saw it.

She pushed her hair behind her ear with her free hand, and with her full lips formed into a pout, she softly asked, "Are you trying to woo me, Jack Maristone?"

"Have been for a long time," he whispered back. His nose practically touching hers, he felt her breath on his lips before he tasted them again. He couldn't stop; he didn't want to. He ran his hand along her smooth cheek, and then into that soft, curly hair.

Pulling her face to his, he moved his lips along her jaw line toward her ear and then down her neck. He pressed his hand onto her bare back to move her closer and began sliding it lower. A part of him warned that he should stop before there was no turning back. At this rate, they wouldn't make it to the New Year's Party, but would instead have their own private party here.

Praise for *GOODBYE GRANNY PANTIES*

"Readers who enjoy a witty heroine and want a glimpse of dating disasters will enjoy this book."
~Renee Ashley Williams, erotic romance author
~*~
"Andrea's unique turn of phrase is sure to produce a smile, or in some cases even a burst of laughter."
~Anne Ashby, author of The CEO Gets Her Man

Goodbye Granny Panties

by

Andrea O'Day

This is a work of fiction. Names, characters, places, and incidents are either the product of the author's imagination or are used fictitiously, and any resemblance to actual persons living or dead, business establishments, events, or locales, is entirely coincidental.

Goodbye Granny Panties

COPYRIGHT © 2014 by Andrea P. O'Day

All rights reserved. No part of this book may be used or reproduced in any manner whatsoever without written permission of the author or The Wild Rose Press, Inc. except in the case of brief quotations embodied in critical articles or reviews.
Contact Information: info@thewildrosepress.com

Cover Art by *Kim Mendoza*

The Wild Rose Press, Inc.
PO Box 708
Adams Basin, NY 14410-0708
Visit us at www.thewildrosepress.com

Publishing History
First *Last Rose of Summer* Edition, 2014
Print ISBN 978-1-62830-435-0
Digital ISBN 978-1-62830-436-7

Dedication

To my late friend Barb Leeman,
who told me to never give up on dreams.

Chapter One

Pushing the frizzy strands of hair off her face, she had only one thought: find and do bodily harm to the person or persons who had scheduled their annual sales conference in Florida in July.

July! That's when families came here and *tolerated* the heat and humidity, but only because they were on vacation. They could escape to the pool where the water was tepid, or to their overly air-conditioned hotel rooms.

But not her. Tess had to sit in the heat and humidity at a table in the far corner of the courtyard, listening to a twenty-year-old up-and-coming brown-noser discuss the attributes of working as a team. Didn't he realize that most of the people in this group he was talking at wrote the book on operating as a team? Obviously not, since he continued to lecture them.

All she wanted to do was go inside where the air conditioning was running at full blast. It would be so cold, she'd get goose bumps, but she didn't care. She just wanted to be out of this heat and not sweating like a goat anymore.

Tess leaned over to Allie and whispered, "I figured it out. Only the Devil could've planned this trip. He wanted us to be hot and miserable, and acclimatized to his environment."

Allie looked up from the tabloid magazine lying

open on her lap, and said, "Sorry, but you're wrong on that one. Look at the knucklehead Doug over there. He looks just as miserable as us. The sweat stains on his shirt qualify as a fashion don't."

Tess quickly glanced behind her and saw their manager, Doug, sitting at another table with a young woman talking to him. She whispered back. "Great. Now he'll cover up his BO with more of his cheap cologne."

"Pssst, look at this." Allie passed the magazine to her.

Tess looked down at the article headline. "Studies Show Women Over the Age of Forty Have a Higher Chance of Being Hit by Lightning Than Finding a Soul Mate."

Tess sighed loudly and felt her shoulders slump. As if this sticky humidity wasn't making her miserable enough, her married friend had to make sure she saw this particular article.

Reading the discourse to distract herself from the speaker, Tess again wiped her hair from her face. It felt like every pore on her face, and then some that she didn't know existed, was open and expelling as much oil as possible.

According to the author, Tess was close to the tipping point of entering spinsterhood. Why couldn't the magazine have talked about how women don't need men to feel complete and successful? Where was the mention that forty was the new thirty? Single moms can be happy and content with their lives, right?

Well, Tess could believe all that, if her friends and her mother weren't constantly reminding her how they worried about her, and about what this was doing to her daughter, Claire.

What Tess *thought* she was doing was showing Claire how to be independent and self-sufficient. Or at least that was what she told herself when someone reminded her that she had been single for a long time. *A very long time,* as if she had forgotten. She no longer remembered what a passionate kiss felt like.

She sighed again before closing the magazine and flipping it back over to Allie.

"Doesn't that depress you?" Allie whispered.

Tucking her hair, which was not cooperating with the humid Florida air, Tess answered, "Nope." She looked away and rolled her eyes. "Depressing is sitting here and working while all those families over there are having fun."

Allie's right upper lip formed into a sarcastic smile. "Come on now, you don't find this fun? I mean what could be better than sweating? I need to completely change clothes after this."

Allie was the only person Tess knew who could say she was sweating when there was never a drop of moisture on her at all. She didn't even glisten. It was as though there was a bubble around her to make her always look put-together.

"I'm not even going to bother answering you." Tess gestured across to the pool. "Fun would be sitting on the other side of the pool with a frozen drink in our hand. Fun is not sitting outside here listening to this pimply-faced boy who just exited puberty rally me into being a team player."

She lifted her frizzy curls. "And to top it off, look at my hair. I have more curls right now than someone with a bad perm."

Allie snickered. "I see someone forgot to get off her broom today. Why don't you just tie it back?"

"I tried," Tess snapped. "Maybe I should just shave my head, like that singer, what's-her-name?"

Allie said, a little above a whisper, "I can't remember her name, but I know she looked good bald. You wouldn't. Your head's not shaped right. It's like...lopsided or something."

"I'm not talking to you anymore."

"Liar," Allie quipped back.

Bill, the twenty-something leading their group cleared his throat, "Excuse me. Tess. Alison. Do you have something to share with the group?"

Tess lifted her chin to scratch her throat, but before she could respond, Allie leaned over and asked, "Did he just call me Alison?"

"I think so."

"Tess? Alison? Did you have something to add?" Bill asked again.

Allie pulled the nametag hanging on a chain around her neck out to look at it. "Um, no, but the name's Allie. Not Alison."

For a very brief second, Tess actually felt sorry for Bill when he turned bright red. Allie could be a bit abrasive, especially when she was called Alison.

He looked down at the sheet of paper in front of him before responding, "My roster states Alison. Not Allie. Now if we can get back to the rules for the team-building exercise this afternoon. We need to learn to work together to get the job done."

Tess shook her head. The words slipped from her mouth louder than she had intended. "It's teaching me I'm too old for this forced-fun crap."

She wanted to be sucked into a giant sinkhole when she realized everyone had heard her. The only sound came from the families playing at the nearby pool. The guy sitting next to her softly chuckled. A few others joined in.

Tess glanced at her ally. His name was "Something" Maristone. For the life of her, she could not remember what the something was. As luck would have it, she couldn't see his name tag. *Gosh, what is his name?* He was the owner of Maristone Management, the company Tullamore had just acquired. She rubbed at her temple as she thought. *Why am I so bad with names?*

Bill continued speaking as he handed out sheets of paper to everyone. "Let's get back to the activity. I've paired you up into five competing teams. As quickly as possible, you are to collect the informational items on your list and bring it back to me. This exercise demonstrates the only way we can win in the real world of business when given a task—teamwork."

Tess leaned over to Allie, "As if we didn't know that. Doesn't junior realize that when he was busy being born, we were graduating from high school and ready to conquer the world?"

"Don't remind me," Allie whispered.

Maristone turned his head, and in a low whisper added, "Speak for yourselves. I'm a few years ahead of both of you and am old enough to be his father."

Both giggled a bit too loudly.

Bill coughed into his hand and cleared his throat again. "Tess. Alison. Since you two seem to be making a mockery out of this, you are assigned to the zoo. You have four things to find."

Tess groaned when she saw the items. Count the number of concession stands. Which exhibit has a new baby? How many gorillas are in the monkey compound? What is next to the amphibian exhibit?

Of course they had to go to the zoo—where it would not only be hot but probably smelly from the animals. Just her luck. Why couldn't they be assigned to the theme park where there was some fun? But of course, this was a sales conference and their *fun* was built into the exercises.

Every year it seemed the activities got more humiliating. This conference's only saving grace was that this was the *off* year from the talent show.

Unlike some of her colleagues, she dreaded these activities. Hated them was more like it. Tess would rather walk into the room naked than get up on the stage and pretend she could dance, act, or sing. She knew, even when she drank, that she couldn't carry a tune. So far she had come up with an excuse not to participate every year.

Allie pushed back her chair so it scraped loudly against the concrete. With not only a very forced smile, but an exaggerated southern accent as well, she said, "Of course, we can handle this, darlin'. Piece of cake."

Looking at Tess, with her normal voice she said, "Come on. Let's get out of here. The sooner we leave, the sooner we can get back and head over to The Bar to meet Tom."

Tess reached under the chair for her bag. She quickly whipped her nametag over her head causing the elastic string to get snagged in her curls. She freed it from her hair by yanking hard at it. When it came loose, it not only pulled several strands of hair, but also smacked the shoulder of her neighbor, Jack. *Jack Maristone.* That was his name. Why did she have to be in a humiliating situation to remember a person's name?

She looked at him sheepishly, and mouthed the word, "Sorry."

If he was annoyed, she couldn't tell from the expression on his face.

As she scurried away, she made her up her mind; she was going to shave her head no matter what its shape was.

Bill shouted as they walked away. "Wait. Don't forget to call my cell phone every thirty minutes with a status update."

Yeah. Whatever, Tess thought, as she and Allie headed to the front of the hotel to catch a taxi to the zoo. She asked the cab driver to put the air on full blast. They leaned back on the seats in the very cool, air-conditioned car.

Getting out of the cab, the hot humid air hit them again at full blast.

They waited patiently while the security guard checked their handbags filled with nothing more harmful than a nail file and lipstick. The way the guard was looking at a trio of girls walking past, Tess decided she could have arsenic-laced animal feed in her bag, and he would never have noticed.

Tess headed straight for the closest gift shop.

"Hey! Whatcha doin'? This is no time to shop for Claire!" Allie shouted.

Tess yelled back, "Getting a map and finding out from them what the new addition is. They'll probably have a zillion of those as stuffed animals!"

Coming out of the shop, Tess pulled her frizzy mass of curls off her face and into a ponytail with a headband with pictures of tigers on it. It would hold for a little while.

"So what'd ya learn?" Allie asked.

Waving the map and two bottled waters in front of her friend, Tess replied, "There was a new baby cheetah born a month ago. Her name—yes, a girl—is Zarah. They are all excited about it."

Allie shook her head. They walked over to a table to study the map and to get away from the mass of people leaving the zoo to escape the heat of the day.

"Hey look at this." Tess pointed at the map. "On one side of the amphibian exhibit is a garden of worldwide exotic plants and flowers and on the other is the education and research center. So now all we need to do is count the number of concession stands and then head over to the primate exhibit to count the gorillas."

Sitting, they each counted fourteen concession stands on the map. They then studied it to find the quickest way to get to their target which, naturally, was in the far corner edge of the zoo. There would be a lot of weaving through people and exhibits to get there. When passing by the garden near the amphibian exhibit, they stopped briefly to look at a magenta-colored orchid.

Feeling gleeful that most of their mission had been accomplished within ten minutes of being in the park, Tess decided they might slow down a little instead of sprinting to get to the gorillas.

"Decided to enjoy your time in the zoo?" Allie asked with a smirk.

"No. I just want to be done with this and on to

something more fun. But we can't be done so quickly that our snot-nosed, pre-pubescent group leader gives us a low rating on the team survey for possible cheating."

Closing the map, Tess pointed to the path they needed to take. "I'm already in the doghouse with Doug. The other day when I was in his office going over my review, did you know he said I wasn't professional enough?"

"You're lying!"

"Nope. Told me a lot of people look up to me, so I needed to promote a more professional image to the out-of-training sales reps. Apparently, I'm too relaxed."

Allie groaned loudly when they saw the line to get to the primate enclosure. She ran her fingers through her black, *very* straight, bobbed hair. Not a strand was out of place, nor kinked up with humidity.

Tess looked at her watch. "Gawd, standing here in this heat is almost worse than having to go to Kevin's wedding and watch him marry the 'love of his life' next month."

Allie raised an eyebrow. "I thought you weren't going."

"Yeah, well, Claire wants me to go. But I'll tell you this. My happy self will be sitting in the back praying he waits at least a month before cheating on his new Mrs. Right."

"Maybe those days are behind him."

"And pigs will fly," Tess said. "That man can't keep his pants zipped up when a pair of long legs walk by. He won't change. Men like him don't. Once a cheater, always a cheater."

They inched forward in the line, and Tess

continued, "I honestly don't think men can commit to just one woman anymore. It's not in them. It seems that they want to get their fill of as many women as they can before they wake up one morning to find out that either it no longer works or they're too old to attract Ms. Perky Boobs."

Allie crossed her arms. "Oh, I so love telling you that you're wrong. Jon has never cheated on me."

"Maybe not physically, but he does in his mind."

"What?"

Tess continued, "Don't tell me he reads those girly magazines for the articles. If that's the case, he'd do just fine with a newspaper."

"Okay. You got me there, but I don't think of him looking at that as"—she made quote signs in the air—"being unfaithful. Plus, unlike you, I wear lacy lingerie that makes me feel sexy and keeps him guessing about what I'm wearing."

"Come on, don't you get wedgies or something?"

"If that's the sacrifice I need to make to keep him from straying, then it's worth it."

Tess snorted. "Whatever."

Allie crossed her arms in front of her, signaling her not giving up. "You need to try it."

"What? There's nothing better than sitting at home on a Friday night watching a romance movie in my sweatpants."

Sighing, Allie responded, "You wear the sexy panties when you're at work, or out in public. They'll make you feel sensuous; and then maybe you'll actually flirt with someone. I heard Dana's trying it with Harry to see if she gets any response from him. She's so sure he's cheating."

"You and I both know work is Harry's lover. Dana is clearly second." Tess sadly thought of her other best friend.

Her sister-in-law's lifestyle was that of a single mom while Tess's brother, Harry, virtually lived at his law firm. Dana had once hired an investigator believing there was no possible way he could be spending so much time at the office. How wrong she was. At least if Harry had been sleeping with another woman, Dana would know how to compete.

Allie placed her hands on her hips. "Let me ask you something. When was the last time you were with a guy?"

"You mean out on a date or sexually?"

"Either," Allie answered.

"Kevin was the last man I dated, and you saw where that got me—knocked up, with him thinking he had to do the right thing. The problem was he wasn't paying attention when the minister mentioned the marriage vow of faithfulness. Last time I had sex was when Claire was four."

Allie said rather loudly, "You mean it has been nine years since you've gotten any?"

Tess looked at the crowd around them, crossed her arms, and leaned forward to whisper, "Can you say that any louder? I don't think the people over on the side of the park near the elephants heard you."

With a dramatic wave of her hand, Allie continued, "You know what your problem is? You need to go on a date, wear a thong, and get laid. You know, I think Claire would understand if you wanted to go out every once in awhile. It might be healthy for her to see you out."

"So now you're a kid expert, huh?" Tess inched forward in the line. "How, exactly, will it be good for her?"

"You need to show her how *relationships* are supposed to work. All you are showing her right now is how to live like a nun."

Her ponytail flopped back and forth as Tess shook her head."Nun? Is that what you think?"

"Yeah. Dana and I both do. We're worried about you. You're not getting any younger, darlin', and according to that article, your pickings are getting slim. You have a better chance of winning a multi-state lottery than finding someone to spend the rest of your life with."

Tucking a strand of hair which had escaped the headband, Tess responded, "First, ya'll need to stop this. My priority right now is raising my daughter, and maintaining a career to be able to provide for the two of us. I don't have a whole lot of free time to be trolling the streets looking for a man who may or may not want a 'til-death-do-us-part relationship. Plus, any unattached man my age isn't looking for someone like me."

Tess crossed her arms and then put a finger to her lip. "Hmm. What would a man prefer? A woman teetering on the age of forty, with child; or a childless twenty-year old with a youthful body and torpedo tits? Oh, what a hard decision that is!" Tess said louder than she intended.

"You're being a cynic," Allie shot back. "If the woman was attractive, the guy might just want a woman who is more experienced."

"I'm being a realist. They want a busload of

younger women where nothing on them has started heading south. The only ones who would be interested in me are the older ones who can't get the twenty-year olds—but they still fantasize about them."

"Well maybe there's someone who wants an older woman for her maturity and sophistication. Be a cougar."

"Look Allie, I'm not into going out and playing the game of 'Are you interested in me? Am I interested in you? Will we be committed, or can we continue to see other people?' It's too much work."

As they rounded the corner in the line, Tess could not believe she was having this conversation while waiting in line at a zoo. "Even if Mr. Hypothetical does say he's committed, he'll be dating me and five others at the same time, *and* able to keep all of us straight. Men seem to have a knack for that. I, on the other hand, have to write everything down, and I still forget where I have to be and when."

"I'm not saying you need to marry the guy. Sheesh!" Allie rolled her eyes. "Listen, in a few months, you're turning forty. Forty stands for *fun* these days. You're still young and in your prime. Sexually, I mean."

She winked at Tess. "You get to do what you want and you have the money to do it. Live a little, Tess. Life is not all about your daughter and work. In a few years, you'll wake up and she'll be off at college. What are you going to do then? Sit at home in your housecoat wearing big cotton panties, collecting cats, and contemplating getting a battery-powered toy to spice up your life?"

"I'm not answering you. I just want to get through

this stupid scavenger hunt and then go to The Bar and hang out with everyone."

"Yes. You want to do that because it's the only time you ever really *go out*. I bet you couldn't go on five dates before the end of this year."

"I could if I wanted." Tess was exasperated with the conversation she was still having.

Allie didn't look convinced. She pointed a finger in Tess's face. "I betcha you can't. And you know it."

"I could, if I put my mind to it."

"You can't," Allie said, looking skyward. After a long pause, she said, "I bet you can't do it before the clock strikes midnight on New Year's Eve."

Holding her shoulders high and forcing her chin out, Tess said, "You're on." She extended her hand to shake Allie's.

Allie grinned slowly and shook back, "Loser sings at next year's talent show."

"What! Sing? Are you kidding me?" Tess asked in horror.

A voice behind them said, "What's so hard about singing?"

Tess whipped around so fast she nearly fell over. She found herself looking into the whitest teeth she had ever seen.

Mr. White Teeth shrugged his shoulders and said, "I've been enjoying your conversation. Y'all have made for some entertaining listening while we've been waiting in line."

Tess blinked a few times. *Listening to their conversation? How much had he heard?* "As much as I would like my friend to play the fool in front of all our co-workers, I'm really not that mean."

"No, but I am," Allie said. She snapped her fingers. "Five dates. If you can't do it, you sing Rod Stewart's 'Do Ya Think I'm Sexy.' If you go on all five dates, then I sing it."

Turning her back to Mr. White-Teeth, Tess shook Allie's hand to seal their bet, and said, "You better start learning the words because you'll be performing it next year."

"That's what you think. I've got a gut feeling you'll be the one up on that stage howling like a dog in pain," Allie said.

Behind them Mr. White Teeth asked, "How many dates was it again?"

Tess looked around at him and the young children next to him. Hesitantly she said, "Five...before the end of the year."

His smile was too big, and too white. The light from his teeth blinded her for a second. "I could help you make it only four," he said. "You sound like you're a hoot. Are you free tomorrow night?"

Is he for real? He has three small children. She studied them a little closer. They all looked to be about the same age, yet none of them looked alike nor resembled him.

He was rather tall and muscular, as if he worked out every day. He had dark eyes and dark hair with very bushy eyebrows. She quickly looked at his finger and didn't see a ring though she knew enough to know that didn't mean he was single.

"I'm not sure," she finally said. She nodded toward the kids. "What would their mother say?"

"Dunno." He shrugged his wide shoulders. "They're not mine. Me and the guys from the firehouse participate in this volunteer program for kids. We're treating them to a day at zoo. So, are you up to going out tomorrow night?"

Tess was speechless. This was a first. As a senior consulting executive, she was never at a loss for something to say. As she adjusted the squeezing headband, she felt Allie poking her thigh.

"Hey, I'm a pretty harmless guy." He leaned close to them. His overly white teeth were not far from her face. She could smell his peppermint gum.

"Let me think about it." As she turned back around, they were finally let into the exhibit.

"Ten minutes only, please," the attendant said. "So the next group can come through."

"How many gorillas are there?" Tess asked him.

"Five. Two males and three females. One is pregnant," he said, nonchalantly, closing the gate.

"Wow, look at that one over there," Allie said, pointing to one. "Seems to be pleasing herself."

"Stop that," Tess said slapping her hand down. "Don't point. There are kids around."

Immediately one little girl saw the same gorilla and asked her mom what it was doing. The mother quickly shuffled the girl to the other side to look at the chimpanzees.

"See what you started?"

Mr. White Teeth walked up to her, asking, "Well?"

"I don't even know your name." She still did not believe this was happening to her.

"Rick. Rick Patterson."

"Nice to meet you, Rick. I'm Tess." she said nervously. She reasoned that she'd never see him again after this. And she'd have one date down. "Okay.

Tomorrow evening, then. How about we meet in front of that piano bar on the boardwalk at seven?"

"Deal. Make sure to dress casual, Tess." As the young children tugged at his arm to go off to see other animals, he said, "See you, then."

As they walked away, Allie whistled, "Wow! I'm surprised. That was a big move on your part." She fanned her hand in front of her face. "Did you see the buns on him? Whew. I know what I'm dreaming about tonight."

Sighing, Tess said, "You're a piece of work, you know that? Now, let's go hand in our stuff. This is too much fun in one day for me. First a scavenger hunt, and now a forced date to look forward to."

What have I gotten myself into? They walked to the zoo's front entrance to catch a ride back to the resort. *Am I nuts to go out with someone I just met? Am I desperate enough to go out with a possible mass-murderer?*

****

After handing in their information from the scavenger hunt, Tess and Allie ran to their rooms to change into bathing suits. On their walk through the resort, they decided to sit by the virtually empty pool and watch the sunset instead of joining the early crowds at The Bar.

Poolside, Tess watched an older couple sipping martinis while reading their books. Every so often one would say something to the other, neither showing annoyance for the interruption in their reading. She wondered if they were one of the exceptions to current society's marital statistics. Perhaps they had been together since high school and were still madly in love with each other.

Allie broke into her daydreaming. "Look. I see some of the other *contestants* coming back. I guess Billy wasn't kidding when he said we were the first ones back. Course I wanted to laugh when he asked if we cheated."

"We didn't cheat. We were creative, and we used the resources available. Plus it was nice that the cab company has that shuttle service area. Who would guess that our same driver would be waiting for us?" Tess never took her eyes from the old couple, sipping on their drinks. What was it like to be that comfortable with someone? She felt a smile crawl across her face when the man held his wife's hand in his.

Tom meandered across the patio toward them. Tess pulled her knees to her chest to allow him to sit at the foot of her lounge chair, as she studied him.

He had started with Tullamore at the same time as she. They had been through everything together—a brief relationship, marriages, and divorces.

Tom was well known for his wandering eyes. He used the *clever* excuse that he was window-shopping. However, at the sales conference three years ago, he actually sampled the merchandise and was caught in bed with a female co-worker by a surprise visit from her fiancé.

He'd thought he was safe from his wife finding out, until he discovered the fiancé was his son's history teacher. The news was out, Tom's marriage was history, and he entered the world of middle-aged divorced men.

Tess had made it clear she wouldn't forgive his actions. She knew what is was like to be cheated on.

Nonetheless, he was still her friend.

"When did you get back?" His rapid speech always reminded her of a firing squad.

"About an hour ago," she answered slowly.

"No way!" Tom exclaimed. "Who did you bribe to get the information for you?" Tom grabbed her drink to take a sip.

Allie got up from the chair to sit at the edge of the pool. "We did more than just get the blasted things on the list. We actually got a date for Tess."

Tess's face felt very warm when Tom quickly turned to look at her.

"What? You? Go out on a date?"

"Thanks for that vote of confidence." Tess tried to disguise that she felt deflated and nervous at the same time about the whole thing.

Completely ignoring Tess, Allie quickly added, "I bet her she can't go on five dates before the end of the year. She's *so* going to lose and will be singing at next year's conference. Wait until you hear—"

Tess grabbed her drink from Tom's hands. "Go get your own. Allie doesn't think I can do it."

Tom agreed, "Neither do I. I can barely believe you have *a* date tomorrow!"

Allie answered, "It's this guy who was behind us in line to get in to see and count the gorillas. Do you want to know how many there are?"

Tom looked back to Tess, "Not really. I'd rather get back to this crazy bet."

Tess looked away, feeling Tom's probing eyes on her. She couldn't look into his big, brown eyes that usually laughed at the world. Since his divorce was finalized, he had made his intentions toward her known.

Once, when he had come to Atlanta on business, after several drinks he had even proposed to her. They *were meant to be together* he had said. She had laughed and told him it wouldn't work. They were just friends who had way too much to drink.

She had seen the flash of hurt in his eyes before he looked away. Tonight, when she finally glanced his way, she saw that same look.

His voice seemed oddly quiet. "You're going out with someone you just met while waiting in line?"

She turned and focused on the older couple. "Stupid of me, huh? I don't know him from Adam. He could be a psycho."

Tom nodded in agreement. "Could be." His still-hurting look told her he wanted to be in the potential psycho's shoes.

She pulled the tiger-laden headband off her head and scratched her scalp to relieve the tightness she felt. The evening air was still humid and a bead of sweat ran down the side of her face. She lifted her hand to brush it away.

More people were returning, including Jack Maristone and Bruce The-Sidekick. She was sure she'd remember Bruce's name after she hit him like she had Jack. With drinks in their hands, Jack and Bruce joined two men sitting at a table on the opposite side of the pool. They too had changed clothes.

"You and I could go out instead," Tom said very quietly.

"I heard that. And, no, *you* don't count." Allie pointed her finger at both of them. "Remember, if you cancel, you're back to five. Plus, you'll be on your way to proving my point. You can't date."

Stretching out her cramping legs, Tess's toes rested against Tom's thigh. "I think I already went through all the reasons I *don't* date."

Tom said, "I can't believe you, of all people, are doing this. It's so unlike you."

"What's that supposed to mean?"

"You think through all the pros and cons before you do anything." Tom rested his hand on her foot.

She sat for a long time, not responding. She looked to the older couple. The man helped the woman from her chair. They walked hand in hand toward the hotel. Had they known hurt and heartbreak? If they had, she'd never have guessed. They were holding hands like lovers.

What was *she* doing with her life? Making excuses. Not wanting to be hurt. It seemed like anytime she had allowed herself to fall in love, she was left with the pain of a broken heart.

First, there was Tom. They'd been immediately attracted to each other when they first met. They were both single and would get together periodically, making special trips to see each other. She could still remember the first time he kissed her. Her heart had beat so fast, she thought she was having a heart attack.

She was more than a little stunned when he announced that he was getting married. It was on the same day she was in Chicago interviewing for a job with another company so she could be closer to him.

When the firm extended her the offer to relocate to the Windy City, she said she needed time to think. As soon as the plane landed in Atlanta, she called to decline. She couldn't live in the same city knowing that Tom went home to someone else every night. They would just be good pals when business caused them to interact.

And then there was Kevin. He was extremely good-looking and could have had anyone he wanted. They had been dating for several months when she discovered she was pregnant, proving the pill was *not* one hundred percent effective. She had truly believed he cared for her when he asked her to marry him.

It was not until after Claire was four that she discovered he *had been* having anyone he wanted, one of whom was their nanny. She learned he'd cheated on her with her midwife while she was pregnant. It nauseated her to think that he had slept with the woman who had helped deliver their daughter.

She ran to her mother, whose sympathy extended to patting her hand and telling her all men were like that. "You have two choices, Tess. Turn a blind eye like I do, or leave him."

Now her heart was doubly broken. She'd never imagined her father in that light. She was not about to ignore what Kevin did. She filed for a divorce, locked up her heart, and threw away the key.

Now, Allie had given her the ultimate challenge. She wasn't known for backing down or giving up. However, this one scared her. Could she allow herself to open up and possibly get close to someone? Or should she start memorizing the words to the song?

"I'm going through with this date tomorrow night," Tess announced in the same determined manner she did when conducting a meeting. "You two can follow me if you'd like to make sure I'm not kidnapped. By the way, if I am kidnapped, my ex does *not* get the house, okay?" She stood up, walked to the pool, and dove in, getting Allie wet in the process.

She felt the warm water lap against her as she swam to the other side of the pool and back. Tom was still sitting at the end of her lounge chair watching her. "So is this bet five dates with five different men, or can it be one man going out five times?" he asked.

Allie responded, "It can be either. However, knowing Tess, it will be five different men. She can't commit either. Yet, she blames it on all men."

Tess ran her fingers through her wet hair. "Hello! I'm right here. And I could commit if I wanted to."

"I just ask that you be careful," Tom said. "I know you. You hate to lose and will do anything to win. Just don't get yourself hurt or hurt anyone else in the process."

"We'll see." She climbed from the pool in search of a dry towel. "I'm looking at tomorrow's date as a practice run. I'll need to figure out where to polish my charm skills for future dates. Now, can we change the topic to something else?"

Tom stood up and handed her a towel. "How about you two get dressed. We'll meet back here and walk down to see the fireworks."

It was the best offer she'd had all day

Chapter Two

The weather was still hot and humid. Tess wondered if she'd melt before she actually made it out on the date with Mr. White Teeth. *Rick!* Etiquette rule number one: Call your date by his given name, not by the name you've given him.

She was sweating. Was it from nerves? She would find a restroom soon and put on more antiperspirant. If he didn't show up soon, she was going to need another shower.

She watched the people walk back and forth or ride bicycles on the boardwalk as she sat on a bench. Her bodyguards, Allie and Tom, were nearby watching her, and she willed herself to not look around for them.

Glancing at her watch, she noted Rick was fifteen minutes late. Great! She was going to be blown off on her first date.

There had to be an easier way to win this bet. Maybe she could look up escort services in the phone book when she got back to Atlanta. She stood up and walked over to the railing to look at the water, trying to appear nonchalant. She could see Allie and Tom feeding the ducks. They were as obvious as clowns at a wedding.

There was a distinct smell in the air. It could only mean one thing; her manager, Doug Smyth, and the cheapest cologne known to mankind, were nearby. He was the last person she wanted to see, or smell right now. Standing in his presence too long always gave her a headache. He would find no humor in the bet, nor would be think it acceptable for her to go out with a complete stranger while she was at sales conference. It *did* sound bizarre, the more she thought about it.

Since transferring from New York City last year, he was constantly on her about something. It did not seem to matter to him that she was consistently in the top five for sales. He found fault with everything she did, even telling her she laughed too often and never took things seriously. What did he know about her, or laughing? He had the sense of humor of a toad.

"Tess? What are you doing here alone?" Doug asked her.

Sure enough, the smell belonged to him. Slowly turning around, she looked at his entourage. There were other regional managers as well as Jack Maristone and Bruce The-Sidekick.

She needed to do a better job of remembering last names. There had to be a name for this idiosyncrasy, but she knew she'd forget that too.

She put her left hand on her hip and ran her right one through her hair. Her fingers snagged in a knot of hair in the back of her neck. The humidity was making it into a rat's nest.

"Oh, hey, Doug." She put a fake smile on her face. "I'm, um, meeting a friend."

The skeptical look on Doug's face, with one eyebrow lifted, showed he didn't believe her. She pushed one curl behind her ear and saw the look of pity on Jack and Bruce's faces. They could see how uncomfortable she was; they just didn't know about what.

"I thought you would be preparing for tomorrow's presentation," Doug said nonchalantly. When he used this tone, it was not a good sign.

"Presentation?" she asked clearing her throat. *What was he talking about?*

"Didn't I tell you?" he said, overly authoritative. "You're helping with the closing tomorrow."

Her mouth went dry. This was *so* him. Dropping things like this on her at the last minute. *Jerk! He wants to see me fail.* She silently yelled obscenities at him, and was worried her mouth would actually say them.

Fortunately, over Doug's shoulder she saw that Rick was walking toward her. She couldn't take her eyes from him. His shirt was a little too tight over his muscular physique. She couldn't be seen with him in front of her management. They would think she was the biggest floozy alive.

She didn't care that her smile was too big. "Not a problem. A, um, friend from school, is here. See ya, tomorrow." She quickly moved around the group of men and toward Rick. She refused to look back at Doug, though she the felt daggers from his eyes piercing her back.

"Sorry I'm late," Mr. White Teeth said when she walked up to him. "I had to wait for my relief at the firehouse before I could leave."

"That's okay." She tugged at his arm to get away from Doug as fast as possible. She couldn't deal with his condescending look or the barrage of questions which she knew would follow.

"So, what do you have in mind?" she asked, counting the minutes until this date was over.

"Miniature golf," he answered. "There's a course not far from here. We can walk."

"Lead the way." She glanced over her shoulder at the group of overly-conservative men still watching her. She knew she was going to hear about this on tomorrow's flight home.

Walking, Rick told her all about his life as a fire fighter and how it put a damper on dating because of the abnormal schedule he worked. She wanted to laugh at him. Damper? Looking the way he did, she would wager money that women purposefully set their homes on fire so he could rescue them. He strutted in such a way as to suggest he knew he was attractive. Okay, *hot* was more like it.

At the golf course, while they picked out their clubs, she asked, "So you don't mind being part of a bet?"

"No way! Listening to the two of you in line was cracking me up," he chuckled. "I hate to inform you, but, you've got us men all wrong. We're not as bad as you made us out to be."

"Then prove it," she replied as she lined up her putt.

Immediately, he was behind her, molding his body around hers as she went to swing her club. Her body immediately tensed. She prayed silently that Tom and Allie were not close by, witnessing this. She would never hear the end of it. Ever! Allie was probably taking pictures, at this moment, to share with the office.

Acutely aware of his body, she asked, "What are you doing?"

He whispered seductively in her ear, "Helping you line up this shot. You want to win, don't you?"

Briefly, she wondered if he meant the game or the bet. Of course, she wanted to win, but she didn't need him hugging his hard body around hers to do it. She let him control her swing and the ball went into the hole.

His mouth was close to her ear. "See? You need us more than you think."

She turned her head to look at him. From the corner of her eye, she saw Allie and Tom with their clubs in hand, staring at her. This was bad. Real bad. "Well, thank you, kind sir," she drawled in an overly-fake southern accent. She felt like a complete flirt. "You do realize that after tonight, we'll probably never see each other again, don't you?"

Arrogantly, he replied, "Yes, but I'd still like to make it a night you'll always remember and compare favorably to others."

Great, he's turning on the charm to get me between the sheets.

When they were at the sixth hole, he said, "Let me ask you something…Why do you think men can't be faithful? Did you get burned or something?"

"You could say that." She swung at the ball too hard. It bounced against the windmill and landed back at her feet. "Let's put it this way. I haven't met too many men who live monogamously. My father had more mistresses than even he can remember. My husband felt it was okay to sleep around, starting when I was pregnant. My good friend Tom cheated on his wife. My neighbor…"

"Okay," Rick said, holding both of his hands up in the air. "I get the point, you're surrounded by cheaters. But that doesn't mean every man's like that," he said with a grin. His too-too white teeth gleamed. He stood very close to her and stroked the bottom of her chin with his thumb. "There are a few of us who are the real thing, you know."

You're smooth. She took a step back so he couldn't touch her anymore. He was beginning to creep her out by turning on the charm full blast.

Tess changed the conversation to his involvement in the underprivileged kids volunteer program. She listened as he talked non-stop about how he, yes he, was making a difference in a child's life.

At the last hole, he asked. "Are you really forty?"

"Why?"

"Because when you made the comment yesterday, I didn't think you looked that old."

Her mind went numb. *What? That old?* "I'll take that as a compliment," she said flatly, as she sank the ball into the last hole. "But yes, I'll be turning the big four-zero in September."

"Get out!" he exclaimed loudly. "I honestly thought you were younger than that. Man, you look good for your age."

"Make-up is known to do wonders," she said. *And so does running at five a.m.* Before she could say any more, he suddenly sprinted away from her toward a young woman who looked to be choking.

She watched as he did the Heimlich maneuver. When the girl, who looked to be about twenty years old, appeared to pass out, he laid her gently to the ground. In disbelief, Tess watched him do mouth-to-mouth on the female. This was unbelievable. The woman, who had not an ounce of fat on her youthful body, was choking, not having a heart attack. Why did he need to put his mouth on hers?

Walking up to Rick, Tess asked, "Do you need me to call 9-1-1?"

He shot her a look of annoyance, "Uh, no! I'm a firefighter, remember? I know what I'm doing."

She shook her head. Oh yeah, he knew what he was doing, all right. Proving her point. Had this woman been eighty years old with wrinkly skin and penciled-in eyebrows, he'd have stopped at the Heimlich. But since it was a twenty year old with a flawless complexion, he had to get some mouth action. Men! Always trying to take advantage of a situation.

Turning around, she saw Tom and Allie a few holes back, again watching her and Rick. She put her hand on her hips and cocked her head to the side. She mouthed the words, "I told you so," and looked back at her date, comforting the waking damsel in distress.

As Rick continued to sit with the young girl, Tess grabbed the two putters and returned them to the rental shop. He had neither moved from his spot, nor appeared concerned that his date was nowhere in sight. He was talking with the girl and her friends, all of whom were life-sized Barbie dolls. Ten minutes passed before he made his way over to Tess sitting on top of a picnic table.

"Sorry about that," he said apologetically, putting his hands in his back pocket.

"Is she all right?" Tess looking him in the eyes seemed to unnerve him.

"Yeah! She and her friends were a little shaken up."

Tess jumped down from the table. "Listen. You're a nice guy, and all, but those girls are more your age than I am." She paused as he looked down at his shoes sheepishly. He had been caught.

"I saw a couple of my coworkers over there. I'm going to walk back to the resort with them, while you go hang out with your new friends." She gestured to the group of girls who had moved over to the snack bar, and were giggling as they glanced her way. "Seriously, I don't mind."

"Are you sure?" he asked, still looking at the ground.

"I'm sure." Before walking away, she said, "And by the way, thank you for being my first date."

He smiled his too-bright white smile as she waved goodbye.

She met Allie and Tom at the rental counter. "I rest my case. A young woman comes in the picture and men become mush." She crossed her arms over her chest.

Allie was laughing so hard, Tess could not understand a word she said. She turned around and saw Rick's arm around the waist of the girl he had rescued from choking.

Tom jumped in, "What did you expect? You just met him."

Tess looped her arm through his as they walked back toward the resort. "Yes. And he just met *her*, and look how chummy they look? He did exactly *what I expected*."

Trying unsuccessfully to suppress her amusement, Allie said, "But he was saving a woman's life."

"Saving a life, my ass. He could've stopped at the Heimlich. But once he saw those collagen lips, he had to get a taste of them. Do you think he would have done that if it was someone's grandmother?"

Tom answered, "I sure as heck wouldn't."

"Exactly. The good thing is, that's one down, and only four to go. At this rate, I'll be done before my birthday." Tess stopped and looked over her shoulder at Allie. "And when you, my dear friend, are singing next year, I'll be sitting in the front row with opera glasses and popcorn."

Chapter Three

He pulled his car into the parking lot. Elizabeth's new white convertible was already there. Hopefully, this would be their last meeting with the lawyers before their divorce was finalized. For the life of him, Jack Maristone couldn't understand why she was dragging this out, especially since she was the one who had asked for the divorce.

Taking his time, he made his way up to her lawyer's office, knowing his attorney was already there. It would be asking too much to think they had started without him; Elizabeth probably insisted they wait. She would use it as leverage to show how he *always* made her wait.

The matronly receptionist looked at him solemnly when he stepped from the elevator. "They're waiting for you Mr. Maristone," she said gravely. "I'll let them know you are here."

He walked to the window and looked out onto the Atlanta skyline. Thunderclouds were rolling into the city. In another hour there would be a downpour of rain, and traffic would be a nightmare. It matched his mood perfectly.

"Jack? Are you ready to go in?" his lawyer asked from behind him.

He nodded at Peter Moore. He knew Moore was fighting hard for him. Though Elizabeth had been the one to take a lover, she now acted like the victim—demanding compensation for the hardship of being married.

She wouldn't accept the fact that she was the one who cheated; that she was the one who had a boy-toy while Jack worked, unknowingly supporting the two of them.

He followed Moore into the conference room where Elizabeth sat with her attorney. Her hair—not a strand out of place—was perfectly styled, her make-up professionally done.

For some reason this made him think of Tess Grayson. In the meeting this morning, he had noted during several instances that she was the complete opposite of his soon-to-be ex-wife.

It was the first time he had seen Tess since the sales conference. He smiled as he remembered how, during the entire meeting she had nonchalantly tried to tuck her long, curly, butter-colored hair behind her ear. She tried to tame the few curls escaping her ponytail, to no avail. He rather liked them.

"I think we should get started," Elizabeth's lawyer said in his whining voice. Jack cringed every time the man spoke. "Before us, I have outlined what we consider to be our best and final terms. I think it is understood that my client has made a number of concessions. I hope you can finally agree to this so my client can get on with her life."

Jack stared incredulously at the lawyer, who made it sound as if he was the one slowing this process down. Elizabeth was the one whose feet had been dragging. Once it had been disclosed what he stood to gain from the sale of Maristone Management to Tullamore, she had purposely waited until the sale was complete before finalizing any of the terms of their divorce.

One thing he knew about Elizabeth, from the day he had met her at a college football game, was that she loved money. Greed should've been her middle name.

He was a senior and she was a freshman. He fell in love with her innocence and, what he thought at the time was, shyness. After they were married, he learned it was pure snobbery.

He had thought they were in love. When had it changed between them? When had she decided she no longer wanted to be with him? It must have been when she began judging everything he did was beneath her, including making money. She clearly categorized him as part of the working class.

Keeping his thoughts to himself, Jack focused on the document in front of him. It was exactly what he had expected from her. She wanted the house in Boca Raton and half of what he made from the sale of his company. Anything less would have surprised him.

When he asked if he could have a moment alone with Elizabeth, she and her lawyer appeared nervous. He rubbed the back of his neck, stiff from tension. "I just want to ask her something. I don't want an audience when I hear the answer. Just give us five minutes. Okay?"

It must have been the gruff way he said it, because both lawyers nodded their heads, stood, and left the room. It was the only thing they had agreed on during the entire process.

Jack looked around the overbearing, too-big room. It suited Elizabeth's style.

He regarded the woman he'd once thought he was

going to spend the rest of his life with. She was definitely not the same person he had proposed to. Then again, neither was he.

"I have just one question, Elizabeth: Why?" He looked straight into her eyes, knowing it unnerved her. She had told so him on many occasions, and then would remind him that she wasn't one of the underlings who worked for him.

There was no need to try to intimidate her. How could she think that was his intention? He learned this was her defense mechanism to distract him from whatever matter was currently before them.

As she got up from her chair, she smoothed her already-perfect hair. She walked to the window to look out, with her back to him. He leaned back in the chair and waited for her answer.

Her back remained rigid. "I'm not happy with my life, Jack. This simply isn't how I wanted to live my life. So…I'm making some changes."

"And being with a younger man is one of those changes?"

"As a matter of fact, yes." She turned away from the window to face him, once again smoothing her hair. "He makes me feel special and beautiful. He notices the little things. He noticed when I had the surgery to remove the lines around my mouth and eyes. Did you?"

Jack looked at her face. It looked the same, her mouth still pulled into its permanent frown. "I think you need to get a refund from that surgeon," he said dryly.

"That's not funny," she spat at him, as she walked to the corner of the room to pour herself a glass of water. "He makes me feel alive. With you, I feel old and confined. If you must know, you lack whatever it takes to make a woman feel special or needed."

Her voice started to get louder and her face turned red. "And all you ever do is work. It's work this, work that. I hate it. Your only hobby is work. You can't even carry on a conversation without turning it into business."

She continued to empty the proverbial worms from their can. "You've become old and boring, and it's aged you. Do you even realize that you look older than you really are? And another thing—"

He stopped her before her tirade worsened. "I was busy working so I could keep you in the lifestyle you've become accustomed to, my dear. What is it you'd have had me do, Elizabeth?" he asked sarcastically. "Color my gray hair so no one can tell I'm about to turn fifty? Wear leather pants?"

"Heaven forbid you do anything to make yourself appealing," she hissed at him. "Incidentally, don't make me out to be the bad person here. I earned everything I'm getting. In fact, I really deserve more, but I'm ready for this to be over."

She continued, "Mark and I want to be together. Can't you just give me that? I only want the house in Florida. You can keep all the other places."

"Mark? I thought his name was Jerry."

"Jerry and I were over months ago. I met Mark in Boca. He makes me feel sexy." She flipped her hair and sat back in the chair she had previously occupied. "But because you work so much, you never even knew or saw the transformation in me."

"When did things stop between us?"

"I can't believe you even have to ask that." She tapped her pen on the desk. The sound echoed in the room. "Soon after your company took off."

"But I don't see you complaining about all the money you're getting from it now," he said angrily. He stood and walked to the door, motioning for the lawyers to come inside.

He looked at Moore. "Is everything in here that I agreed to?"

"Yes."

"Hand me the papers so I can be done with this." He picked up the pen and signed the documents. He glared at her. "Here. You are free to go play with your boy-toy, who is probably the same age as our son."

He then took off his wedding ring and set it in front of his lawyer. "You can throw that out. It's worthless."

Jack Maristone strode from the room and headed to the elevator. Outside, where it was thundering, the rain was not yet coming down hard enough to soak him as he ran to his car.

Her words pierced him to the core. He was who he was. So what if he enjoyed working? What was wrong with that? He provided for his family.

Apparently she didn't remember their first two-room apartment. Now they had a six-bedroom estate in Buckhead, and weekend houses in the North Georgia Mountains and Boca Raton.

One thing was sure. For the first time in a long time, Elizabeth had been honest with him. How sad it was that it had to be at the end of their marriage.

Chapter Four

The flowers filled every inch of the church. The floral scent was so overpowering, it reminded Tess of a funeral rather than a wedding. She looked around to make sure she was in the right place. All the occupants were wearing bright colors and there wasn't a coffin in sight, so apparently she hadn't made a wrong turn that morning.

It was, however, a funeral for her pride and dignity. She planned the eulogy in her mind.

"Here lies the Dignity of Tess Grayson. It was abandoned by her when she accepted the invitation to her ex-husband's wedding. Dignity suffered the ultimate in humiliation when Tess, against all better judgment, said she wanted to see Kevin walk down the aisle with the love of his life. Though Tess and Kevin parted on civil grounds, she wanted to be reminded she had no soulmate. Dignity could not take it, and passed into the next life."

When this was all over, she'd have her head examined.

Sitting in the back of the church, she watched as Kevin's mother was escorted down the aisle. Julianne still didn't have a lick of fashion sense. Her outfit looked to be a leftover from the seventies—a lime green double-knit polyester dress. Her gray hair was coiffed into a beehive—sixties-style.

When the music started, Tess turned to watch Claire walk down the aisle in her white flower girl dress. She felt such a sense of pride. Her daughter had taken the divorce well. Maybe because most of her friends were from broken families, Claire wasn't bothered that her parents weren't together and that one of them was getting re-married.

Although she had begged her mother to be there, Tess knew that her softhearted daughter, had worried how she was going to handle the wedding.

"I want you to be there to see me in my beautiful dress, Mama. I won't be so nervous, if I know you're there."

"Okay, Claire. I'll sit right in the back, so I'll be the first one you see when you walk in."

"Are you sure you're not mad that Daddy has found someone else?"

Tess lied, "No, sweetie, I'm happy for your father." And then she told the truth, "I'm going to love to see you walk down the aisle."

Tess looked over and saw the couple a few rows up across the aisle staring at her. Apparently, they had noticed her resemblance to the flower girl, who happened to be the groom's daughter. She and Claire had the same curly blonde hair, straight nose, and wide lips.

Great! Now the talk of the wedding will be that Kevin's ex-wife is in attendance. She was surely going to need a shot of vodka when she got to the reception. Everyone was going to be whispering behind her back while she was there.

When the bride walked down the aisle, Tess did feel a pang of jealousy tug at her heart. She remembered the day she had taken that long stroll.

Kevin's mother was bawling in the front of the church. Her beloved son was being forced into marriage by *the pregnant girl*. Of course, Julianne never accepted the fact that her son had played a part in Tess's pregnancy.

She couldn't even wear a *real* wedding dress. Besides her already protruding belly, her very proper mother reminded her of all the reasons why a pregnant bride could *not* wear a white, also known as the virginal, wedding dress. Only her sister-in-law, Dana had laughed when Tess suggested a red hooker dress. In the end, she wore a cream-colored dress that felt like a tent.

She listened to the vows being said now. Was it her or did Kevin seem to say the word *faithful* louder than the others he repeated? For Leslie's sake, she hoped that Kevin had changed his ways. Maybe, just maybe, he would keep everything where it belonged. There might be a small chance that he could keep his heat-seeking missile confined to quarters.

In the bright summer sun outside the church, Tess waited while the photographer posed everyone for pictures. Kevin and Leslie looked lovingly at each other while her ex-mother-in-law kept flashing dirty looks toward her.

Tess couldn't remember Kevin looking at her in the manner he now looked at Leslie. It tugged at her heart. Secretly, she wished someone would look at her that way. Then again, she'd need to get past a first date for that to happen.

Okay, so the plan is to go to the reception and tell everyone how happy I am that Kevin has found someone, and that I hope I'll find that special person who will make me just as happy. Then I can go home and throw up.

With a glass of wine in her hand, she counted the minutes before she could grab Claire and make her escape. No way could she heed Dana's advice about looking around for an eligible bachelor. Her ex-husband's wedding was not the ideal setting for her to find date number two.

She danced with her daughter and with some doctor—a friend of a friend of a cousin on someone's side. She didn't care. The reception was almost over and she'd never see him again.

On Monday morning, she would tell everyone the wedding was fine. Just fine. She wouldn't elaborate or give a single clue that it had been the worst event she'd suffered through in a long time.

Chapter Five

Rush hour traffic was horrible. There was a wreck on the perimeter highway, and all five lanes had to merge into one. Tess knew she was going to be late for her dinner with Jerry from the dating service. She had opened a short-term account.

As part of their service, they let each applicant have one trial date. So far, it wasn't going well. In fact, it sucked. The first guy she had found interesting made it clear to the agency he was only interested in someone under the age of thirty-five, and she didn't fit that qualification.

She looked at her watch. There was no way she was going to make it to Monte's Restaurant on time.

Had she not stopped to answer that phone call an hour earlier she would have been punctual. She had been waiting for a call from the Ryhan Corporation after courting them for over a year. They were finally agreeing to let her submit a proposal for Tullamore to handle all their consulting services. All. Ryhan Corporation could be Tullamore's largest client, ever.

She consulted her watch again. All the air escaped from her lungs. Picking up her phone, she tried calling Jerry's cell phone. It rang straight into his voice mail. She left a message. Frantically, she called the restaurant to ask if they could pass along to her date that she was sitting in traffic and hoped to be there in twenty minutes.

Tess tapped her fingers on the steering wheel praying the cars ahead of her would move. She looked in the mirror and saw that not only was her hair a complete mess, but she had licked off all her lipstick. There was no possible way this could get any worse.

Her cell phone broke the silence in the car. It was Allie. Tapping the phone on, she said, "What do you want?"

"Wow! Using your happy voice. I just heard the traffic report and had a feeling you were stuck in the middle of it. Are you going to make it in time?"

"No. I was late before I even left the office," Tess answered. "After this, there is no way Matches Are Made is going to give me another date. They'll probably decline me as a customer."

"Just calm down. I'm sure he'll understand," Allie said. "Freshen up your lipstick, because I know you've licked it all off by now."

"Is that supposed to be funny?"

"No. I'm speaking the truth. Please tell me your hair looks good."

"It doesn't."

"Typical. Hey, I heard about Ryhan Corporation. It would be huge if you could land that. Maybe, then, Doug will finally get off your back."

"Doubt it," Tess responded. "He won't get off my back until he sees me crash and burn. Knowing him, he'll sell tickets to that. Listen, I gotta hang up, I can see cars moving up ahead. I'll call you later and let you know how it goes." She clicked the phone off and threw it into her purse.

After passing the accident, she sped along the

highway, hoping to make up for lost time. She was now forty-five minutes late. Her heart was beating fast and her palms were actually sweaty on the steering wheel. After pulling into the parking lot, she fished in her leather purse for her lipstick and came up empty-handed. She grabbed the over-sized tote and sprinted across the parking lot, praying that Jerry was a patient, and understanding individual.

Her reflection in the restaurant's door revealed a disheveled, wrinkled blue linen dress. That put-together look from earlier today had gone bye-bye. It was as if she had grabbed her clothes from a laundry basket.

She counted to ten before opening the door to escape the hot air. September was right around the corner, and maybe, just maybe, it would start to cool down. Probably not. This was Atlanta, after all.

She strode up to the hostess station while trying to smooth her hair. "Hello. I'm, um, supposed to be meeting someone. Reservations were under the name of Jerry Winters. He's tall with brown hair and glasses?"

The hostess gave her a blank stare.

Tess continued, "I called to pass along a message that I was running a little late."

The hostess finally had a moment of clarity. "Oh yeah," she said snapping her gum. "He was, like, a big jerk. Like, he lied if he told you he was tall, because he definitely suffered from short man syndrome. Between you and me, I think, like, his brown hair was a toupee. I gave him your message and he went, like, berserk. I mean like, *really* berserk. He didn't care that you were, like, stuck in traffic. He said you were, like, really inconsiderate. Like, you know, you should've known there was, like, going to be an accident."

Tess rubbed her hand over her temples; she could feel a headache coming on. Each time the girl said "like", her voice elevated five notches and her statements formed into questions. She made a mental note to talk to Claire about never saying that word. She continued to rub her temple. This was just perfect. There went date number two, before it even happened. This was hopeless.

"Tess?" a deep voice said behind her. "Tess Grayson?"

She spun around, almost losing her balance. Behind her were Jack Maristone and Bruce The-Sidekick. She had seen them, together and separately, almost every day since they moved into the floor just above where she worked.

She had made small chitchat with Bruce when she saw him in the building. Why couldn't she think of his last name? She wondered if it was because he never told her. *Yeah, that was it,* she told herself to feel better.

"Here for dinner?" Jack asked.

While her brain was thinking up a plausible story, her mouth took over. "Uh, no, not really. I'm here for a job. What about you?" She felt herself blush when she saw the look, on both of their faces.

"*Stupid. Stupid. Stupid,*" she silently repeated to herself. Why couldn't her mouth learn not to move until her brain gave an order?

"Well, I can't see you as a waitress. You'd be questioning people on what they ordered," Jack said with a small smile on his face. "You won't make tips that way, so that can't be the position you're inquiring about."

"Yes, well you have a point." She tried to sound

apologetic and light at the same time.

"If your business has concluded, perhaps you would want to join us?" Jack asked. The look he gave reminded her of the one he'd given her last month in Florida, when she was meeting up with Rick.

"If you don't mind, I'd love to. You see, I just got stood up by my date because apparently he thought I was standing him up."

A smile passed over his lips, and his eyes crinkled in the corners.

Jack said, "Poor guy. You probably broke his heart. Bruce, see if they will add another person to our table."

Tess watched Bruce walk up to the hostess to change the reservations. Jack did have a way with ordering people around.

"You're sure I'm not intruding on your dinner?" she asked.

"Not at all. You'll be a welcome addition," he said. "Truth be told, whenever Bruce's wife is out of town, he and I grab something to eat. She's been traveling quite often recently, and we're running short on conversation. He'll never admit it, but he doesn't know his way around a kitchen." Jack leaned forward, "Let that be our secret."

"Mum's the word," she whispered, putting her finger to her lips.

When Bruce Taylor's name was called, Tess told herself to take note. It was an easy-enough last name to remember.

As Bruce followed the hostess, Jack gestured for Tess to go ahead of him. "After you," he said, gentlemanly.

He has manners. His mother must have taught him

well. She wanted to slap her forehead; she was beginning to think like her mother. She had to pay more attention to that.

She studied Jack while they looked at their menus. She figured he was close to six feet, a bit taller than she. His face, with its square jaw, was very striking for an older man. She had trouble trying to guess his age. His hazel eyes looked bright and alive, but his hair was a dark gray. There was an air about him that exuded confidence.

After he set his menu down, the waitress appeared and he ordered a bottle of wine for the table. When the waitress left, he asked Tess, "Have you decided yet?"

"I'm just going to have a boring salad." She placed her menu on the table and picked up her water.

"I take it this was the first date with this guy you stood up?" Jack asked, with amusement in his voice.

She wondered if he was toying with her. "I didn't stand him up. Granted, I left the office later than I wanted, but there was an accident on the Perimeter," she answered defensively. "And, yes, it was our first, and now last, date."

Dryly, Bruce said, "If you knew you had a date, you should have left earlier."

Now why didn't I think of that? She made sure her mouth didn't echo the words. "I tried, but I was on one of those work phone calls that you can't really cut short."

Jack tasted the wine, and signaled for the waitress to pour for Bruce and Tess.

"Care to elaborate?" Bruce asked, sitting back in his chair.

Tess fleshed out the Ryhan phone call, and how—

now it was in reach—a mere date wasn't going to stand in her way.

Jack volunteered his and Bruce's assistance in helping her close the deal. Once their food was served, the conversation turned to more personal matters.

Bruce not only had a wife, but three kids—all in college at the same time. They laughed when he said, "In my next life, I need to plan better so it won't be such a strain."

Jack talked about his son. Joel was presently attending Jack's college alma mater.

The conversation then turned to the men's hobbies, golf—so stereotypical—travel, and Bruce's hang-gliding.

By the time dinner was over and the check delivered, Tess had learned enough to know she liked them as people, not just co-workers.

Chapter Six

During the first part of September Tess felt like she spent every working minute she had with Bruce, Doug, and Jack. Most mornings, they met in Doug's office for a debrief on where each of them stood on their section of the Ryhan proposal.

Every morning she was the last to arrive. She could not leave the house until Claire got on the school bus. This left Tess sitting on the highway during the peak of traffic with her million closest friends.

Some mornings as she neared the office, Tess would call her assistant, Maggie, and ask her to run out for a cup of coffee and a plain wheat bagel and deliver it during their meetings. One morning a cup of coffee and bagel waited for her on the table.

Later that day, she thanked Maggie for having it there prior to her arrival.

Maggie looked puzzled. "It wasn't me. I sat by my phone waiting for your call, but it never came."

The next morning, the steaming hot coffee was once again waiting for her. She looked over the brim of the cup at Bruce as she drank. He seemed oblivious to anything. Her eye caught Jack's wink.

She set the cup down and mouthed the words, "Thank you."

He shook his head and refocused on the conversation at hand.

On the day the proposal was due, Tess was in the office before anyone else. She had conned her mother into spending the night so she could leave the house before her daughter even woke up. She stopped by the first floor cafeteria to pick up two cups of coffee.

She walked down the plushy carpeted hallway to Jack's office.

"He's not in yet, Ms. Grayson," Sandra, his assistant, told her.

"Can I get one of those yellow sticky notes from you?"

Tess wrote, "This is payback. I also owe you lunch. Tess." She attached the note to the cup and handed it to his assistant asking that she leave it on his desk.

Walking down the flight of stairs to her office, she realized she had time to work on returning several emails and phone messages before their scheduled time to meet. Instead she found her mind replaying times she'd spent in Jack's company.

There had been times when she got a feeling in her stomach, as if he was watching her. When she would look up, his eyes were elsewhere. Very rarely did she catch his gaze, but when she did his eyes held hers until *she* looked away. She worried either Bruce or Doug would notice.

The few times they had gone to lunch, Jack always sat next to her. Was it her imagination, or was he showing an interest in her?

He had never mentioned a wife. Maybe, just maybe, he could be dating material.

She was attracted to him. He seemed perfect for dates two through five, and then maybe dates six and seven, too.

I'll have a talk with Dana. She'll search the internet and find out everything there is to learn about him.

What was she thinking? This was clearly daydreaming. He was now part of Tullamore, and there was a strict policy on fraternization. So nothing could happen between them.

The sharp ringing of the phone broke into her thoughts. Picking up the receiver, she said. "Tess Grayson."

Doug's angry voice boomed through the earpiece. "Where are you? We've been waiting for you. Sandra said you were here so we thought we could get started early. In case you forgot, this proposal is due at noon."

"I'm on my way." Tess hung up the phone. *What an ass!* Of course she knew when it was due; this was *her* baby, and she was the one who was going to deliver it.

She hated Doug and the way he constantly belittled her. She had hoped that with them working so closely, he would soften toward her. That hadn't happened. Instead he pushed her until she was ready to blow up at him, like a volcano. Decking her boss would be the end of her career at Tullamore. That didn't keep her from fantasizing about it—daily!

She gathered up the last of her notes and as she entered Jack's office, the overpowering smell of Doug's cheap cologne made her want to gag.

"Thanks for the coffee," Jack said with a wink as he pointed to the cup sitting in front of him.

She shrugged her shoulders. "It was my turn."

Tess stopped when she saw Doug's eyes narrowed at her. She pushed her hair behind her ear and sat down in the empty chair across from Jack, next to Bruce. She pulled out the final version of the proposal. She had spent most of the night re-working it and putting all the pieces together.

Rubbing the back of her neck, she said, "This is it. Jeff helped put together some of the final touches. If you ask me, I think it sounds good."

"Tess, I think this is so much better than good." Jack sat back in his chair and focused all his aura of power on her.

She found his compliment to be beyond her wildest expectations. *Honestly, if he didn't work here, he'd definitely be a candidate for date number two.*

Never taking his eyes from her, he continued, "We'd be in serious trouble here, Tess, if you ever went over to the competition."

"Thanks." She felt the blood rush to her face. "If ya'll think this is good, I have a team downstairs ready to assemble it for me. I can drop it off before the deadline."

Sandra opened the door, "Excuse me, Jack, but your wife is on the phone."

The blood that had rushed into Tess's face now vanished. Was that a guilty look Jack had on his face?

Never taking his eyes from Tess, he said, "Take a message."

"I told her you were in a meeting, but she said it's an emergency," Sandra answered.

Jack's attention shifted to the empty doorway where Sandra had been. Pushing his chair back from the table, he walked to his massive desk to pick up the telephone.

Tess was having problems processing what she had

just heard. So, he was married. Why should she care? She worked well with married men all the time. In fact, she worked better with the married ones than she did with single men.

Why should Jack be any different? So he had paid her a little extra attention that she had taken the wrong way. He was just trying to be friendly and she had misread the signs. But then, why that guilty look? It was as if he had been figuratively caught with his pants down.

She strained to hear the conversation, but he spoke in a low voice with his back to the room.

Doug handed her the papers back. "Yes, Tess, have the package assembled, and deliver it." He nodded his head in such a way to let her know she was dismissed.

She gathered up everything and glanced at Jack. He had turned around and was watching her. She focused her attention back to the papers and headed for the door. She had a job to do and right now it wasn't about finding a date.

****

The binders had been delivered to her office. Tess flipped through to make sure everything was in order. There was that smell again. She looked up to see Doug standing in her doorway.

"You have a second?" he asked.

Tess nodded. *What did he think I was going to say? No?* He was her manager, after all.

"Don't let this go to your head, but you did a better job than I expected," Doug said. "When I came here, I thought of you as nothing but a prima donna."

She gulped not knowing what to say. *Prima donna? Me?* Had he just paid her a compliment or was that an insult? She wasn't sure. She scratched at the back of her head, trying to comprehend what he was getting at.

"Thanks. I think," she finally said, confused by his words.

"You know, if this sells, you're going to be rather busy. How would you feel about working with Bruce? Jack and I talked and thought it would be wise to pair the two of you together."

She nodded.

"Good, because I can't have you throwing a tantrum about having to work with someone. I know you're all about winning, but you need to learn to share the glory." He immediately turned and left the room.

She was speechless, *Was he serious?* She had never thrown a tantrum. Wasn't she always a team player? The man never made any sense.

Though he was gone, the scent of his cheap cologne lingered. Reaching into her bottom drawer, she pulled out a can of air freshener and sprayed. She finished packing her computer into her briefcase and grabbed the binders to be delivered.

She struggled to carry the box while wheeling her computer bag to the elevator. When the elevator doors opened, Jack was there.

"Do you need help with any of this?" he asked.

"Thanks." She placed the box in his outstretched arms.

"What are you doing after you deliver these?"

"Going home to catch up on things that I let slide while I worked on this."

"Oh. I was wondering if you wanted to grab drinks and maybe dinner later on."

Did she hear right? Was he asking her out on a date or was she misinterpreting this? Had he forgotten he was married, or did he not care? *He's just like all the others.*

"Sorry, but I, um. How do I say this? I, um..."

"Have to get home to Claire?"

She paused. It seemed like a plausible excuse. "Yeah. That's it," she said.

"I understand," he said. "When I was building up Maristone, Elizabeth said I neglected Joel."

"What?" She was confused as to what he was saying.

"She said I spent too much time away from him. But, now, it's she who has neglected him."

Putting her hand on his arm, Tess said, "I'm sorry to hear that."

She pulled it quickly away when the elevator doors opened to the lobby. The last thing she wanted was someone to see her standing so close to him—knowing her luck, that *someone* would be Doug. He'd read too much into it

"It's all right now. Joel seems to be well adjusted," Jack said.

When he turned to smile at her, something inside of her flipped. Something that envied what Elizabeth had. Him.

"Thanks for listening," he said, as they walked through the lobby. "If you can't have dinner tonight, how about tomorrow night?"

Her shoes clicked loudly on the marble floor.

They were outside in the afternoon sun walking to the parking garage. She heard the hesitancy in her own voice. "I dunno. I've got to go drop these off."

After placing the box on her back seat, he said, "I'd like us to be friends, Tess."

She didn't turn around hoping he'd think she hadn't heard him. Friends or not, he was married and she wasn't going to be part of that game. Her friendship would only go so far. "Thanks for carrying the box for me, Jack." She opened the driver's side door to crawl inside. "Have a good weekend."

Chapter Seven

The first thing she saw was the sign that read, "Lordy, lordy, Tess is really forty." Then she heard the traditional birthday song, with Allie's voice, of course, louder than everyone else's.

She knew they were planning some sort of birthday surprise, but the last thing she expected was to come home from work and find a party at her house. The flashing camera captured her surprised look.

The house was filled with food and people, many of whom were co-workers. She put her briefcase down in the foyer before joining the festivities. It was Friday, so she didn't care how much she drank. Plus, she was in her own house so she didn't have to worry about driving.

She grabbed some stuffed mushrooms and made her way to the patio, where she saw Doug. Why had *he* been invited? Didn't Allie know it would take a week to get the smell of his cologne out of her house?

Doug's treatment of her, even though she was close to signing the deal with Ryhan, had worsened. At the staff meeting earlier that week, he had demanded to know why she hadn't heard anything.

Nothing like humiliating me in front of everyone. She spent the remainder of the meeting fantasizing about getting even, somehow. Slow-roasting him over an open pit fire seemed too quick.

When Tess re-entered the house, she did a double take. Bruce was talking with her brother, Harry. If Bruce was here, was Jack here as well? The two were always together. She looked around but didn't see him.

Allie came up to her. "I hope you don't mind me inviting Bruce and Doug. I figured since you and Bruce will be working together on Ryhan, you wouldn't mind if he came." She lowered her voice to a whisper, "Doug overheard us talking about your party. When he asked when it was, what could I do but invite him?"

"You could've kept your mouth shut," Tess hissed. "Did you ever think about that?"

"I'm not answering that. I'm going to be nice, but only because it's your birthday. Any other day, I would've told you where to go and what you could do while you're there."

"Yeah, well I'll save you a seat and have the cold drinks ready when you get there, too."

Bruce came up and hugged her. "Happy birthday," he said. "You sure don't look forty. Don't take this the wrong way, but you look great."

"Thanks," she said blushing.

"Jack is going to hate finding out he missed your party." Bruce took a drink of his beer.

"Jack? Oh, Mr. Maristone is 'Jack' now?" Allie asked suspiciously.

Tess caught her eye. "Well, yeah, he worked with us on the Ryhan bid."

Allie nodded and said, "Oh, I forgot. When you are on the verge of bringing in the company's biggest account ever, I guess you *do* get to fraternize with all the big dogs and be on a first name basis."

"You got that right," Bruce added finishing his

drink. "You have a real nice house here, Tess. Met your daughter. Looks like a miniature of you."

"Thanks. And thanks for making the drive out to suburbia," she said. "How did everyone get here before me?"

"We made sure someone scheduled you for a late day call so you'd be stuck on the phone while we sneaked out," Bruce commented. "That incident at Monte's Restaurant, when you got stood up, gave us the idea."

Tess shook her head in disbelief. All this secret planning, and she'd never picked up on it.

"Big plans tomorrow for your birthday?" Bruce swirled the ice around in his empty glass.

"Well…I was planning to—"

"She'll be busy shopping," Allie interrupted. "It's what she always does on her birthday. Have to help the economy now, don't we? If you'll excuse us, Bruce, I need to steal the party girl for a sec."

Allie led her into the kitchen, where they re-filled their drinks and ate some of the chips and guacamole sitting on the counter.

"Was I supposed to invite Jack? I mean, I didn't realize you three were a package deal now."

"No. It's just that I have gotten to know Jack since working with him and Bruce. It's nothing."

Allie said with a sigh of relief. "The way Bruce said it, I got, well…nervous. I kinda got the impression that…well…that it was expected that he be included."

"I said 'it's nothing.' You're reading too much into this," Tess quickly interjected.

"You know, speaking of reading, I remember I read a magazine article last spring, right before we bought his company. There was a picture of Jack and his family at their house in Buckhead. Well, not a house, more like a mansion. I remember thinking when I get to be the age of his wife, I want to look and dress like her. She's classy-looking."

Allie stopped to pop another chip in her mouth. "But you know what is weird, I never see him wearing a ring. From looking at him I would guess him to be one of those guys who has to have a thick band with diamonds inlayed in it."

"Well, guess not," Tess responded.

While she debated telling Allie about her feelings for him, her mouth suddenly took over again. "We've gone to lunch a few times. You know, he kind of reminds me of Tom."

"How so?" Allie asked.

Before Tess could answer, Dana came into the kitchen. "Well, have you asked her?"

Tess's guard immediately went up. They were plotting something, "Asked me what?"

"If you've been practicing your song," Dana answered. "You do realize that tomorrow is October first, and the last date you went on was in July. Have you forgotten you have four more dates to go? The clock is ticking."

"Well, don't forget the Matches Are Made debacle. It's not as if I haven't tried. And I've been a *little* busy at work."

"I knew you were going to say that. You've been busy avoiding the challenge, is more like it." Allie bit into a guacamole-covered chip. "You need to get out there."

"Hey. I will once I've wrapped up the Ryhan

account, which should only take a few weeks. I'll call an escort service and have my dates lined up for me. Problem solved. Next!" Tess snapped her fingers, trying to brush the whole conversation to the side.

"You are such the cheater." Allie tried not to laugh. "That's not in the rule book."

"You got a better idea?"

"As a matter of fact, I do," Dana said. "*We* pick the men."

"Oh no, you don't," Tess said loudly. "That's too scary to even think about."

"No, what will be scarier is what the stakes will be when we decide it's time for you to have sex," Allie giggled. She walked over to the pantry door to open it and pull out a little pink gift bag. "When that time comes, you'll need this."

Hesitantly, Tess took the bag—fearing a box of condoms or a vibrator.

"Oh gawd! It's not going to bite you," Allie sighed.

Pushing the tissue paper away, she peeked in the bag to see a red lace thong.

Dana answered, "We think this may make you feel sexy and give you an easier time on your dates."

"With butt floss?" Tess picked up a shrimp and threw it at her.

Allie's head wobbled from side to side, "Yes! Promise you'll wear it on your next date. Prove us wrong. But you need to get going, my friend."

As much as Tess didn't want to admit it, they were right. She had pushed the bet into the recesses of her mind. Now she had to get working. She was going to call Tom, and get his take on the situation. *After* she had a good time at her party.

Chapter Eight

The air was warm as Jack walked across the street from the Tullamore building to meet Elizabeth for lunch. Inside he felt a chill. He was getting tired of her referring to herself as "his wife" to his assistant, Sandra.

It drove him crazy that Elizabeth continued these urgent phone calls which he had refused to return. Only on this latest call did he finally talk with her, and agree to meet for lunch. What was so important that she needed to see him?

She was waiting for him in front of the sandwich shop and gave him an unnaturally friendly hug. This could only mean one thing; she wanted something.

While they stood in line to order lunch, Jack saw Tess sitting in a corner booth with a somewhat familiar-looking man. He racked his brain trying to figure out where he had seen the guy before.

As soon as their lunch was ordered, he joined Elizabeth at the table she had secured by standing over a young couple finishing their meal.

From where they sat, he had a clear view of the back of Tess's head; he watched as she routinely ran her fingers through the mass of hair. He knew under that mass of hair was a pretty face. When her lips formed a smile, her whole face lit up, making her blue eyes crinkle at the corners. Sometimes her small nose would scrunch up. Other times, she would press her smiling lips together and cock her head to the side.

But behind that pretty face was a serious, hard-working woman, driven to succeed. He had watched as she tapped her index finger on the table while she was thinking. Then she would shoot out a question that would stump everyone, including him.

How many times had he wanted to touch those blonde curls that she continuously pushed off her face? How many times had she joked she was going to shave it all off? She wouldn't; it was part of her lively personality.

He watched as the man sitting across from her now said something that caused Tess to throw back her head to release one of her loud, infectious laughs.

Elizabeth looked around, and said in an annoyed voice, "Some people should learn to control themselves and not be so obnoxiously loud."

Jack came back to the present moment's reality and looked at the woman who used to be his wife. She looked very different. She had had more fountain-of-youth plastic surgery. She looked so unnatural.

He finally asked, "So, why did you want to meet me?"

"Couple of reasons." Her eyes shifted back and forth. "I wanted to see how you were."

He opened his eyes wide. "Would it make you feel better if I said I was wallowing in self-pity? News-flash, Elizabeth, I'm not. In fact, I'm doing just fine and so is Joel. So, what's the real reason you want to see me?"

"I heard you're selling the house."

"I am. With Joel away at school, the place is too

big for me."

"Don't you think that will upset Joel when he comes home for break?" She inspected the sandwiches the waiter put in front of them.

"He's a freshman in college, living in a dorm. He'll be thankful to just have a clean bed to come home to. I think what might concern him more right now is how his mother has vanished from the face of the earth and hasn't even called to see how he's adjusting to school."

"Jack, I'm tired of you trying to make me feel guilty," she hissed. "I'm not the bad person here. Things could've been very different between us if you had tried a little harder."

Ignoring her outburst, he changed the subject. "You said there were a couple of reasons. Now that you've seen I'm doing okay and verified that I'm selling the house, what is it you really want?"

"I'm not happy, Jack."

He chewed his food and looked at her in disbelief. He couldn't remember the last time she was happy or even laughed. "And I'm not surprised."

He was tired of her and the current conversation. He saw Tess pulling her hair into a ponytail on the back of her head. He had a clear view of her slender neck.

She let go of her hair when her companion pointed his fork at her with a serious look on his face. He wondered what they were discussing.

"I hate it when you take that tone with me," Elizabeth said, gritting her teeth. "If you had an ounce of compassion in you, you would understand that I miss Atlanta and my life here."

"You have enough of my money. Buy yourself a place."

She put her sandwich down and looked to the side. "You just said the house was too big. Maybe, you don't sell it and I could move back in. We'd have separate rooms."

She's not serious, is she? He picked up his drink to take a sip.

The next few moments seemed like they happened in slow motion.

He felt Elizabeth grab his hand. He heard her voice, but not the words.

His attention once again focused on Tess. She got up from the booth, turned around facing him, and allowed her luncheon partner to help her with her bright red jacket. Her smile was big and genuine as she accepted his assistance. She flipped her hair out from inside the coat and her eyes met his. It seemed as if everything else stood still as they looked at one another.

Her eyes darted to where Elizabeth's hand was covering his own, then back to his face. She leaned down to grab her purse from her seat. Though she waved and gave him a smile, it almost seemed forced.

She must have said something to the man she was with, because as they walked from the shop he glanced over at Jack and nodded. Jack never took his eyes from her as she hugged her companion goodbye before hurrying across the street.

"Jack, are you listening to me?" Elizabeth pleaded. "I'm trying to tell you I made a mistake. I want to come back to try and make things work."

He looked back at her. His appetite was gone. He covered his plate with his napkin. "You should have thought about that before you decided to sleep with the pool boy, the landscaper, Jerry, Mark, and whomever else I'm leaving out."

He pushed his chair away from the table. "Don't look so surprised. Joel knew what you were doing. He filled me in after you moved out. Elizabeth, I've got to get back to work. We are done here, and forever. Stop your phone calls, and most especially, stop referring to yourself as my wife. I'm serious. I'll bring harassment charges against you."

As he walked across the street in the warm fall air, the elation of freedom filled his chest.

His thoughts returned to Tess. She was obviously seeing someone, so why would she even consider him? As Elizabeth had put it, in the lawyer's office just months before, he was probably "too old and boring" for Tess to consider. She had made it obvious she was not interested when she had rejected his offers for drinks or dinner last week. She would *only* go to lunch with him if Bruce was there too.

Chapter Nine

Maggie poked her head into Tess's office, signaling she had a call holding.

Tess covered the mouthpiece. "Can you take a message?"

"I don't think you want me to. It's Jeannie from Ryhan."

"Okay, tell her I'll be right with her."

Tess finished her conversation with Claire. "Listen to me. I'll be leaving here shortly. As soon as I get home, we'll go to the store and get the Halloween party decorations. Okay? Now I have to go. Make sure your homework is done before I get there or we don't go. Love ya, sweetie."

As soon as she hung up the phone, Jeannie's call rang through. She listened silently to the news she had been waiting to hear. The leadership at Ryhan was impressed with the proposal that she, Jack, and Bruce had laid out. It was official. Tullamore was going to handle *all* consulting services for Ryhan Corporation.

Jeannie boosted her ego further, telling her that it was her persistence and dedication that had sealed the deal. They chatted for some time and set up a meeting for the following week to start working on the transfer of business to Tullamore.

When the phone was back in its cradle, Tess leaped from her chair, put both hands in the air, and yelled,

"Yes!"

Allie walked over from the office next door. "You heard?"

"We'll be the official consulting firm for Ryhan Corporation." She shouted, "Do you know how big this is?" She stretched her arms out. "*Huge!*"

"Congratulations!" Allie exclaimed, hugging her. "You want to go out and celebrate? Dinner's on you!"

Tess hugged her friend back. "No, I can't. First I've got to go break it to Doug the Devil, and then I have to get home to take Claire shopping for Halloween. She wants to dress up like a vampire to hand out candy. She's insistent that all the stuff will be sold out even though it is only the start of October now."

Tess walked quickly down the hall to Doug's corner office, only to be told he was in a meeting upstairs. She practically ran up the stairs and found Bruce's office empty also. His assistant told her to check Jack's.

Sandra's desk was vacant. Was anyone working? Jack's door was open. Tess peeked inside to see him standing at the window while on the phone.

Bruce sat at the table drumming his fingers, but stopped when he saw her. "What's up?" he whispered.

She could barely contain her excitement as she tiptoed up to him. "Ask me if I've heard." She blurted out louder than she intended, "We did it! We got Ryhan's business!"

Bruce's mouth opened wide and his eyes were just as big. He held up his hand to give her a high-five. "Congratulations! That's great."

She was having trouble containing her excitement.

"This is the biggest sale in the company's history, and I played a major role in bringing it in!"

A deep voice behind her said, "You really did it, Tess. We were just there for support. No one else but you could've done it. Congratulations."

Tess turned around and, without thinking, gave Jack an enormous hug. As soon as she wrapped her arms around him, she had an odd feeling. There was something about his one arm against her lower back, pressing her close against him. The feeling surged like electricity through her. Butterflies started flapping in her stomach.

It was wrong to hug a married man *and* for it to feel this good. She immediately stiffened and stepped away. "Sorry about that. I get carried away sometimes," she stammered. She pushed her hair behind her ear. It was hopeless; she knew from the heat she felt in her face, she was blushing.

His gentle eyes sparkled at her. "No harm done," he said softly. In a louder voice, he asked, "Did you tell Doug, yet?"

"Nope," she answered. "I'm trying to find him."

"I think he's in the conference room down the hall," Bruce said. "Come on, I'll go with you."

As she walked down the hall with Bruce, she briefly looked over her shoulder. Jack had moved out of his office to watch her walk away.

"Hey! Maybe the three of us should go out and celebrate," Jack called after her.

She stopped, hesitating before responding. She thought back to the time at the Monte's dinner the three of them had shared. She had thoroughly enjoyed their company.

She had already turned down her close friend, so there was no way she could go out tonight. Besides, she had shopping to do with Claire. "Can I take a rain check? I have to take Claire shopping," she finally answered.

She was relieved when Jack nodded his head. What was it that drew her to him when she shouldn't be? She asked, "How about the three of us go for happy hour tomorrow to celebrate?"

Bruce immediately chimed in, "I'm so up for that. You, Jack?"

He smiled directly at her. "Of course."

When she and Bruce finally found Doug, he asked question after question, most of which she couldn't answer. She reminded him she would learn more next week.

After Doug's interrogation Bruce bid her goodnight before walking down the long hallway back to his office. She slowly walked down the stairs. All her adrenaline had been used up by Doug's cross-examination. He hadn't even bothered to congratulate her.

Back in her office, she found a wrapped gift on her desk. On top if it was a note in Allie's writing. "I bought you this as a congratulatory present. Enjoy it." She unwrapped the CD "Do Ya think I'm Sexy." She didn't know if she should laugh or cry. She tossed it in her brief case, and headed for home.

As she rode the elevator down, her mind replayed the ending of her day, specifically the Jack hug. Could she have done anything more stupid? What was she thinking? What possessed her to hug Jack and not Bruce? Jack must think her a complete idiot.

Who cares? She had won one challenge. Now she could concentrate on her next. Winning the coming one was a matter of life of death. If she had to sing, she would die from the embarrassment.

Chapter Ten

Tess also invited Allie and coworker Jeff for happy hour. When the three showed up at their favorite restaurant and bar, The Tuxedo, Doug was already there with Bruce.

Jack was nowhere to be seen. She felt one part relief, one part thorough disappointment. Yesterday's facial expression led her to believe he'd be looking forward to it. She was reading too much into this. They were destined to be *just friends*.

Doug lifted his beer glass. "Well, here she is, the woman of the hour!"

Tess nodded and sat on the high bar chair diagonally—the farthest away from him and his smelly cologne she could sit, and still remain polite.

"Thanks," she said. Turning to the waitress, she said, "Chocolate martini, please."

Allie said, "Make that two. Nothing like having chocolate to celebrate a big win, huh?" Lowering her voice, she whispered. "Especially since I think this is the last win you're going to celebrate in a while. When I win our bet, I'm going to gorge myself on the biggest box of chocolates I can find."

Tess whispered back. "I'm still going to win that bet."

"Bet?" Doug asked.

Tess kicked Allie under the table. "Private joke,"

she quickly answered, relieved that a few more people from the office were showing up to celebrate and distract Doug.

Their department had always loved happy hour. Doug's predecessor, Mitch, had a sixth sense about stress levels. When they seemed near a breaking point, he would come by each of their offices, tell them to turn off their computers, and meet him at The Tuxedo.

At the beginning of her employment, there was one time when Tess skipped the happy hour because she wanted to finish up something that wasn't due for several more days.

Mitch had called her into his office the next morning. "Tess, working like that is unhealthy. When I call 'happy hour,' you need to show up, and let off some steam. We work as a team, and we party as a team."

It was the only time she felt like she had truly let someone down at work.

"Sorry I'm late." Jack stood between Bruce and Tess's chairs. "I was on the phone with home office filling them in on your success."

Tess smiled sheepishly, "I can't take all the credit. Ya'll are forgetting that Bruce here played a big role, too." She patted his back. He looked embarrassed to be the center of attention.

Jack rested his hand on the opposite side of the back of her chair. To anyone, like Doug, sitting across from her, it might appear that he had his arm around her. She stiffened her body waiting for that drink to arrive.

Jack chuckled. "Sure. If that's what you think. You had the ideas, and we helped put them on paper."

She turned in her chair to face Bruce and crossed her legs as she reached for her martini.

"So did Claire get what she needed last night?" Jack asked.

"Yes, thank God." She sighed before taking a sip of the sweet drink. "We had to go to three stores before we found all the things she wanted for her costume and the Halloween party she and her friends are having. If everything had been sold out, the world would've been close to ending."

He laughed.

Putting her drink on the table, she said, "I'm sure you think that's funny. Count yourself lucky that you have a son, and not a daughter. The drama at times is unbelievable. There's no way I could've been like that when I was younger."

From behind her, Allie answered, "Liar. Someone else may've invented drama, but *you* perfect it when you don't get your way."

Everyone laughed.

"I'm not talking to you," Tess answered over her shoulder.

Jack looked at the waitress. "Scotch on the rocks. What are you two having?"

"Another beer," Bruce responded.

"I'm fine," Tess answered loudly. More people arriving and The Tuxedo's DJ playing 80's music had raised the noise level another notch.

"What are you drinking?" Jack asked.

"Chocolate martini." She raised her glass in a mock toast, "A girl's one true love—chocolate."

"Is that what you call it?" Bruce accepted his beer from the waitress.

Tess flipped her head back quickly. "It is! Ya'll may be married to lovely women, but I need to let you in on a little secret. We love our chocolate. It's always there to comfort us and make us feel better." She stopped to sip her drink. "And it's so faithful. It'll never leave our thighs or butts. Ever."

Jack looked down and then back at her. "Your thighs look okay to me."

She waved one hand to playfully hit his arm. "Why Jack, are you...?"

She stopped herself from saying "flirting with me," and now she was the vixen doing the flirting. Looking across the table, she saw Doug watching her every move.

Suddenly, she became aware of Jack's thumb resting along her back. Every once in awhile it would make a rubbing motion. When it did, shivers ran through her body. If anyone looked closely, they'd see goose bumps on her skin.

The artichoke dip being placed in the center of the table along with other appetizers seemed like the perfect mind distraction. She recovered quickly. "I need to remember to eat something so I'm okay to drive later."

"We can drive you home," Jack said, his thumb rubbing her back again.

Another wave of goose bumps went through her body. Not a good sign. *He's married. Married! Think of something else. Naked fat man. Yuck.* That made the dip in her stomach want to come back up.

"Thanks, but that's out of your way. Plus, wouldn't Elizabeth get upset if she heard you were driving inebriated women home?"

He leaned forward, and laughed with Bruce.

"That's a good one," Bruce said. "Jack, maybe you should've done that to give her a taste of her own medicine."

"True, but knowing her she'd have used it to explain why she needed to do the pool boy."

Tess held up her hand. "Okay, ya'll, why do I feel like I'm missing something here?"

"There's nothing to miss now that she's gone," Jack said. "Tess, you don't know drama until you've met Elizabeth."

He looked at Bruce. "Did I tell you the latest? She's made a mistake, and wants to move back."

"No!" Bruce exclaimed.

"Wants to 'try again.'"

"Okay, I'm still sitting out here in left field," Tess said playfully. "I hate not knowing what's going on."

Jack looked at her with a sadness in his eyes. "This is not a very happy subject. This is to be a time of celebration for you." Quietly—causing her to lean forward to hear—he said, "Maybe I'll fill you in some other time."

Tess heard Allie laughing behind her, and wanted to turn around to find out what was so funny. Yet, something was causing her to not move her attention from Jack's face. *Think naked fat man. Really fat, with a thong!*

She heard her name being called. Across the table, Doug was still looking at her. Had he said something to her?

Omigosh, was I staring at Jack? No, she was zoning out. That's what she'd tell Doug and anyone else who noticed?

Doug cleared his throat. "Tess, another drink?"

She shook her head.

Jack leaned forward, to whisper, "Allie can always drive you home, if you don't want me to."

"Thanks," she replied. Her phone went off. She thought she was saved until she saw Kevin's name and number.

Obviously, something was up for him to call her, and that *something* was probably that he couldn't take Claire for the weekend. She shook her head. He did this about every other one of his weekends.

"Excuse me," she said sliding off the chair.

"What's up?" Allie asked, when Tess accidentally knocked her chair.

"Kevin."

"Jerk. That only means one thing," Allie said.

"Yep." Tess walked near to the door where it was quieter.

She pressed the button on the phone. "What's up?"

"We have a slight problem that I don't know how to handle," he quickly said. "Leslie just called. She said Claire wants to go home. Leslie said she's been grumpy ever since she picked her up at your house. She thinks that maybe Claire got her period."

Tess closed her eyes and counted to ten slowly. She was suddenly angry at him and Leslie. She had wanted to socialize with friends tonight. Tonight was about her. Yet she couldn't because Leslie couldn't handle a little *period problem.*

Maybe this was a sign from somewhere that she shouldn't be attracted to Jack. This was her punishment for flirting.

"Fine," she said, hoping she sounded upset. "I'll

pick her up. Tell Leslie I'll be there, hopefully in the next half hour, depending on traffic."

"Thanks, Tess," Kevin said cheerfully. "I owe you one."

Like I'll ever get paid in this lifetime. She snapped her phone shut.

She called Allie over, explained the situation, and asked her to give her excuse as *a family situation*. "Bye everyone," she yelled over her shoulder, angry at having to leave the fun.

Fuming, she walked across the street to their building to get her car. Inhaling a deep breath, she needed to relax. She was mad at Kevin and Leslie, not Claire.

****

Jack pulled slowly onto Tess's tree-lined street. Big trees masked the fronts of the houses of the older, moneyed neighborhood, and the lives of the people who lived in them. He looked at the numbers on the mailboxes, and stopped when he saw hers.

He had waited awhile before asking Allie the specifics of Tess leaving. Once again Kevin, Tess's ex-husband, was backing out of taking Claire for the weekend. Through the rest of the conversation with Allie and Bruce, he learned Tess's address.

Picking up a bag and balancing the hot pizza box, he walked to her front door. No sooner had he pressed the doorbell than a miniature Tess opened the door. The resemblance between the two was remarkable—the same blonde, curly hair and cream-colored skin housing sharp, blue eyes.

"You must be Claire," he said. "Is your mom here?"

A look of suspicion quickly washed over the girl's face. Like her mother, she didn't hide her emotions well.

Tess appeared over Claire's shoulder. She had changed into jeans and a red pullover shirt.

"Have you eaten yet?" Jack asked, holding up the pizza. "I also picked up chocolate ice cream with chocolate chunks. I heard something about chocolate being a girl's favorite."

She gave him a small smile and took the pizza. "Come in," she said hesitantly, casting a glance in Claire's direction.

He had learned from his time with her that she liked to keep her family life private. She didn't introduce him to Claire immediately. For a brief moment, he felt like he was intruding into her world. Yet, it was a world he wanted to learn more about.

Still standing outside the door, he said, "I can go, if you'd like."

"No, no, no, you're here with food, so how can we turn you down? Come in." She smiled, more broadly this time, and stepped aside to let him pass. "I'm sorry. This is Claire. Claire, this is a friend from work, Jack Maristone."

Claire studied him intently. He wondered how many of her mom's friends she was actually introduced to.

"Claire's not feeling so great," Tess said softly.

"Mom! Please don't tell anyone." Claire blushed and stomped away.

Tess shrugged her shoulders. "This way," she said.

Jack followed her through the dining room to the right of the foyer. Ahead of him the vaulted-ceilinged family room had an entire wall covered with windows. Through the dusk, all he could see outside were large trees.

Off to the right was a large, brightly lit kitchen. Tess set the pizza on the island, and pulled plates from the cabinets.

"You didn't have to do this, you know." She smiled at him. "What do you want to drink? I have water, milk, OJ, Diet Dr Pepper, or I think I might have a bottle of red wine."

Opening the box, he said, "I'll have some wine, but only if you're having some."

As Tess walked into the dining room to get the wine, Claire said, "Cool, mom. He got our favorite with sausage, mushrooms, and spinach."

Tess came back into the kitchen with the bottle and looked at him suspiciously.

He shrugged. "You mentioned this was your favorite at Monte's Restaurant."

"I did?" she asked, handing him two wine glasses.

"Yes, you did." He smiled, not letting on he had picked up this information from Allie. He hoped Tess would soon be at ease.

"Okay, so how did you know where we lived?" She watched Claire carry her plate piled with pizza to the table.

"I got to talking to Allie and Bruce about your early leaving. I fished your address from Allie by pretending I knew someone else who lived up here." Jack poured the wine while she put two slices of pizza on each of their plates, and walked to the table.

"That's sneaky." With eyebrows knitting together, she asked, "So why the delivery guy impersonation?"

"Because Allie said that it seemed as though every time you get a chance to enjoy yourself, something comes up. She said you never have any fun. This was supposed to be your night to celebrate. You had one martini and a handful of chips. That doesn't exactly constitute a celebration."

Tess sipped her wine. She reached across the table and put her warm, soft hand over his. "Thanks for thinking of me, but you know you didn't need to do this. You have your own family to think about. What would they say if they learned you were up here in Roswell eating with me?"

"Nothing," he said. "No one's home."

"Oh."

"Which right now I'd like to *not* talk about." He cast a glance toward Claire and then refocused on Tess. "There are some things best left unsaid, or in private."

"I can relate."

She pulled her hand away. "I know that some people think I'm made of ice because, outside of my dates of late, I don't talk about my home life at work. It's my survival-slash-sanity instincts."

She leaned back in the chair to run her fingers through her hair. Her shirt fit snugly against her chest. Most times, her office clothes, while feminine, hid the figure that Jack wanted to feel against him. Even something as simple as her playing with her hair turned him on.

He turned his attention to his pizza. He couldn't watch Tess anymore. Not in this relaxed setting. His thoughts were taking him other places, and he was thankful when Claire broke his train of thought.

"Mom, can I have some of that ice cream?"

Before Tess could answer, he said, "Go ahead. That's what it's there for."

The corner of Claire's lip turned up in a smile exactly like her mom's. "Thanks, Mr. Maristone," she replied politely.

"Call me Jack," he said. He turned his attention back to Tess, watching her pick the mushrooms off the pizza and pop them into her mouth. "She's very well-mannered."

"I try." Tess covered her mouth to hide the food.

He turned in the chair to look at Claire scooping ice cream into a cup. "Claire, what do I have to bribe you with to get you to tell me some dirt on your mother?"

Without missing a beat, she answered. "Clothes and a kitten."

"A kitten?"

"Yep. I'd rather have a horse, but mom said no. When I asked for a dog, she said no to that, too. I keep going smaller, so now I'm at a kitten."

Tess interrupted, "Which grows into a cat. Look at that cat at the stable. It's almost the same size as a dog."

Claire continued as though her mom hadn't said anything. "I've wanted a pet for as long as I can remember, but mom keeps saying it's too much work. I'd take care of it. She wouldn't have to. And when I ask Nana or Dad they always say it's up to my mom." She rolled her eyes.

"Claire. I'll make you a deal. You help me with your mom, and I'll help you with that kitten."

Her face perked up for the first time since he arrived.

"You will? Cool! You have a deal, Mr. Maristone."

Tess interjected, "Hello! I'm sitting right here!"

Glaring at him when Claire went into the other room to watch TV, she asked, "Jack, what are you doing? I'm never going to hear the end of this now. I can see it already—cat pictures everywhere. I won't be surprised if I come home one day to see a litter box waiting."

"You have anything against cats? Allergic to them?" He stuck the last of his pizza into his mouth.

"No!" She pointed at his plate, "You want more?"

"No thanks," he said. "Don't change the subject. Now why can't she dream and go after something she wants. Isn't that what we do, as adults?" He was thinking about what he wanted.

"I guess." She propped her elbow on the table and rested her chin on her hand. "But a cat? Last thing I need is it dragging a dead animal in here."

She looked at him squarely in the eyes. "I need that as much as I love watching Doug try to find a way to get rid of me."

This was news to him. "What are you talking about?"

She leaned back in the chair. "I know you've been tied up with the transition of Maristone into Tullamore, but are you telling me you can't see how he is toward me?"

He shook his head.

"He's been slowly cleaning house ever since he transferred into our office. Granted, some of the people that are no longer here were dead weight. But others..." She shook her head slowly. "Well, let's just say he let some good people go because they wouldn't completely suck up to him. I know that if I hadn't brought in

Ryhan, I'd be packing my desk."

"Well, I'll put in a good word for you."

"Gee, thanks," she said, standing up to clear the plates. "Not sure how much good that would do? He seems to already think we are too buddy-buddy."

Jack followed her into the kitchen and handed her the plates to put into the dishwasher.

"I shouldn't have said it like that." She turned to look at him. "I just hope that *someone* will have my back if it ever gets bad."

What she didn't realize was just how much he would protect her. He wanted to take care of her, and be with her. "Well, I better get going. Claire looks tired, and you've got to get up in the morning."

As she walked him to the door, Tess said, "Thanks again for coming and feeding us. You know you didn't have to do that."

"I didn't mind. I finally got to see you completely outside of the work environment. And I got to meet Claire, who looks exactly like you, by the way. You're going to have your hands full with that one."

"Thanks…I guess." She stopped at the door.

He was close enough to see her chest rising up and down as she breathed. With him standing so close, she seemed flushed and wouldn't look at his face.

"You won't tell anyone what I said about Doug, will you?" she asked.

He put his finger under her chin, lifted her face, and kissed her warm lips. He saw and felt her surprise. She quickly pulled away.

"As long as you don't tell anyone about that."

Chapter Eleven

The end of October weather was abnormally warm, even for Atlanta. Tess sat by the enclosure in her jeans and cotton shirt watching Claire's horse riding lesson. Typically, she used this time to catch up on her reading. Today she couldn't focus on any of the words. She couldn't stop thinking of Jack's kiss from last night.

What was that all about? How could she possibly go to work on Monday and look him in his married face? Especially after the way his lips on hers made her want even more of him. She had kissed a co-worker. She needed to get a grip and put it out of her mind. *Think of it as just a pleasant dream.*

She had to focus on her other dilemma. *The Bet.* She had a little over two months left in which to go on four more dates or she'd be forced to sing. That was a date every other weekend until the end of the year. Kevin had better not shirk any more of his custodial duties, or she'd really be thrown off course. Even so, with no prospects in sight, it wasn't looking good.

Maybe she could hum the song at the conference. Or, maybe better yet—Doug would fire her by then.

She scratched the back of her head, hoping an idea would pop in. She could go home, call Dana and Allie, and see if they knew anyone. *Think, think, think*! It dawned on her that she had the card from that doctor she'd met at Kevin's wedding. He had said to call anytime. This looked like the time. She just needed to remember where she'd put his number and hoped it was not already thrown into the trash.

"Do you mind if I sit here?" a masculine voice next to her asked.

She looked at the very tall person belonging to the voice. The first thing she noticed was his thick, wavy hair. Really thick, almost unnatural, as if it was a wig.

"No, go ahead." She redirected her attention back to her daughter riding in the ring. Claire was guiding the horse over some jumps.

"Phil Jackson," Mr. Wavy Hair said, extending his hand toward her.

His handshake was so strong and fast, she thought he might pull her arm from its socket. She rubbed her shoulder a bit to make sure nothing had come loose.

"Tess Grayson," she said.

"Nice to meet you. I see you down here quite a bit with your daughter," he said. "My daughter, Emma, also takes lessons. That's her, over there." He pointed to a tall girl sitting very straight on her horse. "If it was up to her, she would live down here twenty-four/seven."

"Mine, too." Tess looked at him more closely. She didn't remember seeing him before. Then, again, she usually was doing other things besides checking out the men at the stable.

"Has your daughter asked for a horse for her birthday?"

"Birthdays, Christmas, and any other opportunity she can take advantage of." She put the magazines down next to her. "What about yours?"

"Oh yeah. She's pushing hard this year," he replied, never taking his eyes from her. "She's not giving up either. Drives me crazy."

"Tell me about it."

"What does your husband say?"

She paused briefly before answering, "I'm not married."

"I'm sorry to hear that." He shook his head and made some popping sounds with his mouth before he asked, "Do you want to get together sometime?"

Her brain perked up. Today might be her lucky day. *You're looking at possible date number two,* her mind yelled.

"Well…" Part of her brain was screaming *corny*!

"Do you like listening to live music? 'Cuz I know this place where people come dressed as their favorite artist to sing. Some of them are really good. Interested?"

"Sounds like fun, as long as I don't have to do the dressing up or singing."

"Nope, you don't have to," he said with a cheesy grin.

"Thank goodness."

"How about tonight?" he asked.

She was sure it was her look of surprise that caused him to look away briefly.

"I mean, um, you don't have to." Phil looked very embarrassed. "I'm usually not this forward. I, um, understand if you're busy."

"No, no, it's fine." She felt bad for him, but was thinking more about how things were looking up for her. Here, she wasn't even looking for a date and one literally fell into her lap. "Give me directions. I'll meet you there."

She wrote down the route he gave her to Trudee's

Ranch. "By the way, my mom, Trudee, owns the place."

At the conclusion of Claire's lesson, Phil walked mother and daughter to Tess's car. "I look forward to seeing you later tonight."

Once inside the car, she called and left a message with both Allie and Dana to say she was going on date number two to some ranch place.

"Claire, call your dad and tell him you're coming over in an hour."

****

Pulling into the dirt parking lot, Tess was convinced she'd made a wrong turn somewhere until the neon sign flashed "Trudee's Ranch."

Dana had called to find out exactly where she would be going that night. The surprise in Dana's voice caught her attention. "Once you see a show at Trudee's Ranch, you'll never forgot it…or the Elvis wanna-be." Dana could barely talk through her laughter. "The man must spend hours in front of his mirror practicing all Elvis's hip moves. He has them down perfectly."

Stepping from her new hybrid luxury car, Tess felt very out of place in her jeans and black top. Now she was having regrets about coming. She was over-dressed compared to the others walking into the place.

A punk rocker quickly overtook her in the parking lot. As she walked up the steps, she stopped to look at the four identically dressed guys. They were supposed to be some southern band. *Gawd, why can't I think of their names?* The beards looked authentic. A girl with short, spiked, pink hair stood on the porch smoking a cigar.

Opening the door, Tess prayed she would

immediately see Phil. She could use some insulation. It was like crashing a party and not knowing costumes were mandatory.

Instead she spied a woman working behind the bar with pink sponge curlers in her hair. Now she had seen everything. The woman poured drinks, oblivious to her own appearance. Tess slowly walked inside the crowded smoky bar, scanning the room for Phil. He was nowhere in sight.

The pink-curlered woman approached her. In a deep, smoker's voice mixed with her thick southern twang she said, "You must be Tess. Phil told me to be on the lookout for a purr-tee woman with curly hair. As soon as you walked in, I recognized ya. I'm Trudee, Phil's mamma."

"Nice to meet you." Tess stared at the curlers instead of making eye contact. She tried to decide who Trudee was dressed as. "Where's Phil?"

"Oh, he'll be out soon. He's getting ready for the show." Trudee yelled at the man behind the bar, "Hey, Barry, help me out, will ya? Stop flirting with 'em girls and get back to pouring drinks. Go heavy on the ice." She turned back to Tess. "Good help is so hard to find these days, don't you agree?"

Still staring at Trudee's curlers, Tess nodded. Her lips wouldn't form any words. Tess studied Trudee's red velour top, eighties-style stirrup pants, and gym shoes. When Tess looked once more back to the curlers, Trudee put her hand on the top of her head.

"Oh, silly me. I keep forgetting to take 'em out." She started unraveling each one and handed them to Tess to hold.

Tess blinked slowly at her. The woman actually

went out in public, wearing curlers. Surely any minute now someone was going to jump out and tell her to smile, that she was on *Candid Camera*. There was no other reason for all this bizarreness.

Trudee continued talking, "Whatta ya use in your hair to make it so curly? Is that a perm? I tried that once. Birdie took the curlers out and there was nothin'—not a single curl. So the two of us jumped in her pickup and drove to the drug store to get more. We bought two boxes and left it in for double the time. Tell ya what, that sure fried my hair. It just broke at the roots. Do ya put beer in your hair and then sleep in curlers? I heard that works. Regular beer or lite?"

Tess answered slowly, "Uh, no, this is natural."

"Aren't you the lucky one? How come all you purty girls get everthing? Life's not fair. Oh well," Trudee sighed. "Follow me. I've reserved a table near the stage for you."

Tess cleared her throat and extended her cupped sponge curler- filled hands toward Trudee.

"Oops. Silly me. Let me take those from you." She scooped them up and deposited them on the side of the busy bar. Surely a health-code violation.

Taking what seemed to be the longest route, Trudee weaved through the crowded room to the only table in the front holding a "Reserved" sign. Trudee shooed away the people sitting at the table. Tess tried to tell her it was okay and that she would prefer to sit at the bar instead. She was shushed and told that classy women don't sit at bars. Tess wanted to laugh.

Sitting at the table with her, Trudee began asking a series of questions. "Where do ya work? Where ya live? Who's your people?"

Tess tried to answer, but Trudee would talk with someone walking by or start another litany of questions. The woman's mouth never stopped moving.

When a waitress appeared, Trudee patted her hand, "It's on the house, dear. Any friend of Phil's is a friend of mine. You look like a wine drinker. We have Chardonnay or I can open up my best bottle of white Zinfandel. That's my favorite."

"I'll have a vodka and tonic, if that's okay?" Tess said.

Trudee silently studied Tess. "In a million years, I'd never take you for a hard drinker. Ya have to be careful." She leaned forward and whispered. "I'd hate for my son to get mixed up with an alcoholic. I mean, after everything he's been through."

Tess hated to admit her interest was piqued. "What do you mean?"

"It's been difficult for him ever since that tart of a wife left him. She run off with the Ferris wheel operator from the county fair last year. Phil's been working two jobs to support him and Emma. I'm so glad he has finally met someone who seems like a nice girl, with good manners."

Tess was thankful when her drink arrived. The woman was talking as if she and Phil were going to walk down the wedding aisle tomorrow afternoon.

"Two jobs?"

"Yeah. His day job as an accountant, and on the weekends he moonlights here as Elvis. He's quite good at it. He's kept this place in business with his impersonation."

Tess practically spit the vodka out all over Trudee's velour top. Surely, she hadn't heard right.

Was Phil the Elvis of Dana's story?

Trudee, still talking, was completely oblivious to Tess's sudden shock. "Wait 'til ya see his new outfit. I helped him sew it. It looks like the real thing, right down to the number of sequins. Ya know, he's finally decided to grow in his sideburns. I'm so tired of helping him glue hair to his face."

This was worse than the proverbial nightmare where she couldn't wake up. She was hoping her face didn't show her true emotions. She wanted to forget the bet and run from this place in terror. She picked up her glass and downed the drink in one gulp. She needed all the help she could get to take the edge off.

Trudee continued to talk while Tess flagged down the waitress and pointed at her empty glass.

When a new glass arrived, Trudee finally stopped talking to stare at Tess and the empty glass. She patted Tess's hand. "Dear, that's two drinks, ya know. You need to slow down so you can enjoy the show. I gotta see if Phil needs help. Please, don't drink too much."

The only way I can enjoy this, Tess thought, *is if I don't remember it. My date is Elvis, who I thought was dead.*

Without warning, the lights dimmed and the audience became silent. When Elvis, aka her date, came onto the stage, the crowd went wild. The noise was deafening. "Thank you. Thank you very much." The audience, minus Tess, whistled and went crazy. She stared at Phil in the white sequined suit that every Elvis look-alike in Vegas wore. Trudee appeared and sat down next to her. "Didn't I tell you the costume looked great?"

Phil continued talking. "I'd like to thank you very

much for coming out tonight. I'm especially grateful for Tess Grayson who came by tonight. Tess is a very special person to me."

Tess hoped to pass out. Had he just said her name aloud? Her first *and* last name? This wasn't happening. Her face grew warm, and she was about to pick up the newest drink the waitress had brought while Trudee was backstage. She felt every eye in the place on her. She looked up to see Phil signaling her to stand up. Her knees were shaking under the table. They wouldn't hold her if she did try to stand.

"I dedicate this song to my Tess." He started singing "Love Me Tender."

That was it. She was at the top of her humiliation ladder, and it was a long way down to normalcy. When his mother's back was turned, she drank the entire glass until the ice was dry. She rubbed her forehead, hoping the pain of the night would go away. She hoped she wouldn't hyperventilate. Though she wasn't an Elvis fan, she had to admit that he sounded halfway decent.

Women flocked to the stage as he started singing "Ain't Nothing But a Hound Dog" gyrating his hips just like the real Elvis. When some of the women touched him, it seemed to feed his enjoyment of his stage performance.

At the end of his set, he jumped off the stage, leaned down, and gave her a quick peck on the cheek. She could see the stage make-up melting from his face.

"Well, what do you think?" he asked with a big grin, taking the seat his mother had just vacated.

Tess shook her head in multiple directions wondering how to answer. Her mouth came through before her brain could integrate. "Not bad." She hoped she sounded convincing. "I have to ask, what got you into this?"

Before he could answer, a woman with as much cleavage as possible showing came running up to Phil and kissed him on the lips. Another, with very large, fake breasts, sat on his lap, and put Phil's hand on top of her large chest. In a soft seductive voice, she cooed, "Oh, Elvis baby, can you feel my heart beating?"

Tess was tempted to say "Honey, he can't feel anything through all the silicon."

Trudee once again materialized from thin air and told the girls to get lost because her son already had a girl.

Tess turned her attention to the punk rocker now on the stage screeching a song she could barely make out the words to. *Now here's someone who sounds worse singing than me.*

Phil sipped on the water his mother had brought over. "To answer your question, I've always been a big fan of Elvis. About a year ago, Momma was close to having to file for bankruptcy on this place. I came up with the idea for having Impersonator Night. We built a makeshift stage and for a while, I was the only act. Word got out and more and more people started to come. Now it's become a landmark place."

Landmark place? Was he kidding or being serious? Tess was thankful when another drink appeared before her. She could feel herself getting tipsy, but not too far gone to notice the woman coming up, handing Phil her card, and saying, "Call me."

As much as she hadn't wanted to admit she was with him, couldn't these women see he had a date? Was she invisible? She watched him smile at the card and then back at the woman as he tucked the *carte de visite* into a pocket. The woman blew an air kiss before wiggling her hips as she walked away.

When she left, Tess asked, "So, I'm guessing you like doing this."

"I do. During the day, Phil Jackson is a boring accountant. But, you know, when I put this outfit on, I feel like a totally different person. I'm no longer seen as a geek. I'm lively and entertaining. Do you think that's weird?"

She didn't trust herself to answer. She shook her head as she sipped slowly on the drink in front of her. In this place, nothing any longer seemed weird. Not even the singer on the stage pretending she was a virgin with her cone-like bra made of tin foil.

Tess half listened as he talked about his shows and how he wanted to further extend his aspirations. He asked her for suggestions. Like his mother, as soon as she started to talk, he interrupted her.

Soon, the crowd started chanting for Elvis. He gave her a look and headed for the stage. She stood up at the same time and asked him for directions to the ladies' room. She felt like she was going to pass out. That would be a blessing.

Once inside the bathroom, she locked herself inside a stall and fished her phone from her purse. Dana picked up on the second ring.

"Come save me," Tess said loudly, knowing she had slurred her words.

She sat on the edge of the toilet and let her face press against the coldness of the tile wall. She was pathetic. Wouldn't management at Tullamore love to see her now? Inebriated *and* on a date with Elvis.

Nothing could possibly top this night.

The door opened and voices on the other side could be heard. One was Trudee's. "Did you see how much vodka she drank? I told the waitress to start watering them down. She really looked like a wine drinker. I offered her white Zinfandel, but she turned her nose up at it. I was even going to offer her my best bottle."

"Maybe she doesn't like it," said an equally thick twang.

"Who don't like white Zinfandel? It's one of the best wines ever made," Trudee said seriously.

Tess pulled her feet off the floor and pushed them on the edge of the toilet stall door hoping in her tipsy state she wouldn't fall into the toilet bowl.

Trudee continued, "Did you see the way Phil looks at her? Anyone can see he's head over heels for her. I saw her get up when Phil headed for the stage. Did you see where she got to?"

"Nope."

"Neither did I. I hope she didn't take off without saying goodbye," Trudee snorted. "I was going to make my meatloaf for dinner tomorrow and invite her."

Tess covered her mouth, hoping they couldn't hear her breathe. She was starting to sober up after hearing Trudee on the other side of the door. The door opened again and the restroom became quiet. Tess leaned down to look out from under the stall door. She couldn't see any legs. She slowly let herself out of the stall.

Tiptoeing to the door, she opened it and peered out. No sign of Trudee or Phil. Attempting to both appear casual *and* walk straight, she headed for the front door. Focused on her efforts, she did not see Trudee until the interception. Sans her outlandish appearance, the woman could be a spy.

"Tess," she yelled over the crowd. "Where were you?"

She lied. "The line for the women's room was too long, so I went into the men's bathroom. The smell in there is nauseating. I'm going outside for some fresh air. Can I get a glass of water?"

Trudee brought her a large glass of ice water.

"Thanks," she said, trying to focus. "Do you mind if I take this outside?"

"Not at all. Don't stay too long. Elvis is going back up on stage. You don't want to miss his finale. It makes the crowd go nuts."

Yeah, and I don't want to get sick all over the place either. Tess looked at the white polyester-suited Phil taking the stage and starting to move his hips. She pushed through the door to breathe in the cool, night air. Taking deep breaths, she walked back and forth in front of the building while drinking her water.

Headlights were coming toward her. They stopped right next to her. Hopefully the aliens had come to return her to her planet of origin—Earth. Better yet, it was her saviors, Dana and Harry. The door opened and Harry jumped from the car. She handed her purse to her brother and pointed to where her vehicle was. She then climbed into the car with Dana.

"Don't ask me. I'll fill you in tomorrow," she said before closing her eyes. "I'm not sure which is going to hurt more tomorrow—my head from the hangover, or my pride just remembering tonight."

The last thing she remembered hearing was Dana's laughter.

Chapter Twelve

The man was sadistic. He was Lucifer in a business suit. Scheduling the monthly staff meeting on a Monday morning at seven-thirty was purely evil and hateful. Doug didn't even provide coffee and pastries like their old manager, Mitch had. Also Mitch's meetings were on Thursdays at eight-thirty—so much more civilized.

If Doug was going to call these meetings so early, why couldn't he respectfully start them on time? No, instead he left plenty of time for small talk. Tess sipped on her hot coffee. In the chair next to her, Allie sat telling everyone about Tess's date, as if she had been there.

Ellen, the department brown-noser, was sitting across the table in a too-sheer blouse. Apparently no one had informed her that a nightclub wasn't opening in their building anytime soon. "She's kidding us, right, Tess? I think you're making this up. I've never heard of anyone dressing like Elvis."

I guess you haven't been to Las Vegas in awhile. "Yes, he was wearing the sequined jackets and glued-on sideburns to look like the King." Tess set her coffee down.

"You ain't nothin' but a hound-dog, cryin' all the time," Jeff Parker sang from the other end of the table.

Tess pretended to rub her cheek, with her middle

finger sticking up.

Ellen looked down her nose. "Where did you meet him?"

"He takes his daughter to the same riding school as mine."

Ellen still looked skeptical. "And you didn't know when he asked you out that he liked to dress like Elvis?"

"No, he was dressed like a normal person in jeans and a sweatshirt. No sideburns or anything." Tess wanted to toss her coffee at Ellen to get her to shut up. The woman was completely annoying.

Allie broke her from that thought when she elbowed her. "Tell them about his mother and the curlers. Oh, never mind, I will."

"Okay, no more about the date from hell," Tess said.

Doug stared at her as if she had just fallen out of a UFO. Clearing his throat, he said, "Obviously, Tess exhibited some bad judgment over the weekend and let's hope she's learned from her mistake. Now, let's get to the business at hand."

"I want to know how it ended," Jack asked from behind her.

She flipped around in her chair so fast, she almost got whiplash. Sitting with their backs against the wall were Jack and Bruce. When had they come in?

Jack must think she was a complete nut job. First Friday night, and now this! Her face felt like it was on fire. There was no way he'd ever take her seriously again.

She turned back to face those at the table, hoping that the redness would quickly disappear from her face.

"I hid in the bathroom and called my sister-in-law to come rescue me."

Allie was trying to stifle a laugh. "Dana told me you broke speed records getting into her SUV."

"Well, I just think it says a lot about a guy who can meet someone and feel comfortable showing his other side right away," Tess's assistant, Maggie, whispered. "I think you are being too hard on him. I need to get directions to this place. It sounds like fun. Maybe I want to meet him."

Tess put her head on the table and hoped the ground would open up and eat her alive. While the rehashing of her fiasco was entertainment for the others, it was torture for her.

Clearly, from the glaring stare Doug gave her, he wasn't amused.

And to top it off, she could feel Jack's gaze searing into the back of her neck.

Chapter Thirteen

"You did tell Jeff to meet us in the lobby, didn't you?" Doug asked impatiently, for the fifth time.

No, you big over-stuffed, cheap-cologne-smelling dummy. I told him to meet us at the clients', while you and I waited here in our building. His cologne was making her sick.

Tess couldn't look at him as she nodded her head. She consulted her watch. There was at least five minutes to go before they were technically scheduled to leave.

When the elevator doors opened, Jeff Parker walked out. "Sorry I'm late." He set the box he was carrying on the ground. "I realized I was a binder short and asked Maggie to make another."

She was about to tell him thanks when she heard a familiar voice call her name. She didn't need to turn around. The shock on Jeff's face told her Phil was dressed as a deceased crooner.

Time shifted into slow motion as she turned to see Elvis in a red sequined suit holding a huge arrangement of roses. He even had on sunglasses resembling those worn by Elvis in his later years.

Her mind emptied of any thought. The lobby became very quiet and still as people stopped and stared.

"Sorry about the other night, sugar. The crowd was

great, don't you think?" he asked.

Did he call her "sugar"? She blinked several times, but he was still there each time she opened her eyes.

Oblivious to all the people watching them, Phil continued, "It wasn't until I finally heard 'last call', that I realized I'd been neglecting you. I brought these to say I'm sorry, and I want to make it up to you."

Speak! Say something!

She saw that Doug looked completely annoyed with her. On her other side were Jeff and Bruce, both of whom were trying not to fall out laughing.

She licked her lips. Her mouth felt like a desert. She had to get out of this. *Focus!* "Phil? Can we talk about this some other time?" she asked. "I, um, am getting ready to head off to a meeting. Um, let me call you, okay?"

"Sure thing, baby," he drawled sounding just like the King. "I'll leave these with the guard and you can get them later."

Baby? Phil. Elvis. Whatever his name was, was calling her "baby"! Now this was too much. Her legs felt like they were going to give way. This had to feel worse than singing on stage at the conference's talent show.

She nodded a few times in bobble-head doll fashion. "Good idea," she finally managed to get her mouth to say.

In a daze, and not really caring if she appeared rude, she walked toward the glass doors that led outside. She needed fresh air to bring her back to reality.

"I take it that was Saturday night's dream date?" Jeff tried not to laugh.

She nodded slowly, not wanting to see the reaction on Doug's face.

"That's pretty funny that he thought he had neglected you when, in fact, you ran away." Jeff, no longer able to control himself, started laughing uncontrollably.

She spun around. "Shut up!" she said, flustered. "My personal life is my own business."

"That's correct," Doug said with unusual firmness. "Let's see what *we* can do to keep it that way in the future, Tess."

She nodded, walked to her car, and handed Jeff the keys. After the lobby episode, there was no way she could concentrate on driving. She needed time to mentally prepare for the meeting ahead. The client was probably not going to take it well that Tess would only be playing a secondary role on their account. She was going to turning over their account to Jeff now that she needed to focus on Ryhan.

Chapter Fourteen

"Tess. Here it is!" Allie exclaimed, holding up a very thin negligee. "This is the one Jon saw in the catalog and made several comments about. I can't believe I finally found it. You don't know how long I've been looking for this."

Tess, along with a few other shoppers in the lingerie store looked at Allie waving the barely-there piece of lace. She looked around and saw that there were nearly as many men in the shop as women.

Some men appeared very cool and right at home in the endless displays of bras, panties, silky nightgowns and teddies. Others looked downright uncomfortable as if, at any moment, one of the sales ladies might be asking them if they would like to try on the garments.

On the other side of the store was a vaguely familiar man thumbing through a rack filled with bathrobes. While Allie skipped off to the changing room, Tess absently flipped through the pajama-laden hangers in front of her. She wracked her brain to figure out where she'd seen him. Maybe he worked at one of the other companies in her building.

A sales lady tapped her on the shoulder. In a very fake British accent, she said, "Your friend would like to see you. Right this way, please."

Holding a pair of pink flannel pajamas, Tess followed the stick-thin woman to the changing room area.

"What is it?" Tess asked Allie from outside the room.

"Is there anyone around?"

Tess looked both ways. "Just me," she answered.

The door popped opened, and Allie stood practically naked in the red lace negligee.

"Isn't it great?" Allie held out her arms, and did a slow, seductive turn. "Don't I look sexy?"

Tess turned her head and closed her eyes. "Ohmigod, Allie, I don't need to see this." Reaching out, she slammed the door. "Get some clothes on."

"You're such a prude. You have the same stuff I've got. It's not like you haven't seen it before!" Allie shouted from behind the closed door. "Just because you're in a dry spell and not even remotely near getting any doesn't mean the rest of us can't dress like this to get ours. Seriously, it wouldn't hurt for you to buy stuff along this line to wear under your work clothes. I'll bet you haven't even worn your birthday thong yet."

"Yeah, I just can't wait to have an all-day wedgie and be completely miserable. The last thing I'd feel is sexy."

"You can't know until you try," Allie said. "I'll meet you out there, but we are not leaving until we update your foundation garments. Should things ever get heated on one of your dates, you won't embarrass yourself by what is underneath your clothes—meaning those ugly granny panties. You need to say goodbye to them. Feel sexy!"

"No one is seeing what I am wearing under my clothes." Tess immediately stopped when she saw a young couple listening to their conversation. She stared back at them before returning to the pajama rack.

"You're looking in the wrong place," Allie said when she finally emerged from the changing room. "Pink *flannel* is not sexy. Come over here to these silk ones. Let's look for your size. Then we're buying you all silk panties. It's like having a secret when you're wearing these."

Tess again saw the man looking through another rack of clothes. Leaning close to Allie, she said, "See that guy over there? He looks familiar."

As if hearing her, he looked at them. They simultaneously looked down at the silk pajamas in front of them.

"He's still looking at us," Allie said in a loud whisper. "I think he heard you. Wait, he's walking toward us."

Tess looked up as he made his way over.

"I know you," he said from the opposite side of the pajama rack. "You were at Kevin and Leslie's wedding, weren't you?"

Suddenly, she remembered the doctor who was a friend of the cousin of someone.

"Mark Raymond," he said, extending his hand toward her.

"Tess Grayson," she said shaking the stretched out appendage.

"Doing some shopping, I see." With a knowing smile on his face, he looked at the negligee draped over Allie's arm and the red silk pajamas in her hands.

"Not really," Tess said.

"Yes, we are," Allie interjected, rather authoritatively. "Tess's closet sustained some water damage, so we have to replace *all* her clothes."

"Water damage?" Mark asked skeptically.

Turning toward Allie, Tess was about to ask the same question.

"Yep. Tess was having a new fire alarm with a sprinkler system installed in the house. The technician accidentally set it off in her bedroom and it soaked everything. Of course, everything was damaged. The alarm company agreed to replace all her clothes and furniture, so here we are," Allie said, as if the lie had actually taken place. "What about you, Mr. Raymond?"

"Just checking out the bathrobes. My sister keeps talking about how she likes the robes here," Mark answered. "I might want to invest in some for my practice."

Tess and Allie didn't say anything.

"See you around, and good luck shopping," he said, with a grin.

"Thanks." Tess felt a sharp jab as Allie kicked her ankle.

He stopped and walked back to them. "By the way," he said, "I remember having a good time with you at the wedding, Tess. I gave you my card, but never heard from you. I was...well, wondering if you wanted to get together sometime?"

Another hard kick to her foot. "Sure, I'd like that."

"Are you free next Saturday evening?" he asked.

"She is," Allie answered.

"Yes, I think I am," Tess replied, feeling another kick. *Okay, that's it. Once he walks away, I'm going to take Allie down, right here in the store.*

"Good." He offered her another of his business cards.

She reached into her purse for one of her own.

Wouldn't Doug love to know she was handing out her card for personal reasons?

"Thanks," she said. "Call me if anything changes."

After he walked away, Tess spun around to look at her friend. "Water damage? Where did you come up with that one? And I better not have any bruises on my leg from you kicking me."

"Oh, and what was I to say? I'm here trying to get my friend out of her granny panties and into something more sexy? Care to comment on which you would prefer to see Tess in? Flannel or silk?" Allie said very melodramatically. "No one will want a second date if you keep wearing old-lady panties. He's really cute, by the way. Really good-looking. I actually think I just came."

"Oh, you're disgusting," Tess said, and started to walk away.

"I'm just being honest. By the way, I'm sure any woman he dates wears either silk or nothing at all. And what was he talking about? His 'practice'?" Allie grabbed his card from Tess's hand. "Oh? A doctor? Maybe a sex therapist? Well, babe, since you have just scored a date with Mr. Sexy Man of the Year, we are absolutely doing away with what you have and replacing all of it. I might even pay Claire to make sure it is all thrown away."

Tess stood with her hands on her hips.

"And I don't want to hear any complaints, or I'll start a nasty rumor about you."

"Yeah? Like what?"

"That you fantasize about doing a threesome with Doug and Elvis."

"I think I'm gonna be sick. You're flipping

unbelievable. No one would ever believe that, anyway."

"Wanna bet?" Allie held up a lacy bra and panty set in front of Tess. "I can sound very convincing. Everyone knows about the tension between you and Doug. I'll just explain it is all sexual."

Tess sighed. At least she was up to date number three, and it was only the first week of November.

****

Pulling into the hospital parking lot, Tess was still confused as to why Mark had called just as she was about to leave home and asked her to meet him there. Yes, he was a doctor, but meeting at the hospital was just weird.

Maybe he was getting off work late, and felt it would be easier for them to go to one of the nearby restaurants. She had seen a new restaurant that she had been wanting to try.

She saw the sign from the parking lot to the lobby, where she was to meet him. She looked down the street, figured the restaurant was about a block-and-a-half away. She could walk it in her new leather boots.

Mark was not in the crowded lobby. She paced by the front corner window, but stopped when she saw an older gentleman watching her intently. She probably seemed like a worried family member. She sat down and flipped through a magazine.

After about fifteen minutes she was starting to feel agitated. She was about to call him, when she saw him walking down the hall toward her. She stood up.

"Sorry, I'm late." He was still wearing his white lab coat. "What a night and day it's been. My relief, Dr. Martin, called in sick. Another doctor and I are splitting his shift."

"So when are you off?" she asked.

"Not 'til midnight." He took her arm and steered her away from the folks listening to their conversation.

"Did you want to reschedule?" she asked.

"No. I need a break and figured we could grab something in the cafeteria."

What? We're going to be eating hospital food for our date?

"Hope you don't mind," he continued. "It's a full moon, so it seems like every pregnant woman in Atlanta wants to deliver right now. The last one didn't seem to want to come. The mother was screaming and cursing at me and everyone else in the room. By the time it was over, I actually felt sorry for the husband."

She looked at him oddly. "You're an OB?" she asked tentatively.

"Yep," he replied.

It wasn't possible! He was too good-looking to be an OB/GYN! They have to be old, or at least just average looking. How could women disrobe and be naked in front of him without feeling self-conscious about it? If he walked into her examination room, she would probably walk out in her paper towel cover-up and demand to see another doctor. She would line them up and take the ugliest one.

Mark handed her a tray at the entrance of the hospital cafeteria.

She shook her head. "I'll just have some sweet tea." She might be desperate for a date to get through the bet, but she had her dignity. She had to draw the line at eating hospital food. She literally couldn't stomach it.

"It's on the house," he said. He pulled a prewrapped sandwich from the cooler, grabbed a cup of coffee, sour cream and onion chips, and red Jell-O. She thought she was going to be sick just looking at the food. She looked at his tray and back to him. *I'm wearing lace underwear for this?*

She followed him to a table in the center of the cafeteria. When they sat down, he took a large bite of food and said, "Thanks for being a good sport about this, Tess. I don't think many women would be, but there's no way I can leave. I have a feeling that as soon as I step outside this building, three women will try to deliver at once and I'll be running between the rooms."

He took another big bite of his sandwich, and stuffed about five chips in his mouth at the same time. He was right. Most women wouldn't put up with this. In fact, if it weren't for that stupid bet, she would have probably laughed in his face at the suggestion of dining in a hospital cafeteria.

Then again, he didn't realize how badly she needed this date. She was over worrying about how this would appear to the average person. She just needed to get through this.

"Have you replaced all your clothes from the sprinkler accident?" he asked, with his mouth full of ham and cheese.

"What?" She realized from the smirk on his face that he was on to Allie's ruse. She sighed. "There, um, really wasn't an accident. You see, my friend made that up. She knew I would be mortified being seen with panties in my hand."

There was mayonnaise at the corner of his mouth, and she had to point several times to the corner of her lips before he understood. He picked up a stack of napkins and wiped.

"I find that hard to believe." He lifted the chip bag and poured the remaining crumbs into his mouth. "I think you're one of the most confident women I've ever met. I mean, how many women would go to their ex-husband's wedding? Not many. And how many can hold a red lace bra and a silk nightgown while carrying on a normal conversation with a man they met only once before? About the same number, I'll tell you that."

She was stumped for an answer, but was rescued when his beeper went off. He pulled it from his hip and looked at it.

"Well, I need to get going. There's six mothers up there, all close to delivering. This is going to be one heck of a night. This one's at ten centimeters and ready to push." He stood and stuffed the last of his sandwich in his mouth.

Now, there's something I didn't need to know.

"We gotta do this again," he said, before rushing out of the cafeteria.

Over my dead body! She slowly walked to the garbage can to throw away her paper cup. She was ready to walk out unnoticed, when she saw Trudee and Phil, coming toward her. *Great!*

"Tess! Is that you?" Phil asked.

No. It's someone who looks exactly like me. She plastered a smile on her face. *Why is this happening to me?*

"What are you doing here?" Phil asked.

The lie poured from her lips. "Visiting a friend."

Phil looked worried. Trudee eyed her suspiciously.

"Are they all right?" Phil asked.

"Yes. After visiting, I got a little hungry so decided

to grab something here before going home," she lied. "What are ya'll doing here?"

Trudee piped up. "We were on the children's floor, trying to bring some cheer. I know. Why don't we go back to my house? I can warm up some leftover meatloaf and mashed potatoes."

Does this woman cook anything besides meatloaf? I want to throw myself on a mound of fire ants. "Maybe some other time, Trudee. I spent more time here than I expected, and I need to get home to Claire." The fibs continued to spew from her mouth. Tonight she appreciated her mouth taking over. Her brain didn't need to work.

Trudee didn't give up. "You can bring Claire."

Tess forced the smile on her face. "Well, no, Claire doesn't like meatloaf. If you don't mind, I'll just take a rain check."

Tess froze in shock as Phil took her hand in his and brought it to his lips. "I'll take you up on it."

"Uh, okay." She turned to walk quickly from the hospital.

As soon as this bet was over, she was definitely giving up on men.

****

"Well, here they all come," Bruce said, pointing to Jeff, Tess, Allie, and another woman Jack was unfamiliar with.

"Every Tuesday morning, they come down here to the cafeteria to catch up. I've had the privilege to join them a time or two. They seem like really good people—people we might have hired at Maristone," Bruce continued.

Jack nodded, pouring milk into his coffee mug.

"Say, Jack, have you noticed how Tess can be so outgoing and personable, and yet so private at other times?"

"Not really," Jack lied. He followed Bruce to a nearby table. They were here to go over some items for the week while he ate his breakfast of yogurt and toast. He needed to get out of his office where the phone constantly rang and people dropped by.

He had a clear view of Tess's profile. He watched her constantly pushing her hair over her shoulder. A woman with bright red hair sat down across from her.

"So, I heard you had another exciting date this weekend," the red-haired woman commented loudly.

Tess's jaw appeared tense as she turned to look at Allie. "Did you put an announcement in the paper? Or is there something posted on the Intranet?"

"Both."

"So tell me about it. Was he cute?" the redhead inquired.

Jack leaned forward to hear what Tess said.

"He was cute, all right. The problem is, he's an OB/GYN."

"Eeww," the redhead shrieked, making a face. "That's gross!"

"Let me put it this way, he was beyond good-looking." Tess picked at the muffin sitting in front of Allie.

"That's even worse." Allie loudly slapped Tess's hand from her food. "OB's shouldn't be good-looking."

"Why do women get freaked out by that?" Jeff asked. "So what if he's good-looking?"

Tess said pointedly, "Would you date a sexy, drop-dead gorgeous lady doctor who told you to 'bend over and cough' in a very seductive voice?"

"Okay. Gotcha!" Jeff exclaimed.

"Thought so." Tess sat back in her chair with a smug look.

Jack wanted to join the laughter at their table once she finished telling about her latest escapade. She seemed to be creating a following who wanted to hear about her dating life, him included.

So why did she avoid him and his dinner invitations? He didn't want to contemplate that maybe she wanted someone her own age.

"Oh, it gets better," Tess added. "On my way out, I ran into Phil and Trudee, who luckily wasn't wearing curlers. They invited me over for leftover meatloaf."

Allie was snickering and holding her sides. "Meatloaf?"

"Who's Phil?" Jeff asked chuckling.

"Elvis."

Everyone at the table said "Oh," in unison, and laughed hard.

Jack studied Tess. It was no wonder she had an active dating life. Men had to not only be drawn to her looks and animated personality, but also her air of confidence. She walked with her shoulders straight and her head held high. She never seemed to accept defeat. When Doug berated her in front of others, she remained calm and composed.

"So, what are you doing for lunch?" the redhead asked. "That new soup-and-salad place opened up down the block from here. I think it's called the Salad Plate. Want to try it?"

Tess tilted her head when she spoke. "Can't. I'm meeting Harry for lunch today."

Allie looked over. "How's that going?"

She sighed loudly. "I don't know sometimes. I'm keeping my fingers crossed that he'll come to his senses and admit how he really feels. I, for one, am not ready to give up. I sure hope he doesn't."

Jack finished his coffee, wondering who Harry was. *What was I thinking? I never stood a chance with Tess.* She might not have a man at her side, but it seemed her heart belonged to someone named Harry. That must be was why she rejected his offers. But then, why go on these dates with these other men? It made no sense.

Chapter Fifteen

Her stomach growled so loudly, Tess was convinced people two towns over could hear it. She looked at her watch. It was barely past eleven o'clock. It was too early for her to be this hungry. Once again, her stomach made a sound to remind her it wanted food. And now!

She was about to pick up the phone and see if Bruce and Jack wanted to go to lunch. It had become routine for her to go with them for lunch every few weeks. The more she worked with Bruce, the more she had liked him.

She'd learned all about his wife, Louisa, who was very involved with special needs children. Also, it had come as a surprise that he liked to rock climb as well as hang glide. He didn't look like the daring type; he looked more along the times of Mr. Ultra Safety.

At first, it had been a bit odd to be around Jack after he had kissed her that night. She didn't feel like she could even look him in the face without blushing. It was hard not to remember how tender his lips were on hers, and how the kiss had sent a jolt of fire through her veins. If Claire hadn't been in the other room, she just might have wrapped her arms around his neck to continue.

She needed to keep her wits about her. He was work, and Doug was once again riding her about everything.

Over time, it became easier to have lunch with him. Jack seemed to recognize it, too. He would talk of Joel and his college classes. He shared stories of the places he sailed and scuba dove. One day at lunch he brought in pictures he had taken on some of his dives.

Next to Jack and Bruce, she felt like a slug. What did she do? Well, she did like to ski and snorkel, but mostly these days there was watching old movies and listening to opera recordings.

Maggie, her assistant, knocked on her doorframe just as Bruce's office phone rang. Before he could answer, Tess hung up the telephone.

"There's a Mr. Phil Jackson at the front desk." Maggie gave her usual inquisitive look. "He said it was personal."

Closing her eyes, Tess tried to picture a happy place and took five deep yoga breaths. *Why is he here?*

"Tess?" Maggie inquired. "I can go down and see him if you want."

She answered quickly. "No, that's fine," she said picking up her purse. "I'll go meet him, and then be back after lunch."

She had one mission: Get him out of the building before they were seen together by too many people. They'd go to the little place around the corner before the lunch crowd started.

Hurrying to the reception area, she prayed, *Please, please, please do not be dressed as Elvis!* As soon as she rounded the corner, her heart sank five floors. At least he was half-normal, wearing jeans with his shiny blue-sequined jacket and those old seventies-style sunglasses.

Snapping her gum, the receptionist stared at him as if the circus had stopped by their office.

Walking calmly up to him, Tess said, "Phil. What a surprise! You want to go outside?"

"Sure thing, baby." He planted a wet kiss on her cheek.

Before she got back that afternoon, the office would be buzzing about her lobby encounter. Walking toward the elevator, she pulled on his sleeve for him to follow.

As soon as the elevator doors closed she whispered. "Stop calling me 'baby'."

"Sure thing, sugar."

Closing her eyes, she shook her head quickly back and forth. Opening one eye a bit, she added, "Don't call me that either."

"What do you want me to call you?"

In exasperation she said, "'Tess' would be a good start." *Why doesn't he get it?*

They remained silent. She glanced up at the overcast skies wondering if it was going to rain as they walked outside and along the path next to the water fountain.

Loudly, he said, "I hope I'm not taking you from anything…Tess."

"You were a welcome interruption. I was hungry and wondered what I was going to do for lunch," she lied. "Do you want to grab something?"

"I'd love to, but I'm afraid, I don't have very much time. I have an appointment in a little bit." He stopped in front of the fountain, stuffing his hands in his pockets and rolling back and forth on the balls of his feet.

She sat on the edge of the fountain and patted the

spot next to her. He continued to stand.

"I need to ask you something," he finally said. "You're a really smart woman with a good head on your shoulders, so I know you'll be honest and upfront with me."

Her mind sent up warning signals. All of her sweat glands went into overdrive. *Oh great! He's going to ask if I like the jacket.*

He slowly licked his lips as he looked at her. "You're the only one who I feel really comfortable discussing this with."

It's the jacket. I know it is.

"I'm thinking about giving up my accounting job to become Elvis full time."

"What?" She hadn't meant to say the word aloud.

"You think it's a bad idea?" His eyes suddenly looked worried.

Was he serious? They'd had one *sort-of* date, and three less-than-five-minute conversations. Was he actually going to let this life decision rest on her? Was he really asking her if he should give up a stable job to play dress-up every day? This wasn't happening.

She watched the fountain's water for a minute before looking back at him. He was patiently waiting for an answer. This was rather comical, and yet he was so earnest.

She swallowed deeply. "You need to follow what is in your heart and what makes you happy. No one can tell you what you should do. Only you know that." She impressed herself with the reply.

"So, you don't think this is a crazy idea?"

"Phil, I didn't say that. I just think you need to weigh the pros and cons before you decide." As usual, her brain seemed to be a few steps behind her mouth. "Can I ask how this crossroads came about?"

"When I first started the Elvis impersonations, I didn't tell a soul. But when you came to see me, it didn't faze you in the least that I was dressed like someone else. After that, I went out a few times in public dressed like this, and you would not believe the reactions. People I don't even know come up and talk to me as if I really am the King. I'm no longer the shy geek down in accounting. I'm a new person. You did that for me," he said.

Her head was spinning. Didn't he realize she had drunk half a bottle of vodka and was therefore unfazed by anything? Heck, her ex-husband could have gotten up on stage dressed in drag, and she wouldn't have batted an eyelash.

"I did this?" She didn't want her name in the paper, should he be deemed unstable.

"Yes, you did," he answered. "I trust you. You don't fly off the handle and call me crazy. You're level-headed."

"No. I'm not." She quietly hoped he hadn't heard. No such luck.

"What?" He sat down next to her.

"Nothing. Just talking to myself," she tried to cover. "So, what happens next?"

"I'm headed to meet with an agent. She gave me her card at the club, the same night you were there. If you'd told me this was crazy, I was going to cancel. But you didn't, so I'm keeping that appointment. If all goes well, I'll become Elvis, and so long boring Phil."

"Just don't be hasty in anything. Think it through carefully," she cautioned.

"Don't worry, I won't." He looked at his watch. "Listen, I've gotta go if I'm going to make it downtown on time. Thanks for being so supportive." He planted another wet kiss on her cheek."

"You're welcome," she muttered as he walked away. Once he was out of view, she rummaged in her purse for a tissue to wipe the slobbery kiss from her face. What had she done? With the help of Demon Alcohol she might have created a monster.

****

He had seen her leaving the building with Elvis as he pulled into the parking garage. Walking in the crosswalk to the building, Jack noticed Tess sitting alone on the edge of the fountain.

He made a detour to where she was. Whatever was waiting for him inside could wait a little longer.

Though she had made it subtly clear she wasn't interested in him, he still found himself drawn to her. He remembered the night he had kissed her that her body had pushed closer to him and then suddenly pulled away. The woman had amazing self-control to pull away and return to acting cool and friendly to him as though nothing had happened.

"Enjoying the afternoon sun?" he asked, clearly startling her.

"I am now." She shielded her eyes with her hand as she smiled up at him. She patted the spot next to her, inviting him to sit.

He wished he could act so nonchalant. What he wanted to do right now was run his fingers through that hair and bring her lips to his.

"I thought I saw you with your boy Elvis."

She leaned her head back to laugh and hit his leg in

a flirty gesture. He had to remind himself, she viewed him as only as a friend.

"You're observant today, Jack," she said. "Yes, he came here to ask my advice. He's planning on giving up his career to pursue this Elvis-gig."

"What did you tell him?" he asked.

"To follow his heart."

"That was a non-answer if I ever heard one."

Her smile was big when she said, "What was I supposed to say? That I think he's nuts and that I'd never do something like that?" She paused to watch some people from their building walk by. "Like I should talk after agreeing to this crazy bet."

"What bet is that?" he asked.

"It's such a silly thing. Back at the conference this summer Allie bet me that I couldn't go on five dates before the end of the year. Now I am wondering why I ever agreed to such a thing. If it wasn't for that, I wouldn't have stalker Elvis."

His mind went crazy. Why would she need to agree to something like this? It seemed she was constantly surrounded by men and going on dates. Before he could think about this further, she continued talking.

"I still have two more dates to go on, and then I'm *so* done."

"Two? It seems like you're going out all the time."

She scrunched her small nose, and again patted his leg. "Sometimes the three I've been on do seem like a hundred."

What about that Harry-guy? And then there was the one he'd seen her having lunch with a few times. He couldn't remember his name, but had finally recognized him from the conference—there had been no "Harrys" there this summer.

"So why, exactly, did you agree to this?" he asked.

She lifted her face toward the sun. "Because Allie was convinced I don't know how to date. I haven't been out since my divorce. And before you ask, I'm not telling you how many *years* that has been."

He was stunned and just stared at her. Part of him wanted to kiss her, right here and now, sitting in front of their office building. The more realistic part of his thought process was busy piecing together that her lack of interest in him wasn't due to her active dating life—she, like him, was out of practice. Maybe there *was* hope. "So what does the loser have to do?"

She shook her head. "Sing at next year's conference. Not only do I not like to lose, but I can't sing. Dogs run in terror."

He wanted to laugh at her statement, but the look on her face was serious. He studied his shoes for awhile.

Breaking the silence, Tess commented, "You're coming in late this morning. Before Elvis showed up, I was going to call to see if you and Bruce wanted to grab lunch."

"Yeah, I just flew back from Chicago this morning," he replied. "You know, if you get in a bind, I could help you out with that bet."

She turned her suddenly rigid body toward him. The tension he felt that night at her house had returned. She was on guard.

She squinted her eyes at him. "That's very sweet of you, Jack, but that can't happen. We work together and because—"

"What?" he asked.

Her smile was genuine. "Well, Tullamore frowns on co-workers dating. You wouldn't believe how many people have resigned or transferred to a different part of the company because they found their significant other here. And you know what a hey-day Doug would have if he heard of me dating someone here."

"Really," he replied flatly.

"The edict has been around for as long as I can remember, but it was kinda loosey-goosey. Then about five years ago one of the top dogs and his wife were a getting a divorce. Even though they worked in different departments, they brought their feud into the office. She did something to get back at him and caused us to lose a pretty big client. So after Tullamore let both of them go, they started imposing the rule strictly. That's why Doug is so insistent that we keep our personal lives out of the office."

It was almost better for Jack to think that she was dating someone else, and not interested in him, than to hear this. Any hope of getting to know her better was dead. He now understood why she kept him at an arm's length and referred to him as a *friend*. It was because they had *to be* only friends.

She narrowed her eyes at him. "So, thanks for your offer, but I need to pass on it."

She paused for a long time before continuing. "Jack, I have to say this because it's been driving me crazy. I know I flirted with you at the Tuxedo and might have led you into thinking I was interested. That was wrong of me."

She stood up and looked at the clear sky for a minute. "Omigod, I'm surprised I haven't been struck by lightning yet. Here I was so mad at my ex-husband

and father for having affairs, and then that night when you came to my house I kissed a *married* man. And I liked it. I should be shot." Quickly, she turned on her heel to walk away from him.

He was dumbfounded. *She thinks I'm married?* He thought back to all the times they'd conversed, and never once had he told her that he was divorced. Loudly he said, "Elizabeth and I are divorced."

Tess stopped dead in her tracks. She looked down at her shoes for awhile before slowly turning. "What?" she asked softly. Walking toward him, she was clearly shocked by the news. "When did this happen?"

"We were officially divorced over the summer." Jack looked intently into her disbelieving eyes. "It came as a big surprise to me."

She sat back down on the fountain, tucking her hands under her legs.

"In retrospect, I guess I shouldn't have been shocked. Elizabeth's never been happy. To make a long story short, the multiple affairs were painful, but the excruciating part of the ordeal was her blatant disregard of our son after she left."

"But," Tess interjected, "Sandra said 'your wife' was calling."

"Yes, I guess she was so used to referring to herself as my wife that she continued to do so. Sandra, who was new, didn't know we were actually divorced. They've both been corrected and they won't make that mistake again."

"So, that wasn't Elizabeth I saw you with at lunch a few weeks ago?"

"Oh yes, that was her. Less than a month after the divorce was final she was unhappy again. She wanted to meet and talk of a reconciliation. She's so self-involved and unaware of the repercussions her actions have. The luncheon ended with her telling me everything that was wrong with our marriage, her life, and of course, me."

"I'm sorry," Tess finally said. "Divorce is never easy, especially when one party was unfaithful."

She put her elbows on her knees and pushed her fingers through her hair. In a low voice she said, "I wish I didn't know. It was easier when I thought you were married. At least then I told myself I couldn't be..."

Jack waited for her to finish. He leaned forward to look into her face. "You 'couldn't be' what?"

"Never mind." She refused to look at him. "I need to grab something to eat and get back to work." She paused, and then shook her head.

He placed his hand over hers and said. "Tess, I'm attracted to you..."

She jumped to her feet. In an angry-sounding voice, she said, "You can't be. We need to forget this conversation ever happened. We are nothing more than good friends, Jack."

He watched her sprint toward the building, clearly embarrassed by his action.

Chapter Sixteen

As they walked toward the newly renovated gym Allie excitedly said to Tess, "I, for one, am so happy that the gym is re-opening. I love that's it right here in the building!"

Tess nodded her head as she shifted her workout bag to her other shoulder. As they walked down the hallway toward the new fitness center, Allie continued bubbling with excitement. *Who in their right mind could be excited about working out?* Tess wondered.

She only did it so she could indulge in desserts when she was in the mood. If pressed, she might confess to not wanting to have to buy supersized cotton panties, but staying attractive and fit for any other reason wasn't a consideration.

"I have a treadmill and recumbent bicycle at home, Allie. Why do I need to join?"

Allie sighed provocatively. "Wait until you see the trainers they have. They'll get your pulse raised before you even start to work out."

"Are you going to have an orgasm right here?" Tess now knew the reason she was being dragged to the fitness center.

Allie pretended to be insulted. It was not working. "Just wait until you see them. Then you'll understand, and thank me. You know, I'm only thinking of you and your health."

"My health? You are *not* serious, Allie McDonald," Tess argued while opening the door. "I work out more than you ever have, which leads me to believe there's someone in here you want me to meet. Am I right?"

"I have no idea what you're talking about." Letting the subject drop, the two made their way to the locker room to change.

Back in the equipment-filled room with the other exercisers, an anorexic-looking girl in tight shorts intercepted them. "Allie, how are you? I see you brought a friend," she said, sizing up Tess.

"I did. She just wants to do a try-before-you-buy workout. She's not *big into commitment*," Allie answered.

The girl looked directly at Tess. "We'll need you to sign a waiver first—for liability reasons—so should you hurt yourself, we're not responsible." The bag of bones continued to talk to her as if she was an idiot the entire time she read the paperwork.

Annoyed, Tess picked up a towel and joined Allie on the bicycles. As she pedaled, she surveyed the room. Though crowded with more women than men, she did notice a body builder-like man working with a woman in the corner on some weight machines. She turned her attention to the TV host in front of her working with a couple who felt the need to share their marital problems with the entire country.

She was startled when a warm male voice next to her said, "You must be Tess." She nodded hesitantly. "I recognized you immediately."

Tess looked over at Allie, doing a lousy job of pretending to be engrossed in the TV. She turned her head back to the man who was about her age. She was right. This had to be a set up. "You did? And *you* are?"

"Mike." He smiled broadly. "I'm one of the trainers here. Allie mentioned a friend of hers that she was trying to coax into working out more. She said you'd be easy to spot, should you ever come in."

Tess scowled at her supposed friend, who was concentrating on the console in front of her, changing the intensity of the bike's workout. "Did she now?"

"She did." He seemed unfazed by Tess's reaction. "You know, I'd be more than happy to work with you if you need some encouragement. I can be a great motivator."

She heard Allie snicker. This time she glared at her friend, her nostrils flaring like a ready-to-charge bull.

"Don't be upset with her," Mike said. "She is just doing what is best for you."

"*Is* she?" Tess asked.

He hesitated and licked his lips. "Yes."

Tess stopped pedaling. "Will you excuse us for a moment, Mike?" She pulled Allie from her bicycle and dragged her friend over near the front reception desk.

"What did you tell him?" Tess demanded to know. Allie had waved a red blanket, and Tess was full-on ready to do her bull imitation.

"I told him I had a friend that I was worried about who needed some help."

She looked everywhere *but at* Tess. "I might have said something to the effect that I'd have to find a way to get you in here without any kicking and screaming, but that you really needed his help. Possibly I mentioned you need a lot of motivation because you get discouraged, so much so, that you give up too easily. I kind of left it like that with him."

"He thinks you're talking about exercise!"

"Hey, I can't control what he's thinking."

Tess blew all the air from her lungs and exclaimed loudly, "Ugh! What am I going to do with you? When you hang me out like this, I can't even remember why we're friends."

"Play along. He's your age and not as into himself as Jose Body-builder over there. He's rather nice-looking, don't you think?"

"Play along?! Fine!" Tess said, as she huffed back to the bicycles.

"Do you want to try out the treadmill?" Mike asked as she came closer.

"Sure." She smiled sweetly. Over her shoulder, she cast a sinister look at Allie.

She jumped onto the treadmill and started to punch in the numbers. Mike brushed her fingers away. "You need to start off slowly," he said. "You don't want to overexert yourself."

The machine was going so slow that Tess thought she was going to fall off. She was going to show him. She pushed the arrow button until she started running. The look on his face was full of shock and dismay.

"Don't worry," she said, winking at him. "I know what I'm doing."

"Tess, don't overdo. When was the last time you worked out?"

"Yesterday morning. I ran for five miles before I came to work."

He stood silently as she settled into a nice rhythm. Cautiously he asked, "How often do you work out?"

"On average, five days a week. Some weeks, I can

only get in four days."

She watched him process this information. He nodded and walked away.

To her, it was unsettling to work out in this room. Anyone exiting the building on their way to the parking garage could see all the occupants panting and sweating. She felt as if she was on display. She preferred working out in the confines of her home, where people couldn't see her sweating like a goat. After finishing her five miles, she headed off to have a shower before going home.

When she and Allie emerged from the locker room, Ms. Anorexic once again intercepted them.

"So how do you feel about joining up, Tess?" she asked.

She looked over the now-crowded room. Opposite sexes eyeballed each other for attention. The pheromones were at a very high level. "I don't think so. This isn't for me."

"But there are so many benefits to getting into an exercise routine," Ms. Anorexic continued with her sales pitch. "I saw Mike talking with you. Why don't you wait right here while I get him?"

"I really don't think that'll be necessary," Tess said, trying to walk to the door.

The girl grabbed Tess's arm. "Are you actually saying that Mike won't be able to—?"

Tess removed the bony hand from her arm. "I don't need Mike or anyone to work—"

"My feelings are hurt," Mike said, standing behind her. "Mindy, you can go. I got it from here."

Tess pushed her shoulders back and held her head a little higher—the stance she always took when in a difficult situation and not ready to back down.

"I meant nothing against you," she said. "I'm just not interested in joining. I think I'm doing a good job on my own."

"I can see that," he assured her. "But everyone can use pointers now and then. I would be more than happy to work with you one-on-one whenever you need it."

"Thank you." She tried to sound friendlier now that he made it clear this was not a pressure sale. "I'll keep that in mind."

She started to walk from him, when he asked. "How about getting together sometime then?"

She wheeled around, incredulous. "I don't think so."

"I wasn't talking about exercise. You seem to be into endurance. Think you could endure an entire afternoon with me?"

She blinked a few times before hearing Allie clear her throat.

"I take it from your silence that's a no?" Mike asked.

"No. I mean it's not a no. Yes." Why could she close a multi-million dollar deal, but she fumbled with the words in accepting a date proposal. "I was just caught off guard," she managed to say. "Sure. We can do that."

"Are you going to be part of the holiday shopping crowd this weekend?" he asked

She shook her head. "Not me. I was going to start decorating the house."

"Good, glad to hear you're not one of those ninja shoppers."

She was unsure how to respond to his statement.

What was wrong with shopping? It was a great way to relax and reduce stress.

"Great. Then how about taking a break on Sunday afternoon? We can walk a trail or two at Stone Mountain and then have a picnic if it's not too chilly."

"Okay." She was still in shock over the course of events. "How about we meet at noon at the train depot?"

"You got it," he said, with a wide smile.

She, too, managed a smile before following Allie, who looked much too pleased with herself, out of the gym.

"Are you happy now?" Tess asked, before they separated in the parking garage.

"Yes, I am. I know you'll find this hard to believe, but I would really love to see you win the bet. All I ever wanted was for you to have some fun."

"You're such a liar. If anything, you're itching to get up on that stage and sing, you attention whore."

"I don't know what makes you think that could be remotely true," Allie exclaimed.

Tess turned to walk down the aisle to her car. She yelled over her shoulder, "I've known you too long, Allie, to think any differently."

Chapter Seventeen

The wind whipped between the buildings as they walked down the street. Tess pulled her red coat around her closer and put her head down as she moved alongside Jack on the sidewalk.

"We could've stayed inside for lunch." Jack dug his hands into his pockets.

The wind blew her hair into her face when she looked over at him. There was a sudden urge to touch the long, blonde curls. However, it vanished when she reached up and pushed her hair away. Her overly expressive face looked at him as if he was an idiot.

Neither one made any reference to the conversation that took place outside their office two weeks earlier. If she had thought about it since, she gave no indication.

She let out a sigh. "Are you kidding me? The cafeteria is *so* not going to have anything decent to eat the day before Thanksgiving. Isn't being caught in this wind tunnel more fun?" Her smile gave him reason to believe she did prefer to be outside walking.

They turned the corner, and silently walked the remainder of the way to the restaurant. The only word exchange was when they walked by a store and she asked if he would mind stopping, on the way back to the office, so she could pick up some candles.

The restaurant was more crowded than usual and they had to wait for a table. Tess leaned close to him, and whispered, "Look at the shopping bags. These people are getting an early jump on Christmas shopping." Her mouth was so close to his face. He felt her warm, minty breath on his skin.

He couldn't think with her being so close. All he had to do was turn his head and their mouths would touch.

As if reading his thoughts, she stepped back. "Yes, well, we're one of the few sadistic ones who decided to work this afternoon. I'll return a few more emails after lunch and then I'm out of there."

"Speaking of which," he said, to banish the thoughts stirring through his head, "why *did* you decide to come in today and not work from home?"

"And miss our regular Wednesday lunch? Of course I forgot Bruce was off today," she said with a bright smile.

Their time together was becoming more difficult for him. The more he was around her, the more he wanted her. He needed to find a way to get her out of his system. Maybe he needed to date like she was.

A woman and her teenage daughter, on their way out of the restaurant, walked by and bumped Tess with their large shopping bags. She fell against him and he instinctively reached out to grab hold of her arms. Her body briefly pressed up against his. He felt her stiffen before she pulled away. "I'm sorry," she said.

They were saved from the moment of awkwardness when the nasal young man acting as their host said, "Follow me to your table, please. Where's your friend, today?"

"He took today off," Tess answered.

They were becoming known to the staff and were

shown to their usual booth. Jack helped Tess with her coat. While he glanced to see what the specials were or to see if anything had changed he saw that she didn't pick up her menu. They had settled into a friendly and comfortable routine. He knew she would order the same thing she did every time—the house soup, and spinach salad. He also knew that on the way out the door, she would grab a handful of mints. Bruce had teased her about being stuck in a routine.

While they waited for their food, she asked about his plans for the holiday weekend.

"Joel's coming home. We're driving up to Knoxville tomorrow to see my brother and his family. My sister and mother, who live in Huntsville, are driving up there today."

"Wow! Full house." She sipped on her sweet tea. "Staying up there all weekend?"

"Just until Saturday evening. If the weather is okay, we'll go golfing. What about you?"

"Another date," she replied. She was about to say more, when she saw a sequin-jacketed man coming straight toward them.

"Tess, you'll never believe it. I took your advice and now I've signed with an agent. Donna Landon."

Jack looked from Tess to the man. He not only slid into the booth beside her, but also draped his arm around her shoulders.

"My advice?" Tess's voice cracked.

"Yeah. You remember, you told me to follow what was in my heart." He stopped, looked across the table to Jack, and extended his hand. "Phil Jackson. Or you can call me Elvis, whichever you prefer."

"Jack Maristone," he replied, shaking the man's

hand.

Tess gingerly set down her glass. She turned her entire body in the booth to face Phil. "What did you do?"

"I signed with Donna, who was at the club that night. She wasn't just another ardent fan who wanted to *do it* with the King after all." He picked up a roll from the basket on the table.

Jack could not believe this guy's manners, or the way he talked as if he really was Elvis with women throwing themselves at him. The look on Tess's face reflected his beliefs.

"And get this. I found out today that Donna has already scheduled me for a few shows. She told me my talents are being wasted."

When the waitress brought their food, he asked for a glass of water before continuing. "Tess, I owe it all to you!" He stopped and looked at Tess in a lovesick-boy kind-of-way. He turned his attention to Jack. "If it wasn't for her, I would've never done this. I'm in love with her."

Jack remained silent. Tess appeared very uncomfortable with Elvis's statement. She managed a weak smile.

Phil looked at Tess. "Tess, will you marry me? You can go with me when I perform."

Jack looked incredulously at the two sitting across from him. Phil appeared to be quite serious, whereas Tess appeared ready to run away in terror.

"Imagine if I make it big. You can go on road shows with me." He was like an excited child.

"Thank you, Phil. That's really sweet of you to ask, but I think I need to decline." She picked up her soup spoon. "I'm not ready to be married to a star."

"Okay," Phil said, as he stood. "You know I'll wait for you. See you around, Jack."

They watched as he walked from the restaurant, waving to the patrons.

Jack turned his attention back to Tess. She looked mortified as some of the other diners glanced her way.

"Wow. So now I've met Elvis. I guess it's never too late." He tried to keep his tone light.

"Let's pretend what you saw and heard just now didn't happen." She looked him in the eyes. "I don't need the folks at the office flapping their lips about this."

Jack reached across the table, resting his hand on top of hers. "It'll be our secret," he said, winking at her. Her eyes looked skeptical, so he squeezed her hand. "I promise."

When she nodded he saw the relief in her eyes. He left his hand on top of hers. It was soft and warm to the touch. When his thumb lightly caressed her fingers, she left her hand there for a few seconds. She pulled it out from under his and looked down at her salad. Several emotions washed over her face, one of which looked to be fear.

They finished their lunch, talking mostly of work. On the way back to the office, Tess told him he didn't need to stop with her at the store if he needed to get back to work. He shook his head and held open the door to the shop she wanted to stop at. He followed her throughout the bustling store as she picked up candles, as well as some holiday dessert plates, napkin rings, and gift-wrap. Soon he was carrying the basket filled with her things so that she could pick other items up and inspect them.

Anything that might be construed as negative from him when she picked up something, and she would quickly put it down. Soon, it became a game. Sometimes they could be so comfortable in each other's company, but then she'd emotionally retreat from him.

As they stood in line, his free hand brushed lightly against hers. The woman in front of them turned around and looked at each of them. Jack groaned inwardly.

It was a woman Elizabeth used to play tennis with. "Jack," she said formally. She then focused on Tess who immediately took the basket from him. "What a surprise. I see you're looking well and carrying on. How is Elizabeth doing?"

He felt Tess move away from him. She didn't want this woman to have the impression they were together.

"I think she's fine. She's in Florida with her sister," he answered.

"Good for her." she said, with her usual haughtiness. "The weather is probably nicer than what we have here." Once again, she focused on Tess. "Are you going to introduce me to your friend?"

"This is Tess."

Tess quickly added, "We work together."

"Really!" The woman continued to size up Tess. "I didn't think you worked anymore now that you sold your business."

Jack felt relief when another cashier offered to help them at the other end of the counter. He put his hand on Tess's lower back to guide her away from this woman. Why should he care what this self-appointed duchess thought? He and Elizabeth were no longer married. He didn't need to answer to anyone.

In silence, he watched Tess pay for her items. When he picked up one of the bags, she grabbed it from him. She didn't want anyone to think they were a couple.

On the walk back to the office, he grabbed her arm. "Tess, let me help you. A gentleman always helps a lady. No one is going to think we are a couple if you let me carry one of your bags."

"Yes, they will. I don't want people to think there is something between us." Her face said something quite the opposite.

Once inside the building, they walked in silence to the elevators. When she got off on her floor, she turned to him. Quietly, she said, "Happy Thanksgiving. Have a safe trip tomorrow."

Before he could answer, the doors shut.

Chapter Eighteen

The weather had not warmed up as much as the weathermen had predicted, though the sun was shining brightly. Tess pulled on her gloves as she walked through the unusually crowded parking lot toward the train depot at the park.

Mike was already there when she reached the depot. He was wearing hiking boots with workout clothes and a heavy-looking windbreaker. She had worn jeans and gym shoes with a fleece jacket. He'd said they were going to walk, not hike. Looks like his plans were different.

He saw her and waved. As she came nearer he said, "I didn't realize it was going to be so crowded."

"Neither did I." She was still not sure what his plans were since he was dressed for extreme exercise.

"I hope you don't mind, but I bought us some tokens so we can ride the train around the mountain."

"That's fine." She took the token from him.

Once they were seated on the crowded train, she asked, "Did Allie put you up to this?"

She saw the perplexed look on his face and wanted to retract her words, realizing it was not true.

"You mean your friend Allie from the gym?"

"The one and only," she said, still looking at him.

"No," he said, more forcefully. "When I was working with her in the gym, she told me I needed to work with you. I thought she meant working out. It wasn't until we met that I realized her connotation."

"When we met?" She stepped from the train at the stop close to the hiking trail. "I'm confused."

Walking next to her in long strides, Mike said, "It was your spunk that appealed to me. The way you wanted to let me know you didn't need any help, and then you ran for close to an hour to prove it. The way you stood up to Mindy when she was trying to sell you a membership made me think 'this is someone I want to get to know.'"

Tess kept her mouth from saying anything, jumping from one large rock to another on the path.

"You didn't try to fall all over yourself to get my attention," he continued, leading the way. "It really gets tiring when woman throw themselves at me."

Egotistical much? They continued up the hill. On the way, he talked about a number of his clients as a personal trainer, stressing the time he had worked with a famous lingerie model. There were other famous people he had worked with to improve their bodies.

Tess wanted to ask why he was no longer worked with them, instead of working at the fitness center. She told herself it would be rude to ask. Her mouth thought differently. "Wow, that's all pretty impressive." They neared the top of the trail. "So, how come you are now working in our building?"

Not showing any embarrassment, he confided, "Caught one too many times in bed with my protégés. One of the husbands actually threw me out of the house before I had a chance to get dressed."

She laughed at the mental picture of him standing on a porch butt-naked, asking for his clothes in his very soft voice. She continued to laugh.

"What's so funny?"

"Nothing." She tried to compose herself. "Didn't you learn anything after being caught the first time?"

"Come on Tess, be real," he said. "When you are working that close, and the women have bodies like that, you can't help but have a little bit of it. Plus, it wasn't always my idea."

"So is that what attracts you to me? The fact I am not drooling all over you?"

"Yeah. You're a challenge that I want to conquer." He helped her up a steep rock. "I know from your friend Allie that you are not into women. Besides, I see you with that older guy all the time."

She stopped. "Older guy?"

He turned to look at her. "Yeah. He's a bit taller than you. Grayish hair. I see you two leaving together at lunchtime with another shorter, bald guy. Your body language suggests you're into the taller one. The way I figure it, you can't be seeing him or you wouldn't be here today. Does he not excite you?"

"Excuse me," she said, angrily, "He and I are just good friends. I haven't even thought of him in the way you are suggesting."

She knew she was lying. When Jack had run his thumb over her fingers all she could think of was him running his hands over her entire body.

"No? I heard he has a lot of money. Is that what you're attracted to?"

Tess was getting madder by the second. "No! A man with money is not on the top of my priority list."

"Ah-ha!" He jumped off the rock. "So it's primal sex. Well, you've come to the right place for that."

"Oh brother." She exhaled all the air from her lungs. The wind whipped her hair around her head. They were finally at the top of Stone Mountain and all she wanted to do at this point was to get on the tram and be away from Mike.

He walked over to her, grabbed her hair, and forced his lips onto hers. They were hard and cold. She felt like she was kissing a granite rock. It didn't feel at all gentle, like Jack's. She pushed him away from her. "What was that about?" She backed away from him.

"I'm showing you what you could be having," he said. "Stop playing hard to get, Tess. I know you want me."

"If your eyes were brown, I'd tell you what you're full of. But I can see you're so full of yourself, there's not even room for that. A little advice, Mike: Women like romance. You know, the chocolates-and-flowers thing?"

"Why waste time on all that when the end results are the same? Tess, I want to feel your tight buns and muscular thighs."

"Why me?" She put her hand up. "Wait, don't tell me. It's because I'm a challenge. You should go after someone much younger than me."

"Younger woman want me to go 'ooh' and 'aah' over their bodies." He closed in again. "You'll just be happy that I want to sleep with you."

"You're so gross, and so wrong." Tess walked quickly to the tram to buy a ticket for the ride down. She had to get away from him. *I should be thrilled to sleep with him? Does he think I'm that desperate?*

He was behind her in line. "Tess," he said. "Don't leave like this."

"Get away from me," she said.

"Mike?" a woman behind him asked. "I thought that was you. Where are you working now?"

He whipped around and hugged the petite woman. "Lydia, you look fabulous," he said. He walked around the woman, put his hands on her behind, and squeezed. "I see you're keeping up on your exercise regimen."

Tess rolled her eyes and walked up to the tram. As the door closed, she watched his hands pat the woman's butt and thighs.

She looked out the tram's window as the vehicle moved slowly down the mountain. *Why do I attract all the freaks?"*

She was thankful she only had one more date left. She could not wait to get home and tell Dana and Allie about this latest washout.

****

Tuesday morning, Tess pulled into the parking garage next to Jack getting out of his car. She gathered up her things to walk into the building with him. *The older man! Sheesh!*

She knew Jack was attracted to her. At least he wasn't trying to get her into bed. She enjoyed his company, until something would happen that would remind her he was single. Why couldn't he be seeing someone so she wouldn't have these thoughts of feeling his lips on hers?

"How was your Thanksgiving?" She pulled her computer case behind her, shifting her purse to the opposite shoulder and realizing it didn't match her outfit. At least this took her mind away from staring at his mouth.

"As good as it can be when you're around family,"

he answered. "Ate too much. How was yours?"

"Relaxing and good—until I had the date from hell on Sunday." She couldn't look at him. She was feeling warm standing so close to him.

"Date number four was that bad?"

"Worse than bad," she said, trying to suppress a smile. "It was right up there with the doctor who took me to the hospital cafeteria for dinner."

"How romantic!" Jack teased.

"Ugh! Why do I try and tell you anything?"

"Sorry. Go on."

"The fitness center instructor asked me out, because he thinks of me as a challenge. Even so, he was quite sure I would be honored to have him sleep with me." She stopped talking as they stepped under the covered walkway in front of the fitness center. She glanced to see if Mike was there. His hands were on a woman's hips as she lifted some weights over her head.

"Well, did you?" he asked quickly.

She stopped and looked at him. "No!" Instinctively, she touched Jack's arm to motion him to keep walking toward the door. "By now, you should know me well enough to realize that I wouldn't do something like that."

"Was he in there just now? Are you reconsidering?" Jack asked. There was something in his voice that she couldn't put her finger on. *Was he jealous?*

"This isn't funny," she said, as he held the door open for her. "This bet sucks! Believe me, it's going to be my death."

"Uh, Tess. My offer still stands," he said.

She felt her phone vibrate in her purse. Flipping the

phone to her ear and pretending to ignore Jack's words she said, "Tess Grayson." This was one time she was thankful for the distraction of the phone.

She couldn't let her mind wander to him and what it'd be like to have dinner with him alone. *That's it. I'll just have to make sure there's always someone around to act as a shield.*

Chapter Nineteen

"Tess?" Maggie knocked on her door as she opened it.

"What?" Tess was irritated at the interruption. She had to go over the financials one more time before her meeting the next day. *Why does no one pay attention to a closed door?*

"I know you're busy, but...security called. There's a woman downstairs in the lobby demanding to see you. They called instead of sending her up."

Tess squinted her eyes. *Why would they do that?* "Did they get a name?"

"No, but they said she's wearing pink curlers."

Great—Trudee. She packed up her papers and computer. At this rate, she was not going to be able to get any work done here. She'd take it home, where it was quieter.

Maggie continued to stand at the door. "Do you need help? I can go down with you."

"No, the woman is quite harmless, I assure you." Tess put her computer in her carrying case. "Can you just hand me that box of binders?"

Once loaded down, Tess walked to the elevator. Bruce was standing inside with what looked like most of the people who had come from Maristone. "I'll take the next one," she said.

"Don't be silly. Get on." Bruce moved back to

make room for her. "Where are you going?"

"Home, where there'll be a lot fewer interruptions," she said. "But before I go, I have to deal with Elvis's mother."

She heard several snickers behind her. She bit her tongue to not say anything further.

"Isn't she the one who wears the pink curlers?" Bruce questioned.

"Yep." Tess heard more giggles. She wished she were in their shoes instead of her own. Then she could do the laughing and whispering.

When the elevator opened, there was Trudee—curlers in hair, yellow leggings, an oversized red sweatshirt with a Christmas tree on the front, and blue tennis shoes. Obviously, the woman never bothered with mirrors. Either that or she was seriously color-blind.

Tess breathed deeply and walked confidently up to the waiting woman.

Trudee looked ready to explode. "What did you tell my son?" she demanded.

Tess used the calming voice reserved for agitated clients. "I'm afraid I don't know what you're referring to."

"Don't play your games with me, missy," Trudee spat. "Did you tell him to pursue a singing career?"

Tess shifted the box resting on her hip. "I told him to follow his dreams. Isn't that what every mother wants for her child?"

"Well, he did, all right. Now he has quit his job and moved in with me." Her anger and voice grew by the second. "But he did tell me he would not be staying long, as he was going to move in with you after you marry."

The sound of Tess dropping the box of binders echoed in the lobby. It was when she was picking up the contents that she noticed Bruce by her side. Obviously, he was getting a kick out of this.

"I'm sorry. He said *what*?"

"That you're his inspiration, and he's going to marry you."

Bruce cleared his throat. "I heard that you turned him down when he asked you."

"Who are you?" Trudee focused on Bruce. Her attention quickly turned back to Tess. "So you turned my boy down? Why would you do that?"

Can this woman get any more confusing? First, she's angry at the possibility of me marrying her son, and now for my refusal to do so.

"Phil is nice, Trudee, but we only went out once. There's no chemistry between us."

"You prefer the business type, don't you?" Trudee's eyes narrowed at Tess. The stale smell of cigarettes hung in the air between them. "Phil used to be a businessman until you told him to give it up and act like Elvis full time."

"I didn't tell him to quit his job."

"Yes, you did," Trudee barked, with tears running down her cheek. "You stay away from me and my son. You've brought us nothing but grief. I knew you were bad from the minute I laid my eyes on you. All I can say is that I am thankful I never voted for your father when he was a senator."

Tess felt like she had no adrenaline left in her body as she watched Trudee stomp away. The woman was as whacked as her son. She straightened her coat, resettled the box on her hip and without looking at Bruce left the building to go to the quietness and normalcy of her home.

It would only be a matter of time before the news of the lobby freak-show traveled the grapevine to management. Her one prayer was that Claire would not follow in her footsteps and would be able to stay away from weirdos like this.

Chapter Twenty

Tess walked toward the building that housed Harry's law firm. She was thankful her Ryhan meeting had gone well and ended earlier than expected. Harry had confirmed he was free to meet for lunch, as long as they met in the restaurant in his building.

As she walked up the steps, she heard Phil calling her name. She saw from the reflection in the glass, he was wearing his Elvis costume.

"Stay away from me, Phil. If your mother finds out we've talked, she'll have me arrested."

"I heard about your encounter. I've come to tell you she was out of line."

Tess crossed her arms and stared at the man whose mother had humiliated her in her building's lobby. "You don't say? Here I thought she was inviting me to tea."

"Tess, don't be upset. Let me treat you to lunch, baby, so I can show you how sorry I am."

"Let's get this straight"—Tess started counting off with her fingers—"I'm *not* your baby. I'm *not* going to marry you. I *didn't* tell you to quit your day job. And, lastly, I *will not* go to lunch with you dressed like that."

"Are you saying this is not right for me?"

"No, Phil. *You* are saying that. I told you to follow your dreams, but I don't have to eat lunch with someone who dresses like Elvis."

"But I *am* Elvis. That's who I am."

Talking to him and his mother was useless. The more they talked, the more confused she became.

"You're right. You're Elvis, but here is the thing, I was never into him, his music, or his movies. I prefer the opera and classical music. Now, if you'll excuse me, I'm meeting my brother for lunch."

She walked away. In the window's reflection she saw people walk up to speak with Elvis. Apparently, he was not the only occupant of his fantasy land.

Inside the restaurant she didn't see any sign of Harry. As usual, he would be late. She sat down on the bench near the hostess station.

Out of the corner of her eye, she glimpsed someone who looked like Jack's wife. *Oops, ex-wife.*

Tess slid down the bench seat a little and saw that it was Jack having lunch with Elizabeth. From where she was sitting, she was able to observe both of them. She thought it ironic how she had again run into them in an out-of-the-way place.

Whatever their conversation concerned, neither appeared happy. Jack's usual quick smile and the sparkle in his eyes were missing. He looked upset, almost mad. His mouth was pressed into a frown.

This was not the person she was accustomed to seeing. If he was unhappy when he had lunch with Elizabeth, why did they continue to meet? Did he still have feelings for his ex?

Elizabeth's countenance was similar. Even from here, Tess could see her frown pulling against her all-too-evident face-lift. When she talked, she waved her hands in frustration at him. There was something odd about her hands Tess couldn't put her finger on it.

Could it be she had surgery there, too?

Whatever Elizabeth was saying, Jack looked ready to explode. Tess couldn't tear her gaze from the two of them.

When the waitress brought their check, she saw how Jack grabbed it and signed his name. They both stood up, clearly angry at each other.

Another thing that caught her attention was how he didn't help Elizabeth with her coat. He had always done that with Tess. When Elizabeth put on her coat, it hit her. There was a large diamond on her ring finger.

She stood as Elizabeth huffed by without so much as a glance. It didn't surprise her. Elizabeth had no idea whom she was.

Jack walked out of the restaurant more slowly. She startled him when she stepped in front of him. A smile spread over his face, and the sparkle suddenly appeared in his tired eyes.

"Is everything okay?" Tess worried she might have overstepped the line with that question.

"Having lunch with Elizabeth is always stressful. With her, nothing is ever *okay*, but let's not talk about that right now." He stood closer to her. "What are you doing here?"

"Meeting my brother. He's a partner in one of the law firms upstairs. We get together once a month for lunch."

"Oh." He appeared distracted.

"You know what's funny? The last time we went to lunch, we ran into you and Elizabeth." Her announcement seemed to break his trance.

"What did you just say?" Jack asked.

"It seems that I run into you and Elizabeth when

Harry and I go to lunch."

"Harry?"

"Yeah. Harry. My brother," she said hesitantly. *Why was he acting so strange all of a sudden?* "Do you know him?"

He shook his head, but seemed to be concentrating on what she was saying. *Does he actually look relieved about something?*

She looked around to make sure Harry was not around. "He married my best friend from school. Dana always had a big crush on him. I think it started in first grade when he pulled her pigtails."

Tess pulled him aside from the other entering diners. "Harry's a workaholic and Dana's at her wit's end. There are times she wants to call it quits. I know it's none of my business, but I think that if someone could knock some sense into him, he might see how his wife feels. Last week I pointed out that he spends more time conversing with *me* than with his wife. Dana wanted to know what I said, because he was attentive to her all weekend. I just want things to be better, for them and their kids."

"I take it this is him coming down the hall? There is a slight resemblance."

She poked him with her elbow. "Don't tell him that. He wants to forget his blond, super-curly-haired youth. Luckily, his darkened and only has a wave now."

Jack nodded, and moved even closer to her. Tess introduced the two men and watched as they shook hands. Pleasantries aside, Jack excused himself to walk back to the office.

After he left, Tess wondered why Jack had seemed so relieved after she said Harry was her brother. Odd.

Chapter Twenty-One

Nothing could be worse than having to Christmas shop for her ex-husband and his new wife; but for Claire's sake, Tess had agreed to this torture. There was nothing more she'd like to get them than a calendar for next year in which all the weekends they were supposed to spend time with Claire were circled with a thick red marker.

Since Kevin's late summer wedding, Claire had only spent two weekends with him. His excuse was always Leslie. She wasn't feeling well. Or she had booked a weekend away. Or she had planned a dinner-party. The list of excuses was endless.

Tess could tell it was starting to affect Claire, who up until today hadn't mentioned anything about it. This morning at breakfast she had broken into a tirade about how Leslie had changed now that she and Kevin were married. Leslie made it plainly obvious she didn't want her step-daughter around, but wanted her own family. She announced she was only going to buy her dad a Christmas gift, but not one for the wicked witch.

Before Christmas break, Tess would have to have that hard conversation with Kevin. The poor schmuck probably didn't even know what was going on. If she found he did, Tess was going to sprinkle his present with itching powder.

Tess stopped in front of a boutique store and

pointed at a purple scarf and matching gloves. "How about this for Leslie? They look to be her colors." Tess hoped they'd find something soon, she was hungry. After standing in the checkout line for over fifteen minutes at one store for Harry's brandy snifters and then twenty minutes in another for Kevin's ski-sweater, Tess wanted to scream. She felt sure these stores had not hired extra staff for the holiday shoppers.

"I dunno," Claire grumbled. "How about we get her a new broom and a matching witch's hat?"

Tess wanted to laugh, because her daughter echoed her own thoughts. A part of her nagged to *say something nice*, but she couldn't come up with anything. "Let's go in and see what we can buy here."

"I don't want you to spend a lot of money on her, mom."

Tess smiled, "Believe me, I won't. We'll go to the sales rack and pick out the most hideous thing. If she makes a fuss, you can blame it on me. Okay?"

"Sure," Claire responded, following Tess into the store. "How can you be so cool about it?"

"About what?" Tess flipped through the sales rack sweaters.

"About buying Leslie something for Christmas."

"Sweetie, we all have to do things we don't like."

"Like going on those five dates?"

Tess held a white sweater up to Claire. "Yes, like those dates. Don't you think this will look cute for your ski trip?"

"I don't want to go," Claire said. "I'd rather stay here with my friends."

Tess stopped. "The two of you have been going skiing for a long time now. Your father would be heartbroken if you didn't go. Listen, I'm going to have a little chat with him about this Leslie situation. I doubt the big klutz even realizes what's going on."

"But then Leslie will get mad, and make things worse."

"I'll make sure they don't." Tess held up a hideous brown, purple, and orange sweater. *No wonder it's on sale*, she thought. *Whoever made this was color-blind.*

"We're buying this," she announced. A warm feeling passed through her when Claire smiled and scrunched her nose.

She followed Tess to the register. "Aren't you going to be lonely if I go?"

Tess mussed Claire's hair. "Sure, I'll miss you. But don't worry yourself about it. I'll do the same thing I do every year. Buy trashy books, and watch chick-flicks. But this time, I'll also be looking for my fifth date."

"Why don't you ask Mr. Maristone?" Claire asked.

Tess paused momentarily before accepting the receipt to sign. "Noooo."

"I saw him kiss you that night, you know. Don't you like him?"

Tess took the bags from the clerk, not sure what to say.

"You know, Mom, it's not a big deal or anything. It was just a kiss."

"It *is* a big deal. We work together." Tess walked to the front of the store.

"Whatever!" Claire said, as they walked outside into the chilly air. "Hey, speaking of him, mom...there he is."

Tess stopped, along with her heart. Except for the sales conference in Florida, she realized she'd never seen Jack in nonbusiness clothes. His jeans fit him just right—showing the outline of his legs and butt. He also had on a pullover golf sweater with a turtleneck underneath. With his thick, gray hair, and his firm lips pressed together in his square jaw, he certainly was attractive. His hazel eyes sparkled with light when he looked up and recognized her and Claire.

Tess caught her breath and felt flushed, despite the chilly air.

"This is a nice surprise." Jack opened the back door to his car to place the bag he was carrying inside. "Doing your own last minute shopping?" he asked. He came over to them and kissed Tess on her cheek.

Her entire body caught on fire from that simple peck. She couldn't look at Claire, who had just witnessed this "friends-only" kiss. She was such a hypocrite. She wanted to be more than friends, but it would never be possible.

Claire answered, "We just finished shopping for my step-monster."

Tess smiled and looked just to the side of Jack's face. There was no way she could look into his eyes. "She means that we have finished up our Christmas shopping. These last gifts were for Kevin and his new wife."

"The step-monster, eh?" Jack took Tess's hand to pull her out of the way of a passing family.

"The one and only," Claire answered, sidling up next to Tess.

Tess nodded. Electricity surged through her body from this simple contact. She couldn't keep a clear thought with him here. Her stomach was doing flip-flops.

"Yep. So what are you doing up here?" Tess tried to be nonchalant though her heart was racing.

"Same as you. The last of the Christmas shopping. Now I am officially done."

"Have you eaten yet?" Tess wondered if it was her imagination, or if her voice was shaking. "We're going to walk over to the sandwich shop to get an early dinner. You could come along."

"Love to." He smiled warmly at her, still holding her hand tightly.

As they walked down the sidewalk, Claire pointed out a poster of a cat with a Santa's hat.

"Still haven't got that kitten yet, have you?" Jack commented.

"Nope," Claire answered, casting a glance at her mom. "If you want some scoop to blackmail my mom into getting me one, I have some."

Tess's insides were in knots, wondering what her daughter could possibly say,

Jack let go of Tess's hand to open the door for them, "What's the scoop?"

Once they were in line, Claire finally answered. "That she likes you, but won't admit it. Mom, I want the curry chicken salad on whole grain."

Tess felt her face turn a bright red. She looked down at the floor. She felt Jack take her hand again and squeeze it. There went the surge of tingles through her body to her toes.

"Is that so? I never knew that," he commented with laughter in his voice.

"And you want to know what else?" Claire mischievously turned to look at Tess.

"As soon as you come back from your ski trip, I'll

promise you we'll get that kitten. But you have to go skiing with your dad and step-monster. I mean Leslie. If you want two kittens then you better stop talking now!"

He winked at Claire. "Look how easy that was. Anything else you need?"

"A new smart phone would be nice. My friend Mare has one."

Tess answered firmly, "I told you before. The answer is no."

Claire started to giggle. "Mr. Maristone, do you want to know where my mom is ticklish? She's..."

"Stop," Tess quickly said, looking at both of them.

Jack leaned forward and whispered loudly, "I've never seen your mom squirm so much. Tell me where."

"On her sides," Claire announced, and then started laughing.

Tess freed her hand from Jack's to cross her arms, trying to appear angry. She could tell from the looks on both of their faces that they didn't believe her.

"Are you two done now, so we can order?"

When Claire turned around to give her order to the teenage girl working the counter, Jack put his arm around her waist. "Your secrets are safe with me," Jack breathed softly in her ear. With him so close, a tingle of goose bumps went down her neck.

She needed to focus. She moved ahead when the teenager looked at her. "Two curry chicken salad sandwiches on whole grain." The only saving grace was that no one here knew them.

"Make that three, I'll have the same," Jack said. He released his arm to pull out his wallet.

"What are you doing?" Tess opened her purse.

"My treat. And don't argue." He leaned closer. "I

know where you're ticklish, remember?"

"Don't remind me." She glanced over her shoulder and saw a booth near the window opening up. She pointed at Claire to grab it before anyone else could.

She waited while Jack paid, trying to ignore what she was feeling inside—the warmth, her racing heart. She studied his mouth, and had to shake away the thoughts.

Tess picked up the paper cups to fill them with fountain drinks. As soon as she started to fill Jack's with caffeine-free soda, she froze. She'd been with him so often, she knew exactly what he drank. Balancing the three cups, she carried them to the booth.

Jack stood to let her sit on the inside of the bench. She'd been planning to sit with Claire, whom she noticed hadn't moved from the center of her bench when she came to the table.

While they waited for their order to be called, Jack put his arm on the back of the booth, his fingers dangling on her shoulders.

With all the lunches they had shared, she should have no problem being around him, but today was different. Today, she was aware of everything about him—his aftershave, his jeans, his nearness to her, his familiarity, the charge in the air.

When he left to pick up the order, she felt like she could finally breathe.

Claire looked across the table, "I think he wants to be more than friends, Mom." She sipped on her drink. "I like him, and it's okay with me if you want to date him."

Tess nodded her head sarcastically. "Well, thank you for your permission. I feel so much better now. But like your phone request, the answer is no."

"Whatever. It's obvious you like each other. So what's the big deal?"

"Work. I may have to report to him after the first of the year," Tess replied.

Jack set the tray on the table. "More rumors on the re-org, huh?"

"Yes. The rumors are running wild." Tess, picked up her sandwich.

"Well, nothing will happen until the middle of January. They'll let everyone get settled back in from the holidays."

"Of course you'd be in the know," Tess said, with her mouth full.

"Enough about work." He said took a big bite of his own sandwich. "What are your plans for later?"

Claire said, "We were going to wrap presents while we watch a James Bond movie. Do you want to watch it with us?"

Nothing could surprise Tess anymore. Typically Claire was shy around people she hardly knew. What was with her today?

Tess put her sandwich down. "I'm sure Jack has other plans and doesn't want to spend the evening with us, wrapping presents." She looked at Jack. "Right?"

"I'm up for it," Jack replied.

"Mom, that'd be perfect. This could be like a date or something, and then you'd win the bet with Allie. How cool would that be?"

"Sounds like a plan, or a date, to me," Jack added.

"Well, it's not," Tess said, putting her sandwich down. "It's just a plain watching-a-movie while-we-wrap-gifts night. It'll be boring." Having Jack in her house, with her feeling like this, was dangerous. Her brain rationalized that she'd been man-less for so long, she'd make a fool of herself if he tried to do anything more than kiss her.

Her heart and the warmness running through her were calling her brain a liar. They knew what to do—get him into the house.

Claire suddenly announced, "I think my mom is scared of dating, and that's why Allie made this bet. Do you know she doesn't even know when men are flirting with her? And I've seen a lot of men flirt with her."

Tess was too stunned to speak.

"Really?" Jack said, with too much interest. "And you know this how?"

"Well my dad flirted with women all the time. He still does. Or he did the last time I was with him. I know when a man is flirting with a woman. But my mom doesn't see it."

Tess pulled herself together. "I do too notice. I just ignore it."

Jack raised an eyebrow in her direction, "You do?"

Glaring at Claire, Tess replied, "I do. Now can we drop this subject?"

Claire blushed and picked at her sandwich. "Sorry," she said contritely.

Jack looked at Tess. "I'm sorry, too, since I'm the one who started this. So am I not invited anymore?"

The looks on Claire's and Jack's faces left no doubt in her mind what they both wanted the answer to be. If she said no, she'd look like the biggest wimp alive. Only appropriate, since, in reality, she was.

This would just further convolute an already-complicated situation. How in her right mind was she going to be able to sit and watch a movie with Jack while what would be running through her mind was x-rated? She couldn't be in the same room with him anymore without feeling that all-over tingling and racing-heart feeling.

She was falling for him, and while she'd told herself she'd have to have people around while she was with him, Claire wasn't the best person. Her own daughter was pushing her toward him!

They were waiting for her answer. "Sure," she said, shrugging her shoulders. "But it's not a date."

****

This was harder than Tess expected. For the first half of the movie, she sat on the floor wrapping gifts until both Claire and Jack told her she was making too much noise. She needed the diversion of wrapping to take her mind off the electricity coming from Jack.

She was thankful when he moved from the couch and sat in the chair with his feet propped up on the ottoman. She secretly studied him and became aware of how comfortable he looked. Too comfortable, as if he belonged. It scared her. For as long as she could remember—even when she was married—it seemed to be just her and Claire. Now there was this man who wanted to be part of her life.

She wanted him to kiss her on the lips and, for the kiss to not end. She shook her head. Why was she thinking like this? She picked up the empty popcorn bowl from the table between Jack and Claire.

"Does anyone want anything to drink?" she asked, wanting to leave the room.

"I'll just have water," Claire immediately answered.

"Same for me," Jack replied. "Here let me help you."

Absently, she rested her hand on his shoulder. "You don't have to, I've got this." She pulled away.

Tess threw the kernels in the trash, and turned to put the bowl in the sink when she sensed Jack standing behind her.

"Did you need something besides the water?" she asked.

"I need you to calm down," he said. "I won't do anything you don't want me to do."

"What are you talking about?" She moved around him to the sink to rinse the bowl.

"I know you weren't too keen with the idea of me coming over. But how is this any different from when it's just the two of us at lunch?"

"Because then we're in the middle of a very bright, lighted room filled with a bunch of people. Right now it's just the three of us in my house watching a movie with only the Christmas lights on."

"I can go now if you want," he said.

"No, stay to the end of the movie. It'll make Claire happy."

"What about you?" He ran the back of his fingers along her jaw.

She was having trouble breathing when she looked into his face. The gentleness she saw around his eyes caused her to catch her breath even more. Was she breathing at all? She finally exhaled.

She smiled and walked to the refrigerator to fill Claire's glass with water.

"Stay," she whispered, against her better judgment. She handed him his water-filled glass.

When she walked back into the living room, she saw that Claire had moved to the chair vacated by Jack. That meant she could be cold and sit in the opposite chair or sit on the couch. She handed the glass to Claire, and put her own on the table behind the couch next to the poinsettias. As expected, Jack sat down near her on the couch at a safe distance.

As long as he stayed arm's length away, she'd be fine—which is what he did, and she still wasn't fine.

Chapter Twenty-Two

"Harry, I need your help," Tess pleaded, standing in his kitchen. Harry's sleeves were rolled up as he and the kids washed dishes. Dana was out shopping with Claire.

"What is it now?"

"Fine," she said lightly. She picked up her glass and set it down next to the sink. "After all the help I gave you with Dana, this is how you treat me?"

"Pouting didn't work when we were younger, and it's not going to work now, sis. What do you need?" Harry rinsed out the glass and placed it in the dishwasher.

"Do you know anyone single? I need *one* more date, and there are only fifteen days left until the end of the year."

"This is what you get for procrastinating."

She sighed. "This is not the time for a lecture. I seriously need a date," she implored. She knew she sounded desperate. "You must know *someone* single. My company holiday party is Saturday. I can take 'em, and then be done with all this."

"Why can't you call someone you already went out with?"

"And why don't I check myself into a funny farm while I'm at it? I've been told I look good in white."

"Why not what's-his-name from your office? The

one I met last week at lunch? He seemed interested in you."

"Don't go there."

"Aha! I knew I felt something between the two of you."

She shook her head in disbelief. "Oh yeah. Mr. Observant. This is coming from the man whose wife spent thousands of dollars on naughty nightwear so you would notice her? Give me a break!"

He stopped washing the dishes, and looked at her with a very serious look. "I know what I saw. There was a spark there."

She punched him on the arm. "Well, you're wrong. Please don't ruin my perception of him as a great friend and co-worker."

"I hate to burst your bubble, sis." Harry leaned his back against the sink. "Your overstated denial says that you have feelings for him."

He began to chuckle. "Are you thinking about going to the dark side?" He lowered his voice. "Not following the rules set by Tullamore?"

She narrowed her eyes at him. He was not amusing in the least. She dipped her fingers in the dishwater and flipped a few soap bubbles at him. "No. I'm thinking I need to find another date. Are you going to help me, or not?"

"I know one of the guys I played golf with recently is separated. Rob Turner. I think you may have met him on the Fourth of July."

Tess tried to remember, but the name did not sound remotely familiar. She pressed her lips together and shook her head.

"I'll give him a call," Harry announced.

Tess walked up and gave her brother a light peck on the cheek. "I knew I could count on you." She picked up her coat and headed out the back door. She cut through the neighbor's yard to get to her house.

Chapter Twenty-Three

"I'm real sorry, Tess," Rob said, through the crackly phone reception. "Something came up, and I can't go tonight."

She felt like the wind had been sucked from her lungs. This was supposed to be date number five! When she had invited her brother's golf buddy, he had repeatedly assured her that he didn't mind going to her company party. It seemed odd that with only a few hours to go, he would suddenly cancel.

"Is everything, okay?" She hoped to sound convincing.

"Suzanne isn't going out with her friends tonight. She suggested we go to a dinner and movie," he said very matter-of-factly. "What was I supposed to say?"

"Suzanne?" she asked.

"Yeah. My wife."

She was taken aback by this admission. "You're still married? Harry said you were separated."

There was a long silence. She looked at the phone wondering if the connection was lost.

"Well, we've talked about getting divorced, but neither of us is ready to make that commitment," Rob said sheepishly.

There's an oxymoron if she ever heard one; making a commitment to divorce. "Yet, you saw nothing wrong with going out to a party tonight while you're still married?" Tess was unable to believe she was actually having to ask.

"No," he answered. "Harry has told me all about you, and I remembered you from last summer. You were kinda funny. I was actually looking forward to tonight."

She rubbed at the spot between her eyes, feeling a headache coming. Had someone sprinkled voodoo dust around her?

Closing her eyes, she remembered many years ago her sales training instructor telling her, "Even when you hear bad news, put a smile in your voice."

Forcing her mouth into a smile, she said, "Thanks for calling and good luck to you and Suzanne. I hope it works out between you two."

"Thanks for being understanding, Tess. And if doesn't, I know the first person I'll call."

As if I'd answer that call. She pressed the off button on the phone and fell back onto her bed to scream. She had twelve days left until the end of the year to get in one more date, as in the twelve days of Christmas. How was she, with everyone's busy holiday schedules, going to come up with a date? She was doomed. She was going to have to sing.

Sing—that's it. She rolled to the edge of the bed to grab the phone to call Elvis. He had called her enough lately, to keep her updated on his life transformation, that she had his number memorized from it popping up on caller ID.

She was thankful when he, and not Trudee, picked up on the first ring.

"Tess," he said, sounding overly cheerful. "What's up?"

"Hey, I know this is last minute, but whatcha doing tonight?" she asked quickly. At this point, she was beyond desperate. She needed a date and didn't care if she showed up with him.

"Oh, baby"—she cringed her eyes shut whenever he called her that—"I've got a gig by the Perimeter tonight. How about tomorrow?"

Her brain did some quick thinking. Tomorrow night she was supposed to go to the ballet with Dana and Allie. Maybe they would understand if she canceled so she could get this done.

"Wait a minute, darlin'," he interrupted. "I'm supposed to be down at the Children's Hospital, all day. Being down there makes me depressed, so I'm sure I won't be good company tomorrow night."

Who cares about good company? I need a date! Her mouth took over again without consulting her brain. "That's okay. We'll try another time," she said.

Her brain was mad at her mouth for speaking without thinking. She was going to lose the bet, her common sense had deserted her, and she had just renewed Phil's interest.

****

Tess walked into the hotel ballroom alone, like she did every year. It had never bothered her before, but this year showing up single weighed heavily on her.

She was about to scan the crowd to look for a familiar face when Elvis took the microphone and told everyone he was taking requests for both holiday and Elvis songs. This was the *gig* he was playing? Her company party? Couldn't someone have told her beforehand? No, of course they wouldn't. After all the talk, her co-workers would love to see her in this predicament.

She spied Allie and her husband Jon talking with Jeff and his deep-voiced wife. Before making her way to them, she breathed deeply and felt a hand on her shoulder. It was Bruce's. "Tess," he said. "I want you to meet my wife, Louisa."

Though Tess she had seen pictures of her, she was amazed at Louisa's appearance. The woman was much prettier and more elegant in person. Tall, like her husband, her movements reminded Tess of a ballet dancer.

Even in her black silk pants and red silk blouse, Tess felt like a frump standing next to Louisa. She tried to smooth her hair, clipped back at the base of her neck.

How people would laugh to know that sometimes the "cool and collected Tess" was nothing but a big fraud. This was one of those moments. She didn't belong here. Not only did she feel underdressed, but she had seriously considered showing up with Elvis! She needed counseling, and lots of it.

"It's a pleasure to finally meet you." Louisa extended her hand after shifting her wine glass to the other. "I've heard so much about you."

"Likewise," said Tess grabbing a glass of wine from one of the passing waiters. "Have you been here long?"

"Got here right before you," Bruce said, with a big Cheshire grin on his face. "I see an old friend of yours is performing tonight."

She looked over at Elvis, aka Phil, crooning a tune. In a million years, she would never admit that she had called him earlier to see if he would accompany her tonight. They'd laugh and never let her forget she had asked "Elvis" for a date.

"Yep," she said, turning back to them. "He does have a way of showing up when I least expect it, doesn't he?"

Louisa looked at Tess. "You know him?" she asked nonjudgmentally.

"Went on a date with him. Let me just say, it was before he was officially the reincarnated Elvis. It was only once, but since then I keep crossing paths with him or his curler-wearing mother." Tess gulped her wine. "I spend a lot of time waiting for Elvis to leave the building."

After they laughed at her comment, Louisa said to Bruce, "Don't let me forget to ask Jack if he's still coming tomorrow. Sharon's coming over and I want to introduce them. I think they'll hit it off swimmingly."

Tess managed a weak smile. To change the topic, she asked about Louisa's work with children. The conversation turned to holiday plans, vacation and then, Tess's favorite topic, shopping. During a lull in the conversation, Tess excused herself to hunt down Allie, to share her latest news on her noticeably absent date.

Walking through the crowded room, she couldn't help but come to the realization that everyone here was with a spouse, girlfriend, boyfriend, whatever. She was once again the only one showing up single.

She was thankful when she finally found Allie and Jon. They joked about her luck, or lack thereof, in securing a date. After the laughter subsided, she said, "I only care about winning. Right now I don't care about the person I need to use and abuse to win."

Jon rolled with laughter again, "And with that attitude, you want to know why you're still single?"

Tess rolled her eyes. On the far side of the room, she spied Doug with his arm around his wife. How could it be that mean, condescending Doug was married while she wasn't? She was far more personable and likeable than he could be in this lifetime and the next. Right now, she figured the only thing that could completely top this feeling would be to emerge from the bathroom trailing toilet paper on her shoe.

Ellen and her "significant other" stopped to chat with Allie and Tess. "I hate the word 'boyfriend.' It sounds too high school-ish."

As the woman droned on about who knows what, Tess started planning her escape. Allie and Jon had already disappeared leaving her stuck listening to the boor. Ellen kept invading Tess's space as she talked. Tess backed up, coming to a sudden stop when she felt a human body behind her. She spun around to offer an apology and ended up spilling her drink on Jack's sleeve.

"I'm so sorry." She immediately handed her glass to Ellen, and looked around for some napkins. "Come with me," she said, pulling on his sleeve. "We have to dry this so it doesn't stain."

"It's okay."

Tess dragged him to the corner of the room where a bar was set up, picked up a pile of napkins, and started pressing them onto his sleeve to soak up the liquid. "This is my fault," she said. "I should've been watching where I was going. You know what? Just bring the jacket to me on Monday and I'll have it dry-cleaned." She continued to grab napkin after napkin.

"It's fine." He calmly took her hand to make her stop.

She flushed with embarrassment. *What is wrong with me? I'm never like this around other people. Only when I'm around him. My heart is beating five hundred miles a minute. I'm going to have a heart attack.* "Let me pay to have it cleaned," she stammered, looking up at him. "Can I get you a drink?" She pointed to the bar.

"Sure. Whatever you're having," he answered, with amusement in his voice.

Is he laughing at me? Probably.

Jack casually ushered her aside after the bartender handed them two glasses of red wine. "Are you okay?' he asked.

She looked around to make sure no one was taking notice of the two of them. She was certain everyone could read her face and somehow know that they had watched a movie together last weekend at her house. Tongues would start wagging. "I'm fine."

He leaned his head close to hers. "Did you come alone?"

"I come alone every year. If I showed up with someone, the world might actually end."

"Tess, I've been thinking of last weekend. It was clear that Claire wanted me there. She and you need to have someone in your lives." He paused. "I can be there for you, but you need to let me in."

Tess felt like she was going to spit the wine out of her mouth all over the part of his jacket that was still dry. She swallowed and walked to the corner bench.

Jack followed, sat next to her, and looked at his wine glass before facing her. He looked tense; his jaw was rigid.

A bolt of something went through her as his knee pressed against hers when he shifted on the bench. Her heart beat quickened. Instinctively, she put her hand on top of his. It felt warm and big. That feeling ran through her again when she touched him. The hairs on the back of her neck were standing up.

This is crazy, she thought. *I'm sitting across the room from my devil-boss getting turned on by my soon-to-be-boss. On top of that he's analyzing my life while I'm getting a mini-high from touching him.* It was official; she needed therapy.

"You don't know how many times I've thought about you. About us. I like being with you, Tess, and want to be a part of your life." He looked directly into her eyes. "Then I think you've made it clear that we're nothing more than friends. I can't have just that any longer."

She looked down and saw her hand still on top of his. She made no motion to move it. She studied him and his words. "I don't understand." Tess looked into his eyes, and then away.

She felt him turn his hand over to grasp hers in his. Once she saw there was no one close enough to hear, she looked back at him and stared at his lips.

"If we didn't work together, would you have gone to dinner with me if I asked, Tess? Just you and me?"

She nodded. She was short of breath. She needed to take a crash course on picking up the signal "I'm single and interested." She breathed deeply and nodded again. "I'd like nothing more than that, Jack, except for you to kiss me and not stop. But you see, that can't happen. I'd be the one to get fired when we get caught." Tess sighed, not believing she had actually said the words.

His thumb rubbed against the back of her fingers. She could only imagine what his hands could do to the rest of her. A tingling sensation moved rapidly through her body. She clenched her thighs together. She found she had trouble breathing again.

He leaned a bit closer to her. His breathing was just as shallow as hers. She could see the look of desire in his eyes.

"I'd really like to take you out to dinner one night. I promise we'll go somewhere quiet, where no one will see us. And you'll get that kiss. I want to kiss your entire body."

She felt her face flush. "Really?" Her bottom lip tingled with excitement.

"What are you two whispering about over here?" Doug made a sudden appearance.

Tess pushed a few strands of hair off her face, Jack's hand was no longer on her. *Whew!* She hoped the light was dim enough that Doug couldn't see her face flushing.

"Work," she said, rather quickly.

Jack nodded in agreement.

Inwardly, she moaned when Doug pulled up a chair and actually began talking about work and potential clients she should consider bringing into the company next year. Jack's hand brushed against her shoulder as he got up, excused himself, and walked away. It was several minutes before she was able to make her escape from Doug as gracefully as possible.

When Phil took a break, Tess spent a little time chatting with him. In mere moments some of the ardent female Elvis fans from the office had gathered around him vying for attention. He took her hand and kissed her on the cheek before she could make her escape. It reminded her of a big, slobbery dog.

Tess could feel Jack's eyes tracking her through the room. The few times she found herself near him, her breathing changed and her heart beat faster.

At one point she stood next to him talking with Bruce and Louisa. His hand brushed lightly against hers. And she thought she was going to spontaneously combust. She felt like everyone saw and knew what was in her head. Tess excused herself before anyone else took notice.

After tonight's conversation, there was no way she could go back to having casual lunches with him. She could no longer ignore the definite chemistry between them. She couldn't go on this proposed date with him either. She'd have to avoid him and hurt his feelings. *Okay, problem solved,* she told herself. Her heart felt heavy and sad.

She made her way to Allie, and told her she was leaving.

As she walked through the Villa Christina parking lot, she heard that deep voice call her name. She could pretend she didn't hear, but that wouldn't solve anything. Tess stopped and waited for him to catch up to her. She could see his breath in the cold air.

"That was close," she said when he near. "Doug questioned me in more detail about what we were discussing."

"I need to see you, Tess."

Looking sadly into his eyes, she swallowed hard and forced out the words. "We can't, Jack." His eyes. Eyes that always seemed to be watching her, and now she knew why.

He took her hand in his and pulled her close. With his other hand he cupped the side of her face, and leaned down to kiss her.

Her heart was banging hard against her rib cage, trying to get out. She leaned in closer to him, and kissed him back with the same fervent demand. He released her hand and slid his arm around her to move her even closer to him.

Her body trembled as his mouth hungrily covered hers. She opened her mouth to accept his tongue. Her free hand made its way to the back of his neck to pull him to her, to maintain the contact, to not let this moment end.

The sound of someone's throat clearing brought them back to reality. She closed her eyes, and prayed that the *someone* didn't work for Tullamore. She kept her face downcast, and let Jack guide her to her car, parked a few rows over.

"Tess, it's okay," he whispered. "They didn't look familiar. It was an older couple." He chuckled. "Well, someone closer to my age than yours anyway."

"That's not funny," she said, looking up at him. "And that was *too close*."

"Tess, there's got to be a way around this situation. I want to hold your hand, and not have you nervous about being seen with me." He leaned closer to her. "I want to taste your lips, again. And your neck, and..."

She placed her finger on his lips, feeling her stomach tighten. "Sssh. Not here. We can't afford for someone to walk out and see us. If anyone asks, you were walking me to my car."

The corner of his lip turned into a smile. "I can help you win that bet."

"You can't," she answered, feeling her heart turning to stone. "I don't know what—"

His mouth was back on hers, and she kissed him despite her brain telling her this was wrong on so many different levels. Her heart told her brain to shut up and enjoy it.

Chapter Twenty-Four

Tess was glad Claire was skiing with her father in Colorado. She'd didn't want any witnesses for her nervous breakdown. She was so stressed out that she did truly worry that had Claire been there, she'd probably snap at her over nothing.

Since the company holiday party she had been trying, unsuccessfully, to find a date and avoid Jack at the same time.

And now time was running out. Today was December thirty-first.

At the Ryhan holiday luncheon, Jack mentioned he was taking his son skiing, but hadn't said when he was coming back.

Picking up the phone, she called his office only to hear he was not expected back until after the first of the year. Then she dialed his cell phone, but hung up without leaving a message when he didn't answer.

When shopping at the grocery store, picking up things for Dana and Harry's New Year's Party, Tess found herself checking out the men shopping or waiting in the checkout line. She knew she was truly pathetic.

As soon as she got home and put the food away, she opened the phone book to "dating services." Desperate times called for heinous measures. She was going to pay for her date, no matter what the cost. At this point, she'd take anything.

Though it was only noon time, she opened up a bottle of wine to calm her nerves.

Before she had a chance to decide on which service she was going to call, the telephone rang. Figuring it to be either Allie or Dana, she picked up the phone saying, "What?"

"Well, hello to you, too," Jack's deep voice said through the phone.

Mortified, she covered her mouth with her hand. She chided Claire all the time on the proper way to answer the phones, and here she wasn't any better.

"Sorry, Jack. I thought it was someone else."

"Well, I hope so," he chuckled. "I saw you called. What's up?"

"Aren't you skiing?"

"We had to come back early. Joel took a bad spill the first day and sprained his ankle."

"I'm sorry," she answered. "How is he?"

"Besides the bruising of the ego, okay, I guess." His voice sounded very patient and calming on the phone. "I don't think you called to find about my ski trip, did you?"

"Not really. I'm, um, in a little bit of a bind, and, well, I was, um, wondering what you're doing tonight?" Her hands were sweating, and before she let him answer, she continued, "I know it's last minute, but Harry's having this New Year's Party. I usually go by myself and well, how do I put this? Um. I know you said, um…"

"You need your fifth date."

"Yes," she said, knowing it sounded pitiful.

"I told you I was here to help," he responded

"So you don't mind doing it?" she asked.

"I can't believe you even had to ask that," he said, cutting her off.

"That's great," she said with a huge sigh of relief. Of course, her hands were so sweaty she was about to drop the phone. "You know, Allie's going to be there from work. She doesn't know anything except that we do lunch every once in awhile."

"So she doesn't know you have an amazingly hot mouth?"

Pulling her hair into a ponytail, she realized she was getting turned on by his voice. *So this is phone sex?* "It's not something we necessarily talk about," Tess replied.

"Okay, then I'll be sure not to bring it up tonight."

"Thank you, Jack. I owe you big time for this. See you at eight."

She felt relieved for the first time in a week. She was going to win! More importantly, she wasn't going to sing!

But possibly best of all, she was going to see Jack.

Chapter Twenty-Five

When Jack pulled into Tess's driveway, he noticed the outside Christmas lights were off.

He picked up the two bottles of champagne and headed toward the double front doors. Through the clear panes on either side, he saw her walk by in a T-shirt and gray sweat pants. She stopped and turned toward the door when the chimes rang.

Her hair was hanging loose around her shoulders. He wondered if it was his imagination that her face seemed to light up when she saw him.

"Hey!" She opened the door wider to let him in. "You're early."

He walked into the foyer. "Oh, I thought you meant the party started at eight, so I figured we needed some travel time."

"No, I guess I wasn't very clear. The official start time is eight, but most people are at least a half hour to hour late." She closed the door to the frosty December air. "I figured we didn't need to be there until nine. I should have clarified that you didn't need to show up until eight-thirty. I figured I still had another hour to get ready," she said, pulling at her T-shirt.

"Do you want me to go?"

She smiled, warm and friendly. "Of course not. Let me take your coat." She held out her hand for his wool coat. She pointed at his torso. "I like a man who wears a sweater vest. It's such a good look for you."

"Thank you," he replied.

She motioned for him to follow her as she walked toward the open living room.

The Christmas decorations had all been taken down and the poinsettias were moved along the back windows, but the house still smelled of pine and Christmas.

As if reading his mind, she said. "After I talked with you, I spent the rest of the day un-decorating the house. I just dragged the Christmas tree out onto the back porch a little while ago. You can still smell it, can't you?"

As she walked into the kitchen she said, "Make yourself at home, Do you want something to drink?"

"Sure, what are you having?" he asked, still following her.

She stopped suddenly and looked over her shoulder at him. "Promise not to laugh?"

She was always full of surprises. This was going to be good. He nodded.

"Water," she commented, as she poured a glass. "I figure if I fill up on it, then I won't over-drink the punch at Dana's tonight."

She was close enough that he could smell her perfume. This was the first time he had been really alone with her. There was no one here to make her pull back. Now with her standing so close, all he wanted to do was reach out and touch her.

Tess continued to talk. "I don't feel like nursing a hangover at my parents' dinner party tomorrow. Last year, I was supposed to have dinner here, and I felt like crap. I spent most of the day in bed. All I ended up making were the collard greens, and black eyed peas. Nothing else. I'm not making the same mistake this year."

Jack went to reach for her at the same time she turned to place the empty glass on the counter, leaving her just out of his reach.

"Listen, are you sure you don't want anything while I go finish getting ready?" She walked by and playfully hit him on the arm. "Help yourself to anything in the fridge."

He walked over to the table next to the couch and picked up a photo of her and Claire. It looked to be recently taken.

Out the window, through the trees and into the dark night, Jack could see the lights of the neighboring houses. The music stopped playing. He looked around the room for the tell-tale speakers located in the bookcases on both sides of the fireplace. The CD player must be somewhere nearby.

He opened the first cabinet door next to the bookshelf and found it neatly stacked with CDs and movies. He thumbed through them. She was a fan of opera as well as old, romantic movies. He went to the next cabinet and hit the play button.

Once the music started, he went into the kitchen and opened the fridge. He took out the half bottle of wine, and called loudly, "Where are the wine glasses?"

Tess shouted back from the other room, "In the dining room."

He stood in front of the china cabinet. Instead of getting the wine glasses, he pulled out the champagne flutes. He carried them to the kitchen and pulled out one of the bottles he had brought. He uncorked it over the sink and poured them each a glass.

He sat down on the bar stool at the breakfast counter just as she came out of the room across from the living room. This was not the person he normally saw at work nor the person who had answered the door in sweat pants.

While Jack had always thought she was very pretty, tonight Tess was stunningly beautiful. As she walked toward him in her black silky pants and matching halter-like top, he saw a sparkle in her eye as she scrunched her nose at him.

There was something completely different about her tonight. It suddenly occurred to him. *She appears relaxed.*

Tess stood directly in front of him "Can you help me with this necklace? I bought it for myself for Christmas, but I'm having the worst time with the clasp." She placed the chained opal pendant in his open hand. "Do you mind?"

"Not at all," he answered. This was the perfect opportunity to touch her, to feel her skin beneath his fingers.

She flipped around and lifted her hair, exposing her neck. The upper part of her back was bare. The temptation to slide his hand through the open side of her top to feel her skin was strong.

"Can you see? Do you need more light?" She turned her head slightly when he hadn't made an effort to put the necklace on.

He leaned forward to whisper into her ear, watching her body go completely still. "No. I need you to stay still."

He put the necklace around her neck and fastened

it. When he was done, his fingers stayed along the side of her neck. He leaned forward and pressed his lips against the skin of her shoulder. He felt her breathing stop.

She slowly turned her head while still holding her hair. His lips traced her neck. One hand traveled along the back edge of her top, and he felt the goose bumps on her skin. Her entire body shivered beneath his touch. Slowly, he turned her around to face him.

She was looking into his eyes. The eyes that before he had seen full of laughter, surprise, and determination, now only had heat. They didn't look away from his.

Her hands slid up his chest and around his neck. He reached around her to pull her body into his.

Kissing her lips slowly, he said "There's no one around to see us. You don't need to run away."

"I won't," she breathed. Instantly, her lips and mouth were on his.

When he kissed her, he felt a burning sensation run through him that he hadn't felt in a long time. A yearning and need had awakened within him. He pulled her tighter against him. Her fingers splayed through his hair, which only intensified his feelings.

Their mouths moved together in unison, wanting each other. When he heard a small moan escaping from her, his pressure against her mouth increased. Her body leaned into his just before she pulled her mouth away. They breathed quick gasps of air as if they had just finished a marathon run.

He put his mouth back over hers and kissed her deeply, his tongue exploring her. He didn't want the tasting to stop. When he did finally pull away, he looked into her shocked eyes.

Her one hand remained on the back of his neck while the other covered her red, swollen lips. She stared at him. "Wow," she whispered behind her hand. "That was...that was incredible."

He took her hand away from her mouth and kissed each finger. She exhaled deeply and looked away, possibly embarrassed at what she had said. He had never been complimented on the way he kissed before.

"You don't know how long I've wanted to do that. Kiss you and not have you run in fear." He kissed the palm of her hand. "You're amazing, Tess Grayson."

A slow smile spread across her face. He had seen the look before, and it melted him every time he saw it.

She pushed her hair behind her ear with her free hand, and with her full lips formed into a pout, she softly asked, "Are you trying to woo me, Jack Maristone?"

"Have been for a long time," he whispered back. His nose practically touching hers, he felt her breath on his lips before he tasted them again. He couldn't stop; he didn't want to. He ran his hand along her smooth cheek, and then into that soft, curly hair.

Pulling her face to his, he moved his lips along her jaw line toward her ear and then down her neck. He pressed his hand onto her bare back to move her closer and began sliding it lower. A part of him warned that he should stop before there was no turning back. At this rate, they wouldn't make it to the New Year's Party, but would instead have their own private party here.

Her eyes searched his to find the reason for his hesitation. When he didn't say anything, she tried to step out of his embrace. He moved one hand up against the lower part of her bare back. With the other, he reached to hand her a glass of champagne. He picked up his and clinked glasses.

"Here's to this year that is passing by, and to the next, and what it will bring."

She nodded and he saw the mischief in her eyes as she sipped from the glass.

"Oh, that's good." She rolled her eyes to the ceiling before looking back to him. "Very deep and thought provoking."

"Are you making fun of me?" he asked playfully.

"Uh, yep." She started to giggle.

He smiled. For a brief second he thought of how he and Elizabeth had never teased like this. She was too stiff. She said *he* was too serious. His mind quickly turned back to the woman in front of him, whom he had been infatuated with over the last few months.

With her free hand, Tess smoothed out his hair. "You know, when you first arrived, you looked so handsome and put together," she teased. "Now. Well, you should see yourself in the mirror. You're a mess. You should really invest in a brush, you know."

He tousled the top of her head. Her smile was infectious as she ran her fingers through the loosened strands and attempted to pull them back into a ponytail. "You do realize no one is going to notice anything wrong with mine. It looks like it always does."

She kissed him once again on the lips. He could taste the sweetness of the champagne.

"Now, go straighten yourself up before we walk over there. Allie's going to be there, and you don't need her flapping her lips on how Jack Maristone looked when he arrived. We can't have people thinking we were lip-locking, can we? I have a reputation to maintain."

"Can I be part of destroying it?"

She let out a long sigh. "No, you may not. We have to be careful tonight."

"I know." His lips continued to brush lightly against hers.

She pulled back to put her empty glass on the counter and pretended the collar of his shirt needed straightening. When she was done, she looked him directly in his eyes. The sparkle was still there. "Because…we are co-workers…who happen to be friends…going to a New Year's Party." She kissed her index finger and placed it on his lips. "That's my story, and I'm sticking to it."

He grabbed her hand. "That doesn't mean I have to." He put her index finger into his mouth sucking it with his tongue. He watched as she tried to keep her breathing normal. He could only imagine how she'd react when he tasted the rest of her.

"Yes…you…do." She could barely say the words. At that point, he knew he had her.

Though he released her, she didn't move from the spot where she was standing. She looked down at the floor before returning his gaze. Her voice shook. "I think we need to go."

"Are you sure you want to?"

"No. I mean yes. We have to go, or people will talk. Besides, Ally or Dana or both would come by to check on me."

She unexpectedly put her hands on either side of his face and kissed him passionately. He kissed her back, and heard the moan escape her lips as her hands moved behind his neck. He pulled her closer until they were practically one person.

She pulled away. "I...no...we shouldn't be doing this."

"It's up to you." He put his finger under her chin and lifted her face to his. He lightly brushed his lips against hers and felt her body stiffen once again. "What do you want?"

She opened her eyes and licked her lips. "I can't have what I want."

****

They walked hand-in-hand down the sidewalk to her brother's house. This night was going to kill Tess. She could no longer pretend that they were just friends, when in actuality each wanted more.

Her mind wandered back to half an hour ago when they were preparing to leave for the party. All Jack had done was help her with her coat. That's when she lost control.

Of their own free will, her hands had pushed his sweater vest off, and undone all the buttons to his shirt. When she tore off his undershirt, she was practically orgasmic running her fingers through the gray hairs on his chest. Realizing anyone could see them through the front door's side windows she guided him to her bedroom.

He had pushed her onto the bed, undone the back clasp at the neck of her halter-top, and pulled it to her waist. His tongue ran along the top of her breast while she fumbled with the zipper on his pants.

It was at that exact moment the phone had rung. Instinct told her to ignore it. They heard Dana's voice on the answering machine saying Dad was on his way to pick up her wine opener since Harry had just broken theirs. Tess decided to pick up the phone. It was hard to carry on a normal-sounding conversation when Jack's mouth was doing amazing things to her breast. His hand was traveling south. Thank goodness, she had listened to Allie and had bought those silk panties.

She had apologized for running late and promised Dana they'd be right over. She knew a Malone New Year's Party could not be without wine.

Like a true gentleman, Jack had helped her get her top back in its place and made sure she looked presentable before the doorbell rang.

Now, walking in the cold air, Tess wondered how they could manage to hide the attraction between the two of them. Surely, if her brother had sensed it, Allie would, too.

Tess had already confided to Dana about the events of the Christmas party. It was Dana who helped convince her, just this afternoon, to relax and go ahead with this. "It's just one night, and there's no way for this to make its way back to work. Allie will keep quiet. Hopefully."

One slip and one of their careers could be ruined. More than likely Doug would see to it that it was hers.

"Penny for your thoughts," Jack said, bringing her back to the present.

"You really don't want to know." She unclasped her hand, and looped her arm around his.

What words could she use to tell him that she wanted him, but at the same time was worried about the repercussions of giving in to their desires? How to say she was trying to relax and enjoy the evening, but her worry-wart gene was kicking into high gear?

His silence as they continued to walk made her wonder what he was thinking. Probably that she needed to be put in a loony bin.

Before opening the door to Harry and Dana's, she looked at him. "Remember our story for tonight, okay?"

Instead of showing a sign that he agreed with her story, he quickly cupped her face in his gloved hands and assaulted her mouth. Her entire body responded with a tingling that went all the way to her toes. *Oh yeah, I want him.*

When the door opened, they looked guiltily at Dana standing before them with her mouth gaped open. Tess brushed her gloved hand through her hair and walked past Dana. With gritted teeth, she said, "Don't breathe a word to anyone about what you just saw. Got it?"

Once inside, with a bright, forced smile Tess said, "Dana, this is Jack Maristone. We work together. Jack, this is Dana Malone, my sister-in-law, and long-time friend"—as she hugged Dana, she whispered—"who will remain so as long as she keeps her lips sealed."

The sexual tension was overwhelming. Tess wasn't going to make it through the night.

Dana took their coats and deposited them in the library. The living room was filled with people. Tess took Jack's hand, and was walking with him toward the kitchen when she saw Allie and Jon looking at them.

We're friends, she kept repeating in her head as she walked toward the back of the house. Once in the kitchen, she acted as if there was nothing unusual and made light conversation with Dana and Allie while filling wine glasses for herself and Jack.

She introduced Jack to several of the partiers, all

the time referring to him as *a friend*, though he kept one hand at her waist or lightly held her hand.

While Jack and Harry were in the other room talking with her dad, Allie grabbed Tess's hand and dragged her to the dining room. Picking up a plate, Allie started to pile it high with food.

"Do you know who's in the other room?" Allie asked in a low voice. She slapped Tess's hand when she stole a meatball. "Get your own plate."

"It's more fun to eat off yours."

"Answer me," Allie said, holding her plate out of Tess's reach. "Is he your *date* for the night?"

"Yes, but before your little brain goes into overdrive, we're just friends." Tess nibbled at a cracker and cheese from Allie's plate.

Jon came into the room, apparently to eavesdrop

"He's going to be our boss!" Allie said in a high-pitched whisper.

"We're friends, Allie. He's agreed to be my date for tonight only. He wanted to help me win that stupid bet of ours."

"Well, let me tell you, you sure look like more than friends walking around here. Holding hands...and the flushed look on your face when you came in didn't look like it was from the cold." She stopped and looked hard at Tess. "What are you *really* doing?"

Blushing, Tess stopped picking at the hot cheese spread, and moved to the shrimp. "It *was* cold outside. I can't lose this bet. I took him up on his offer so I could win. You know me, I hate to lose."

Allie stared at her. "That's a given. Your duplicity is not flying with me. When did this more-than-a-friendship start?"

Tess studied the food for awhile. "You might say it's been building up. At first I thought it was a little flirtation on his part, you know, wondering if he still had it. I brushed it aside, and kept telling myself it was nothing. But evidentially, it was something. The night of the Christmas party was the turning point."

Allie stood gaping at her, stunned by the news.

"I couldn't ignore it anymore, Allie. Not saying I am an expert, but let me tell you. What he does with his mouth is unbelievable. He kisses so much better than Kevin ever could. And his hands—"

Jon interrupted. "Yeah, sounds like a friend zone violation to me."

Tess picked at the shrimp cocktail in the center of the table.

Allie stared at her for a long time. "So what happens on Wednesday morning when we are all back in the office. What then? You're just going to end this and pretend nothing happened?"

Tess slumped into a chair in the corner and buried her face in her hands. "I don't know."

Allie shooed Jon out of the room. "You've fallen for him, haven't you?" She waited for an answer that never came.

"Tess, this is so dangerous. What if this gets out? Have you thought about that? Doug will throw that behind of yours out on the street so fast, you won't have time to blink. He's threatened by you. I think he's mad that you brought Ryhan in and that they want nothing to do with him."

Standing up and crossing her arms, Tess whispered loudly, "First of all, the only one from work who knows about this is you. So if anyone finds out, I'll know where it came from. Second, believe me, I know there can't be anything more to it. Jack and I are to be only friends. Apparently, no one seems to be talking when he and I go to lunch together. Even you didn't have a clue."

Allie shook her head in disbelief. "You wanna bet? Mike in the fitness center made a comment to me after your date with him. He said that you weren't interested in him because 'you wanted the old guy.' At first, I had no idea who he was talking about, until I saw the two of you walking back from lunch one day."

Setting her plate on the table, Allie continued, "Honestly, Tess, you should see the way you two try *not* to look at each other. If anyone had suspicions about you, all they needed to do was to pay close attention at the company party. I was trying to make my way to the two of you before Doug could, but he beat me to it. Then you walking in here tonight holding hands confirmed it. Good grief, missy, what are you thinking?"

"Someone referred to me as 'the old guy'?" Jack leaned against the wall, pretending to be insulted by the comment.

Tess spun around. Her heart was pounding, hard and fast. *How much did he hear?*

He walked up to the table and picked up a plate. "I'm not *that* old. I'm only turning fifty next month."

Tess realized he hadn't heard enough, since he only commented on what Allie said at the end.

Allie shook her head, and said, "Well, you both have my word that I won't say anything. So long as it's *just* tonight."

"Maybe," Jack answered.

Tess looked down at her feet. She thought she was going to be sick. She kept repeating "friends" in her mind.

Allie narrowed her eyes. On her way out of the room she whispered to Tess, "We'll talk later. Alone."

Jack's eyes followed her. "Is everything okay between you two?"

"She's just worried about me bringing you here. She thinks I'll fall head over heels and do something stupid."

"Will you?" He stood close to her and brushed his hands against hers.

"What do you think?" Tess took a step back from him. "Remember, we have to keep our wits about us."

"I *think* you worry too much." He placed his hand on her bare shoulder. The tingling started all over again. "Just enjoy yourself tonight, because I plan to."

He was right. She and Allie were probably just overreacting.

She smiled up at him. She couldn't resist the urge to reach up and touch his face, to feel his warm skin beneath her fingers.

She was glad she hadn't told Allie what had transpired in her bedroom, hadn't told her that it was incredible. Beyond anything she had ever imagined or experienced.

Tess felt him lean into her hands. *Keep your wits about you*, she told herself mentally. *Yeah, that's really gonna happen.* She knew she was way too attracted to him, and wanted to be near him—to have him touch her like he had an hour earlier.

****

At midnight, with champagne flute in hand, Tess

found herself sandwiched between Allie and Jack while they counted down the seconds. He leaned over and kissed her lightly on the lips when the clock struck midnight. He was keeping up his end of the bargain.

She looked into his eyes and realized they needed to leave here…and soon. She had already planned the escape route. It was faster if they cut through the backyard to get to hers.

She turned to Allie and hugged her, wishing her a Happy New Year before doing the same to Dana and Harry standing nearby.

Once all the hugs and cheers were given, Jon said in a loud, drunken voice, "Well, I didn't think the Ol' Ice Princess had it in her. Now I've lost a hundred dollars in a bet I had with Harry here." He started to sway as his wife jabbed him in the ribs with her elbow.

Tess raised her eyebrows to look back and forth between her brother and Jon. The room felt rather warm as she realized Harry and Jon had bet on her inability to date. Sister-in-law Dana looked away guiltily.

"Who else has been betting on my social life?"

Jon started to answer. Allie tackled him and clamped her hand on his mouth with full force. He swaggered back and crashed onto the couch, taking Allie with him.

"What the *hell*?" Tess asked.

The absence of speech was deafening. Everyone stared at Jon and Allie heaped on the couch, and then back to Tess. Allie responded, "Jeff and the team at work had a pool going. There's about fifty dollars in it saying you wouldn't make it to the five dates. Jeff was the only one who thought you could do it."

"What? No one had faith in me?" Tess's voice was

getting louder. "And *Ice Princess*? Which one of you jackasses dubbed me with that title?"

Dana picked up the last of Jon's spilled food from the floor. "I guess you can blame me and Harry for that, Tess. Don't be angry. You know we're just jangling your cage."

"I'm not *angry*—" she said.

Dana quickly changed the subject. "So what's everyone's New Year's Resolution?"

Allie had risen from the couch. She whispered quietly for only Tess to hear, "I know what it better *not* be."

Jack looked at Tess and said, "I think I know what my mine is."

Allie again whispered, "Bad answer." She stared at Tess.

Grabbing Allie's hand, Tess said, "Follow me." They went into Harry's office. "What is going on? Can't you just be happy for me?"

"Not with him, I can't. I can't let you commit career suicide. That's exactly what's happening here."

"We're just having a good time."

Dana walked into the room. "Does *he* think the same thing? Because I don't think he does."

Allie grabbed Tess by her shoulders. "Please don't do anything with him. You're not into casual relationships or one night stands. You don't have the ability to just walk away from him."

"As much as I hate to be a killjoy," Dana said, "Allie's right. You'll put your heart into this and it'll get broken. Then what?"

Tess wrapped her arms around herself. As much as she hated what she was hearing, she knew they were right. She just didn't want to accept it.

Allie said, "I'm sorry, Tess, you suck at playing poker. Doug's been watching you, and he'll pick up on this in an instant. I can't bear to see you get hurt *and* be unemployed at the same time."

Tess felt the pain in her stomach growing bigger and bigger by the second. There were too many thoughts running through her brain. *The bets. Ice Princess. Reorganization. Jack. Career-suicide.*

She'd have to be a complete idiot to not see where this was headed. What had she done? *Stupid, stupid, stupid!*

Dana interrupted her thoughts "Tess? He seems like a nice guy. But you've got to see that with Tullamore's non-fraternization policy, there can be nothing between you."

Allie commented, "Well, at least you didn't sleep with him."

"I almost did," Tess meekly answered.

"What?" Dana and Allie exclaimed in unison.

"I need to go." Tess looked around and the room was spinning. She was going to be sick. *Air.* She needed some quickly before she passed out.

Dana grabbed her hand. "Don't throw it away."

Tess looked at her, not understanding what "it" was, but figuring it was her career. She walked quickly to the foyer to grab her coat from the rack. Before her arms were in the sleeves, she knew Jack was behind her.

"I have to go…and you have to leave."

He gently took her hand and pulled her to him. She could feel his heat. He put his finger under her chin to lift her face. "What is it?" he asked softly.

She tried with all her might to sound calm when she answered, but her words came out harshly, "It's late. You need to head home. You've got a long drive."

She saw the confusion on his face when he let go of her hand to reach for his coat. She felt an abyss grow between them.

From the office doorway Dana's eyes seemed sad as she watched the interchange between them.

Tess and Jack walked silently to her house. She felt as lonely and empty as some of the dark houses they passed.

How had she let this happen? If it hadn't been for Allie's stupid bet, she would still be living in her "ice princess realm." Now her heart and that stupid warm tingling she felt inside wanted her to put her career on the line.

Jack's eyes were watching her as they moved along the sidewalk back to her house.

Quickly she built up the ice wall around her. She could feel it. Just like she could feel his confusion over her sudden change of behavior.

He tried once to take her gloved hand in his, but she pulled away and put it in her coat pocket.

The thought that Jack might be using her to make himself feel like a man again grew more and more in her mind. She remembered a couple of years ago hearing Dana's brother discuss how devastated he was after his divorce. He'd slept with the first woman he dated just to make sure he still *had it*.

Fine. If he's using me, than I'm surely using him as well. She could handle that. As her brain tossed this around this rationale, she didn't realize they'd arrived at her house and were standing by his car in the driveway.

"Tess, what happened?" he asked.

His face was half shadowed by her front porch light. She saw his bewilderment. Something squeezed at her heart, and she wanted to touch his face. She pushed her hands deeper in her pockets to resist the urge.

She looked up at the night sky's stars. "I used you," she lied. She licked her lips. "I knew how you felt about me, and because I wanted to win this bet I called you...and used you."

She could sense his body tensing. He shoved his hands into his coat pockets.

Gruffly, he said, "Wait! I thought based on what happened in there, you were—"

She interrupted, "It was wrong of me. But we both know there can never be anything between us," she said. "This was a mistake."

She looked at his chin so as not to look into his eyes. She counted to ten as she always did when there was a hard message to deliver and she needed to sound confident and detached. *Ice Princess*—how appropriate. She wasn't quite able to pull off the persona. At that moment she hated herself more than she hated anything else. She'd been cruel and hurtful.

His eyes narrowed. "Is that what this was? A mistake?"

Instead of answering, she nodded.

Jack stared at her before roughly grabbing her shoulders. His voice was barely a whisper. "Was it *nothing* when you moaned while we were on your bed?"

She remained silent while his eyes searched hers.

"Is *this* a mistake?" He lowered his mouth to hers.

It took all the willpower she could muster not to respond or react. She clamped her lips tightly together.

He stepped back. She saw the anger building up in his face.

"Jack, it is a mistake to pretend we can be a couple. We need to go back to how things were—"

He cut her off, "Don't give me that, Tess. That's BS. What about what you said that day at the fountain, and at the Christmas party?"

He stopped and shook his head. "I believed I was actually falling in love with you, and you with me. And I believed our passion tonight was genuine. Are you telling me I was wrong?"

She nodded her answer.

Her legs began to shake when he opened his car door and got inside.

"I can't be friends with you, Tess. Friends don't lie to each other like this."

She remained still as she watched him pull out of her driveway and down her street. Her chest felt heavy. It was hard to breathe. When his taillights disappeared she turned to walk into her house on wobbly legs. She had never felt so hollow inside.

Maybe this was why she never trusted herself to date, or to care. It was too painful and too much work.

Chapter Twenty-Six

Tess lay in bed, pulled the covers over her head, and relived the night before. It had started so well, but ended so badly.

She picked up the phone to dial Jack's number. She listened to his outgoing recording and left a message that she needed to talk with him. She had to apologize. What if she had just thrown away the best thing that happened? She didn't have to ask *what if.* She had thrown him away, and he had loved her.

After he had left, she went into the house and cried. When was the last time she had done that? She hadn't shed a tear when she discovered Kevin cheating on her. A tear didn't fall when her divorce was finalized, yet here she was, crying over her horrible treatment of Jack. He would never have mistreated her likewise. She had lost a trusted friend, and it was all her stupid fault.

She crawled out of bed and walked to the kitchen to make a pot of coffee. Could she drown her misery with a caffeine high? She searched for some coffee liqueur to add to it. Once she had poured herself a large mug, she walked over to the window and looked out.

The bright, sunny day was the opposite of how she felt inside. She wiped away the tear that snaked down her cheek. She had to pull herself together before Claire came home.

There was a loud banging on her front door as if

whoever was there frantically wanted to be let inside. It would be expecting too much if she opened the door to see Jack standing there. *Completely unreasonable.* She had hurt him too badly.

Opening the door, she saw both Allie and Dana standing there. Dana held a pastry box. Without a word, Tess walked to the couch.

She heard the front door shut. She listened as they made their way into the kitchen to help themselves to coffee and the bottle of liqueur.

"How are you?" Allie called from the kitchen.

"How do you think?" Tess glanced behind her. She knew they could see her red, wet eyes.

"Sorry. Stupid question on my part," Allie said sympathetically. She sat down on the opposite side of the couch. "Tess, we're sorry. You know we were just looking out for you and your career, don't you?"

Dana sat on the loveseat after placing the box of jelly donuts on the coffee table.

"Is that supposed to make me feel better? Is that supposed to make any of this go away?" Tess heard her voice shaking. "I think I fell in love with him. I was so verbally brutal after we left your house that now he's not even willing to be my friend."

Dana pushed the box of donuts to Tess. "He won't even be your friend?" she asked.

"No. I wanted to make him not feel for me so that it could end before it got a good foothold." Tess pushed the box away. "The worst part is how I feel inside. I hurt him so badly and now *I'm* aching inside." She stopped when her voice started shaking again.

Dana asked sympathetically, "So what's going to happen when you see him at work?"

"Nothing," Tess answered. "He'll probably pretend I don't exist."

Allie shook her head, "I'm sorry, Tess. I really am, but you know what has to be."

Nodding, Tess stood to walk to the window. Outside the trees swayed in the wind. She watched leaves on the ground blow across the yard. Taking a deep breath, she said softly, "I know. How could I have been so naïve?"

Allie answered, "You weren't. Look on the bright side. We stopped you before it got too far out of hand."

Closing her eyes, Tess ran her fingers through her hair and scratched her scalp. "At least I won't be in the office that much."

"What are you talking about?" Dana asked.

When Tess didn't answer, Allie responded. "Ryhan wants Tess, Bruce, and Jeff on-site for the next few months as they work to get them on-track."

"I'll be in the office on Monday for our monthly staff meeting and to gather some stuff up. After that I'll only go into the office when I need to."

"That may make it easier to get over this then," Dana commented.

Wiping at her eyes, Tess continued to look out the window. "Why does this hurt so much? Will this emptiness inside me *ever* go away?" Tess asked, brushing tears away.

"You know time is healing," Allie said, putting her arm around Tess. "You need this time and the space of working outside the office and not seeing him. It's going to be hard, but we're here for you."

The room was silent as Tess once again wiped her eyes and blew her nose. What was she going to do next? She had her daughter to think of. At least Claire wasn't here to witness how foolish her mother had been. She had to pull herself together before her baby came home at noon from her ski trip.

"I guess the one bright thing from last night is that at least I won the bet and won't have to sing." She stopped to look up at the ceiling. "Plus I'll carry the memory of how it felt orgasmic when he kissed me."

Tess looked at her friends. "I guess the only thing I can do now is carry on like I did before any of this started. One day we'll laugh about all this and the outrageous dates. Right? This just isn't a good time. In the meantime, I'm going to pretend none of this ever happened. I just ask that this *Jack thing* stays between us."

"You can't go back to the way you were, Tess," Dana said sadly. "Your heart was closed back then."

"Yes, I can. The heart goes back into the vault." Tess reached into the box for a donut. "It worked for me before, and it will work for me going forward."

****

Allie had suggested that the best way for Tess to beat her depression was to shop. And the best kind of shopping on a day like today was for shoes. This was the perfect time since stores were having their boot clearance sales.

Leaving Allie at the front of the store looking at a pair of leopard-print shoes, Tess walked down the aisle and spied the pair of leather boots she'd been eyeing since the fall. Nothing would stop her from getting them today. She grabbed the boots just as another woman was reaching for them. Tess kicked off her shoes, put the soft boots on, and admired them in the floor mirror; they felt like butter on her feet.

Allie sauntered down the aisle with a shopping bag over her shoulder. "Why do you always get short boots?"

"Because the tall ones never fit over my calves." Tess picked up her purse and the boot box from the floor.

"Huh! Follow me. We're going to find a pair that will work." Making their way down the next aisle, Allie continued, "I found the perfect way to get back at Jon for making a complete ass of himself on New Year's."

Running her hand along the boots, Tess asked, "What'd you do now? Tell him he is *cut off*?"

"Much more drastic than that." Allie stopped in front of a pair of camel-colored leather boots. "What size are you?"

"Seven. Let me guess—you started wearing cotton panties?"

"No, I have my limits." Allie pulled out a box marked size seven. "Here, try these. I cancelled his girlie magazine subscription. Not getting his girlie mag fix is worse than not getting sex. You should have seen his face when I told him."

Tess chuckled as she sat down on the bench, kicking off her shoes and pulling up her pants leg to put the boots on.

"How do those feel?"

Tess held up one leg. "My leg feels like it is choking. Do they make the leg part bigger?"

"Man, you do have big calves. Take those off and we'll find another pair," Allie said, looking around.

Tess tugged the boot, but it wouldn't budge. "I can't get it off."

Allie tried to push the leather top down. It was suctioned onto Tess's leg. "Okay, hold your leg up and I'll try to pull it off." Allie grabbed the boot heel to pull while Tess held onto the side of the bench. The boot didn't move.

"I think it's stuck." Allie kept pulling at the bottom of the boot, which didn't want to loosen from Tess's leg. "I hate to admit it, but I think you were right last summer when you said he fantasizes about the women in them during our lovemaking."

Trying to take her mind off the boot stuck to her leg, Tess asked, "Did he tell you this?"

Still pulling, Allie said, "Not in so many words."

"What did he say?"

Allie face turned red as she gave the boot a hard yank. "That he liked to take a quick peek before we fooled around."

Allie's anger seemed to loosen the boot. She fell backward onto her bottom, and Tess was pulled off the bench. The two women sat sprawled on the floor's aisle. Both sat up at the same time with looks of surprise on their faces.

Allie held the boot in front of her. "No more of these for you."

Tess released a bubble of laughter. "See? I'm always right," she said. "I told you men cannot commit to one woman, and I told you I can't wear those."

"I guess you're *right*." Allie burst into a guffaw. They sat on the floor laughing, while the other shoppers stared at them.

Tess didn't care; she needed the tension release.

Chapter Twenty-Seven

As hard as it was for Jack to admit, Tess had been right to end anything between them. Ever since the discussions had started about him being in charge of Tullamore's Eastern Division, he knew she'd ultimately report to him.

The hard part was not just the words she'd used, but that she had treated the break-off like business, removing all emotions. She was well-known at the company for looking at a situation objectively and making recommendations for changes. But outside of work, he had seen her warm and compassionate side.

Remembering the hardness of her mouth during that last kiss was the worst. It was excruciating hearing her say what had happened between them was a mistake. He had never felt more alive than when he was with her. She had looked into his face earlier that same evening and told him he was incredible. It was hard to believe that less than a week had passed since their near-lovemaking evening.

Jack sat in his office watching people meander into the building after the weekend. Today everyone would learn the details of the new personnel structure. Some would learn they had new managers or directors. Others would be told their positions were being restructured and that the company would help them look for a new job. A number of early retirements would be announced as well.

He was thankful Bruce was willing to step down to a senior consultant. Bruce wanted to get away from managing people and return to managing projects. He admitted that working with Tess on Ryhan had made him realize he missed consulting.

Jack looked at the email draft he was going to send to the staff, after the various managers had a chance to talk with their employees this morning.

A part of him wanted to sit in Doug's monthly team meeting just so he could see Tess. However, he knew she'd avoid making any eye contact with him, and he wasn't ready to put himself through that.

He looked at his watch. She was probably pulling into the parking garage right now. She'd stop at the coffee cart before running into the meeting. Doug would make some comment, to which she'd roll her eyes.

Jack stared at his computer screen for a long time before reading the company-wide email sent by Tullamore President Richard Brown. The email talked about changes needed to stay competitive in the industry as well as to incorporate some recent acquisitions. It continued into the necessity of consolidating into fewer geographical segments and getting back to managing clients rather than creating many layers within the organization.

He halted his reading when a cancelled meeting notification appeared in his email. Tess had deleted their reoccurring bi-weekly Wednesday lunch meeting from her calendar.

Now he regretted telling her they couldn't be friends. Being her cool business self, it wouldn't have surprised him if she had kept the luncheon dates. She'd pull herself up and hold her chin high. Now there was no going back.

They were through before they started.

Chapter Twenty-Eight

"You look like you're miles away." Phil sat on the bench next to her at the horse corral.

"Hello, stranger," Tess said, giving him a wan smile.

She wasn't in the mood to be light and gay. She was tired of pretending that nothing was wrong with her life. Only recently had she realized that Claire was picking up on her mood. She had lied to her daughter and told her it was hormonal. This seemed to work.

"Haven't seen you here in awhile," she told Phil.

"Needed to take some time off from lessons until I could sort out a few things financially." He didn't look the least bit embarrassed by confiding money troubles.

"I read an article last weekend in the paper about you." Tess looked to see that his sideburns had grown and were abnormally thick. "That should help you out."

"Honestly, I have been busy since the middle of December. I even went to Graceland last week, networked and made a few more business connections."

"Good for you." Tess looked to the ring where Claire was guiding her horse through a series of high jumps.

Patting her knee, Phil said, "You look tired."

"Just been busy," she said, not meeting his eyes. "I've spent the last two weeks at a client site that needs a lot of help getting on track. The thought of traveling the next few weeks to some of their large sites is not at the top of my list of fun things right now."

"Anything else going on? You look more sad than tired."

She chewed on her nail, ignoring the remark. "Hey! I hear you're seeing Maggie. She's a real nice girl."

"You're not jealous, are you?"

Tess cracked a smile. "No," she said, looking at him. His eyes reflected concern.

"What is going on, Tess?"

"I don't think I have been a nice person. I did something real stupid. I thought I was protecting myself. Instead I ended up hurting someone—someone who was a friend."

Trying to get a grip on her raw emotions, she sighed and ran her fingers through her hair. "I said something that I shouldn't have, and I doubt he'll ever trust me again. Not that I blame him. I hate what I did, and I hate me more for it."

"Have you told that someone how you feel?"

"No. He made it clear we're not friends anymore. Plus I found out yesterday, he's seeing someone."

She turned to look to the far end of the indoor arena. Claire and her horse were gracefully sailing over each jump. Maybe she'd break down and enter Claire into the upcoming competition that her instructor had been talking about. They would have more time on their hands now that she was swearing off men again.

Yesterday at lunch, Bruce, unaware of Tess and Jack's prior involvement, had shared some information with her. His wife Louisa had introduced Jack to a widowed friend of hers before Christmas. It seemed that they had hit it off immediately. They had gotten together a second time on New Year's Day when Jack went over to watch college football.

Bruce had said, "The four of us are having dinner tonight at Midtown Diner. We've got tickets to an upcoming show at the Fox. I'm just happy that Jack's finally putting the divorce behind him and getting out to live a little."

The words slapped at her. The realization that Jack was seeing someone so soon after their fallout only strengthened her belief that she had done the right thing. Maybe she *had* been the stepping stone to see if he was still attractive to the opposite sex.

Bruce continued, "You know, Tess, Elizabeth was not a warm person. After the divorce Jack was very distrustful of women in general."

Tess laughed nervously. "I thought Jack and I got along fine."

"That's because it's purely business between you, and nothing else. You're harmless and non-threatening."

Last night Tess had rationalized that Jack could at least take this woman out in public and be seen. With her any outings had to be secret and hidden—like her silk panties. No one but her ever saw them. She should've stayed with the cotton granny ones.

"I take it you wanted it to be more than friends," Phil commented—bringing her back to the present.

"It never would've worked. We probably shouldn't have crossed the friendship line," she admitted.

She saw Phil waiting for her to continue her woeful tale. It hurt too much to share that Jack had moved on while she was a tangled mess inside. "I guess that's what happens when you take a risk. If it doesn't work out, someone can get hurt." She sat on her hands and made circles with her boot toe on the floor.

"That's a strange statement, coming from you." Phil's voice was full of sympathy. "If it wasn't for you, I wouldn't have taken the risk and followed my dreams. I'm *much* happier now, thanks to you."

She looked at him and felt moistness in her eyes. "Yeah, well, I betcha if I ran into him today, he'd look right through me."

"You just need to get his attention. Do something drastic. Make him notice you."

She stopped staring at her feet and looked into space. "I can't. I just keep telling myself to forget about what happened and move forward. I need to be happy for him finding someone else."

Phil hugged her close to his body. Maybe he was hoping to ease some of the hurt. "Well, you're going to need to do something about it, Tess," he said firmly. "You'll figure something out."

Chapter Twenty-Nine

Being forty sucked. Sometime in the last week, Tess's eyes had decided they couldn't read the words on the paper without reading glasses. She hated having to pull them out to read something. Once she had them on the words on the paper no longer seemed so small, but she would never openly admit this to anyone.

She took off her glasses to rub her eyes. Figuring out what Ryhan's problems were was easy. Getting their executives to approve her recommendations was another thing.

The company valued its employees very little. Sure, they conducted an employee survey on an annual basis, but then threw the results in a bottom file cabinet drawer. Turnover was at an all-time high.

Expenses were through the roof, and, due to their turnover, the company hadn't introduced a new quality product in over two years. They tried to throw money at their employees for new product and sales ideas, but at the same time treated them like they were less than human.

"How about we call it a day and go to lunch?" Bruce asked.

Jeff looked at his watch. "Geez. I can't believe it's already one o'clock. If it's a liquid lunch—and I don't mean coffee or one of those energy shakes we've been drinking lately—then I'm all over it."

Tess leaned her head against the back of the chair and closed her eyes. She couldn't believe how tired she was. In her estimation, the money they were making from this project wasn't enough. Maybe they could add an "obstinate client charge" to their fees to pay for long and needed vacations for the three of them.

Lifting her head from the back of the chair to look at Bruce, she said, "Tell me again why you wanted to become a consultant."

"The challenge of it all," he answered with a big smile.

"You're sadistic," Jeff replied.

"Shut the computers down and let's call it a day. There's always tomorrow." Bruce closed his laptop. "Let's go."

"You're right." Tess smiled big. "Hey, you know where we haven't been in awhile? The Tuxedo. I can get a salad, and you"—she looked at Jeff—"can get that beer."

"Way to go, Tess," Jeff said. "I like your style."

****

They arrived at The Tuxedo at the tail end of the lunch hour. While being escorted to a table near the window, Bruce pointed out Jack, Doug and a few other department heads from the office were on the opposite side of the restaurant. The last thing they needed was to see, or be seen by, upper management.

"Wait until they leave before you order that beer," Tess said to Jeff as they sat down.

Jack was in her direct line of sight. This was the first time in a month she'd seen him. Seeing his gray hair, that square jaw, his full lips gave her stomach butterflies. *If he looks at me with those warm hazel eyes, I'll be done with.* No sooner had the thought appeared in her head then Jack glanced her way and caught her looking at him.

She looked down at the menu, completely embarrassed at being discovered. *If he comes over,* she told herself, *just act cool and polite. He's my boss's boss, and that's all.* If that didn't work, thinking of Doug naked should do it. This, however, caused her mind to wander to memories of Jack: nearly naked in her bed, running her fingers through his gray chest hair and being turned on, and his hands exploring her body.

"Tess. Are you okay?" Jeff asked, studying her.

Great, she'd been caught having x-rated thoughts at lunch by a co-worker. "Is it me, or does it feel like they have the heat cranked up?" she asked, trying to recover.

Bruce responded, "It's a little warm, but then it's cold outside."

They sat in silence and studied their menus. When the waitress came to take their orders, Tess asked for water. Bruce and Jeff asked the waitress to bring straws for their light beers—to make them look like ginger ale. Tess and the waitress laughed at the idea.

Tess saw Jack watching her as her hand pushed a mass of hair off her face. She immediately looked away. She wasn't going to look in his direction no matter how much effort it required on her part.

The three chatted about the cold weather. After the waitress returned with their drinks, Bruce dropped a bomb in Tess's lap. "The other night Louisa and I were talking about going to Grand Cayman in March. We're waiting to see if Jack and Sharon are going to join us."

"Sharon?" Tess put her glass down when she felt her hand tremble.

"Remember? She's Louisa's friend that we introduced Jack to?"

Tess's smile was forced. She had to remember it was over. She had used him to help her win a bet. She couldn't have feelings for him.

"You're right. I forgot."

Jeff asked, "Are ya'll talking about Jack Maristone?"

Tess felt it was best to change the subject. "Yep. Do you have any plans for a vacation, Jeff?" She picked up her glass and was happy that the shaking hands were gone.

"Taking the kids to Florida for spring break. What about you?" Jeff asked.

"My parents have a place down at Seagrove Beach. Claire and I may go down there for spring break."

"Where at in Seagrove?" a familiar deep voice asked.

Tess's head snapped to look at the owner of the voice. Jack.

"About two miles east of downtown," she answered. She was somewhat surprised that anyone could hear her voice over the pounding of her heart which seemed to echo through the room.

Doug jumped in. "What are you three doing here?"

Tess quickly answered, "Taking a late lunch to talk about our next steps with Ryhan."

"This seems out of the way from their office," Doug countered.

"Yes, well our strategy is to not have anyone from there overhear our discussion," Tess answered coolly.

Jack pulled a chair out and sat down across from Tess. She could only imagine what she looked like to him—tired eyes, messed up hair, and probably smudged make-up after this morning's frustrations. Thank goodness her big-buttoned red jacket with the scooped collar looked attractive on her.

"Let me talk with the team here," Jack said, dismissing Doug and the others. "I'll meet you back at the office."

Bruce and Tess watched Doug leave. When the waitress came with their food, she asked Jack what he wanted to drink. Jeff gulped when Jack said he'd have what everyone was having.

Jack looked at both Tess and Jeff, but focused his attention on her. "I haven't seen you in awhile," he said. "How are things going?"

"Been keeping busy at Ryhan," Tess answered for the group. She was surprised at her even voice.

"That's what Bruce tells me," Jack responded. "I also heard that you were pretty straightforward with their HR folks on a few things last week when they shot down some of your recommendations."

She wanted to slap her head. Of course, Bruce would keep him in the loop on what was happening at Ryhan. They got together socially outside of work.

"We have a Monday morning meeting to go over our entire proposal. If they start making the recommended changes next month, it will still take them a full year before they see any improvements. The issue is getting management to buy into this, because their president doesn't see the value of treating employees with dignity."

Leaning back to let the waitress put her salad down, Tess continued, "Management is expected to be on call twenty-four/seven, and that tends to filter down to all their employees. One of the IT architects told me after he missed his daughter's birth he thought about quitting, but he needs the job because his wife is going to stay at home. That's just one of many horror stories we've heard. Yet all the president cares about is the bottom line."

"I'm meeting tomorrow afternoon with the HR Director and the Assistant to the CFO to go over our plan before we collectively present it to the management team."

Bruce's fork stopped halfway to his mouth. "You got in with the CFO's office? When did that happen?"

"Just as we were leaving. I ran into him when I was coming out of the ladies' room. I told him we were leaving for lunch to go over a few things. I pitched him some of our ideas with a dollar value tied to each, and he fell for it."

Bruce lifted his hand and gave her a high five. Jeff did the same.

"When I grow up, I want to be just like you," Bruce said, before putting his fork full of turkey salad in his mouth.

"Doesn't everyone?" Jeff took a drink of his beer.

Tess smiled at the two. For the first time in a month, she felt good about herself.

The feeling didn't last long as she glanced at Jack and saw his eyes were on her. *It will never be the same between us,* her brain told her. Success and recognition at work was what drove and motivated her. It was her comfort zone. Men and relationships were foreign to her.

She rested her chin on her folded hands and considered some of the suggestions Jack raised. It felt like the old days when she first met Bruce and Jack. She was Tess the businesswoman...and ice princess. And it felt good.

****

Tess dreaded going into the office. Doug had left her a voice mail stating that he wanted a private meeting. She had about as much time for this as she did for being stuck in traffic. She had learned from Allie that when Doug came back from lunch yesterday he was fit to be tied and on a rampage.

She stopped by the coffee cart near the elevator and saw Jack walking from the direction of the fitness center. She put her head down and rummaged through her bag, hoping he wouldn't see her.

"Tess, what are you doing here?" He approached, invading her space.

God, he smells good. "Doug wants to see me. He left messages on my cell and home phones. When I called him back, he wouldn't elaborate except to tell me to be in his office first thing this morning."

Jack shook his head. "I'll walk with you."

This was work, and she knew she couldn't refuse him. Being around him stirred up something that she thought had been suppressed. Obviously not.

They walked onto the elevator. Soon it filled with other people, causing them to move to the back corner. Try as she might not to touch him, her efforts were futile. She felt his hand brush along hers. Bad move. The tingling shot through her body like wildfire.

She closed her eyes and counted to twenty this time. Ten surely was not enough. Why did she have to run into him, of all people? Could this day get any worse?

Making small talk, he asked, "Did Claire ever get her kitten?"

She smiled, "Yes. Two as a matter of fact."

"Two! You *are* a sucker. " He smiled at her. "So how's that going?"

"You mean besides the fact that one likes playing with my hair while I'm sleeping? Then when she's done playing, she thinks it's her bed. Other than that, real good," Tess answered.

When he laughed, she realized how much she missed his company. Maybe, just maybe, they *could* be friends. His hand brushed against hers again as they maneuvered through the people to exit the elevator. That simple touch caused her pulse to quicken. *Wait! He's dating Sharon. Simply because he's a gentleman— I'm reading the signals all wrong.*

After dropping her bag and coat off in her office, she walked up the stairs to Doug's new quarters right down the hall from Jack's. She stopped outside the door. Judith from Human Resources sat in one of the chairs at the small conference table.

Okay, this isn't good. They only bring in HR if something is bad. Really bad. Quickly, Tess scanned through the list. She had not killed anyone, stolen from the company, or committed sexual harassment.

"Hey, Tess. It's been a long time," Judith said in her too-calming voice.

Tess wondered if the woman ever showed an excitable emotion.

"Judith." Tess stared as she took the chair next to her. Judith turned her attention back to Doug cleaning under his nails with a letter opener. *Disgusting!*

Tess took several deep breaths.

"You're the Senior Consulting Executive on the Ryhan project, Tess, correct?" Doug looked at the pad of paper in front of him.

Her mouth wanted to say, "Well, duh?" but her brain kept her lips clamped shut. She needed to see where he was going first.

"What example are you setting when you skip out of a client's office early and have drinks on company time?" he asked, glaring at her. "I don't see where any of you asked for personal time off yesterday."

She looked at the two faces staring at her. *What's going on here?* "We needed to go over a few things that we didn't want to discuss in Ryhan's offices." She paused to gather her thoughts before continuing. "It was late, we were hungry, so we decided go out of the building for lunch instead of using their cafeteria."

Doug added, "*And* have a beer. Basically, drinking on the job. You know the rules, Tess, and you blatantly disregard them like you do everything else here."

Tess quickly said, "Wait a minute. Let's take a step back. Yes, we did discuss Ryhan. Jack even offered up a few suggestions after you left."

She sighed and kept going, "As for taking personal time, we're working over sixty hours a week that included a late night the night before. So, yes, we left a little early in the business day. We don't exactly keep nine-to-five hours. Maybe we were tired and needed a break."

Doug pointed at her. "You have a tendency to get away with things here, Tess, that others can't. It has become more so now that Ryhan has asked for you by name. Well, it's not going to be tolerated anymore. You work a full day, like everyone else, or you put in for personal time."

"What about the hours I put in at night after my daughter goes to bed. Don't those count?"

"If you are having to work that much, maybe you're not right for this client. Maybe your thoughts are elsewhere during the day."

What was he saying?

Judith cleared her throat. "Perhaps we should all take a step back, and calm down a bit before things are said that aren't meant." She looked back and forth from Tess to Doug.

Doug backed down only slightly, "I don't disagree that people should blow off some steam, but they need to ask for the time off just like all their co-workers who are putting in just as many hours. As the senior person, you should have done that for your team."

How she hated this man. He treated her like a five year old!

Judith spoke. "Drinking during work hours is not permitted, unless the person is entertaining a client who is also drinking, or if the person is on personal time off. My understanding is that was not the case yesterday. Tess, you didn't ask for the time off *and* you permitted drinking. There are consequences to that."

Doug added, "There are rules within the company which must be followed. There are no exceptions to these, at any level. We will take the appropriate actions for you allowing your team to drink on the job. That will be written up and placed in your file. That will obviously negate any salary increase you were scheduled for this year."

Tess stopped breathing. Her world was crashing around her. Her hands, clasped together in her lap, were wet from nervous sweating. She couldn't even look at Doug. She blinked several times. In all her years at Tullamore, she had never been treated like this. She was respected, both internally and by the clients. Her back stiffened.

"There are also consequences to something else that has been brought to our attention. We are here to speak to you about this also," Judith said in her monotone. "We have heard of some inappropriate interactions between you and Jack Maristone."

That's it. I'm going to throw up on the table. Life was happening in slow motion as she looked back and forth from Doug to Judith. "What?" Tess asked.

"I'll be meeting with him later this morning." Judith leaned forward with her ramrod straight back to look over at her. "Tess, you have been with the company for a long time and should know the rules."

"It is clearly a lack of judgment on your part, Tess," Doug interjected. "This is just part of a series of misjudgments that have been ongoing. You've brought an Elvis-look-alike, whom you were dating, into our building. There were a number of instances in which you exhibited inappropriate behavior toward Jack. A number of people have taken notice of the two of you going to lunch together. The topper was what you did in the parking lot at the Christmas party."

She looked at Doug and felt the blood rush from her face. Jack had approached her! "Exactly what was it *I did* in the parking lot?" Tess wanted to know exactly what had been seen.

Doug interrupted, "You were seen together in the corner of the room talking very closely. You were seen by several leaving together, and were observed in a very passionate embrace in the parking lot. Then there was the way you were looking at him at lunch yesterday. I wasn't the only one to notice. Howard commented on it when we left the restaurant."

Who had ratted her out?

Tess put her elbow on the table and pointed at Doug. "I left that party alone and I resent someone making an accusation like this. Who is saying this?"

"There was more than one person who saw the two of you in the parking lot," Judith said.

"Who?" Tess was so scared at this point, she was sweating. If she rubbed her brow she'd look even guiltier. Her days were over. This was going to be career deaths for both her and Jack It was ridiculous. He was already dating someone else.

"They have come forward anonymously," Judith responded.

Doug added, "I've seen, however, with my own eyes your flirtations with Jack. It's been pretty obvious. It must be pretty uncomfortable for him to have you acting like this."

She felt like she was in the twilight zone. If there was one thing that she was cognizant of, it was that *anything* could be perceived as flirting from Doug's perspective. Then she remembered Allie's New Year's Eve words about how a blind person could see the attraction between her and Jack.

"What does Jack say about this?" Tess asked.

"I'll be talking with him later this morning and letting him know we've taken care of this situation," Judith responded.

Jack knew about this, and yet acted friendly in the elevator toward her? Was this his way of getting back at her for what she had done to his ego? If so, he was a real bastard. He'd ruined her life. He was the one who kissed her!

Allie was right. The woman was always the one who was hung out to dry.

"Tess, your behavior is a detriment to this organization and what we stand for." Doug focused his attention on her. "You played a nice game here. First you aligned yourself with someone whom you report to. Then you think you're above everyone else and the rules don't apply to you. Is this how you think you can advance in this world?"

She swallowed. Her mouth felt dry. "I'll not sit here and have someone say I did something that I didn't. I did not flirt with Jack Maristone to boost my career. I've advanced by career over the last eighteen years because of hard work, and commitment to this company and the clients we serve."

"What about the parking lot witnesses?" Judith asked.

"It was dark. How do they know I was in an embrace with Jack Maristone, like you say?"

Doug answered too calmly. "Because people who know both of you say it was you?"

"What I do on my personal time isn't your business," she finally said. "I can tell you this. I don't have relationships like you are implying with my co-workers."

Doug slid a paper across the table to her. "If what you are saying is accurate, then we'll need you to sign this document which attests to that. If you don't sign, consider this your two week's notice. This will allow time for you to present your recommendations to

Ryhan's executives next week and then turn the project over to Bruce. I'll be with you and Bruce at the meeting to ensure this happens."

She grabbed the paper, glancing at it, and knowing she couldn't sign *and* be truthful.

Quickly she stood and took the paper that would end her Tullamore career. "You'll have to excuse me. I've got to prepare for a meeting. I'll get back to you on this."

With her head held figuratively higher than the ceiling, she walked from the office. As soon as she hit the stairwell, however, she ran for her office.

****

Tess's brain was a jumbled mess by the time she made it to her office. Allie was right— getting mixed up with Jack had been a monumental mistake. Yet, was her eighteen years of good service to the company valueless because of this one mistake?

She closed the door to her office and left Allie a voice mail on her cell phone, briefly describing the last thirty minutes' events and asking for her help. If there was anyone who could quickly find out the scoop, it was Allie.

As she waited for her computer to boot up, she rationalized the decision she was going to have to make.

She had never been treated like this in her career. Things had started going downhill when Doug arrived, the same month she had appeared in the national Human Resources magazine. A few months later she'd been featured in a national weekly news magazine. While it had been her time to celebrate, Doug found every opportunity to try and beat her down. He had never credited those two articles for helping to bring additional business to their company.

She quickly answered a few emails, and wrote on a scrap of paper the calls she needed to make from the car on her way to Ryhan.

She glanced at the line of pictures on her desk—Allie, Dana, and her on her fortieth birthday; Claire's birthday; she and Claire at the beach; and the one taken of Bruce, Louisa, Jack, and her at the Christmas party.

Looking back, Tess realized she'd skirted some of the questions so as not to lie. She just left out some facts. If she had said he came on to her, then they both would be escorted out; she, of course, before him.

She owed him nothing. Sure, he'd made her feel like a woman again, but that was about it. He had moved on to his next victim and let her take the fall. Selfish bastard!

She wanted to beat her head on the computer as she internally argued with herself on what to do.

Judith knocked on the door and came inside before Tess could answer. It was the enemy.

"I don't want you to think we were ganging up on you," Judith said as she sat in the chair opposite Tess.

"What would you call it?"

"We had to remind you of company policy."

Tess sighed and looked away from the overly-calm Judith. The woman must take heavy doses of drugs to maintain such a dispassionate air.

Still not looking at her, Tess said, "I keep wondering what I've done to be treated liked this, and for the life of me I can't figure it out." She stopped and looked at Judith. "I never flirted with Jack."

"I told Doug after you left that I didn't think you

flirted with him. There was the shocked look on your face. I also told him that I thought you valued your career too much to throw it away on a man. However, I do think with your personality some men—Doug, and even Jack—may have misinterpreted you."

"Doug and I mix like oil and vinegar."

"Yes, I know that, too."

Tess leaned forward to prop her elbows on the desk. She folded her fingers together as if praying, and rested her chin on top. "What if I don't do anything? What then?"

"We have two people who witnessed the parking lot incident between you and Jack." Judith fidgeted in the chair and licked her lips. "Several people have seen the two of you together at other times. And then there were Doug's and Howard's interpretations of you looking at Jack yesterday."

"Hypothetically, what would happen to Jack if this turned out to be true, but he was just as much a part of it as I was?"

"Nothing."

"Why does that not surprise me?" Tess reached into her bottom desk drawer and pulled out a water.

Judith picked up the picture of Claire from her desk. "Beautiful girl. I heard from Bruce how well-mannered she is. You must be proud of how you raised her—you know, being a single mom."

Tess tucked her hair behind her ear, then immediately clasped her hands together. Her computer beeped indicating she had an instant message. She flicked the mouse onto the icon.

It was from Jack, and he wanted to talk right away. He was the enemy that knew why she was in the office.

She typed, "No." She then clicked to sign-off so he couldn't send her another.

"I've done nothing wrong, Judith."

"Then sign the paper and the matter will be closed," she responded.

Tess rubbed her temples. "I'll let you know by the close of business today what my decision will be."

"I know you'll do the right thing, Tess." Judith stood up and walked to the door. She stopped. "I've looked through your file and it has been impeccable until now."

"Thanks." Tess turned toward her computer. She quickly drafted an email that she might, or might not, send by the end of the day. If she pushed the send button, she'd need to let Bruce, Jeff, and Jeannie from Ryhan Corporation know what was happening, before all hell broke loose. She stared at the screen a long time before saving it as a draft.

As she logged off, Allie called on her cell. Tess talked with her while gathering her stuff. She looked at the pictures on her desk and threw them into her briefcase.

Tess continued talking in a low voice with Allie as she stepped onto the elevator. When the doors closed, she saw the doors of the opposite elevator opening. Inside was Jack. He was coming to find her. Well, she wasn't ready to talk with him after what he'd done.

****

By the time Tess pulled into her driveway, she felt like a huge weight had lifted. Even traffic on the highway hadn't bothered her. It was one of the few times she actually listened to the music on the radio instead of talking on her cell phone, which had been ringing non-stop.

She had also stopped by the hairdresser to get her hair taken care of. It was long overdue.

Dana, Allie, Harry and Claire were sitting at the kitchen table eating a large pizza topped with sausage, spinach and mushrooms. Harry poured her a glass of wine

"I can't believe you did it!" Allie handed Tess a plate. "And I like the hair. Very chic."

"Mom, what's going to happen to us?" There was no mistaking the worry in Claire's voice. She had known nothing but her mother working all her life. Her mother, their sole financial provider, who'd always taken care of her.

"We'll be fine, sweetie," Tess answered. "I'll still have a job. It just may not be with Tullamore anymore. In fact, now that I'm away from Doug, I may be happier."

Her cell phone rang. She walked to her purse and looked at the number. She was expecting this, but was not ready to deal with him tonight. She would wait until tomorrow to hear what he had to say.

"Who was that?" Dana asked.

"None other than The Devil himself. Doug. Screw him. Let's celebrate a new beginning."

****

This was the part of the day Jack liked best; the early morning before the swarms of people arrived to bring the building to life.

Since the first of the year, he had arrived most mornings at five-thirty, when the fitness center opened. It was habit among the early exercisers to nod to each other as they made their way to the various machines.

He had no idea who they were or where they worked, and he didn't care.

At this hour in the morning, he reveled in the peace and quiet of not talking or being talked to. This was his time to think, before the bustle started upstairs—before the telephone rang, before people overran him waiting for directions, before reports had to be read, before decisions had to be made.

Jack stretched his muscles before getting on the recumbent bicycle. He caught a glimpse of the one fitness center instructor present at this hour. He wondered if this was the guy Tess had used for a date, the one who had commented to Allie about Tess not being interested in him because she wanted "the old guy." He was curious if this guy knew about the bet—the childish bet, in which he was nothing but a pawn in a game. He had to stop thinking about her. He tried to focus on the TV in front of him.

His mind wandered back to Tess. He had tried calling her yesterday after hearing from Sandra that Tess had been ambushed by Doug for drinking at lunch. There was also something about "inappropriate behavior" at work. That was all Sandra had been able to pick up, except for the expression on Tess's face when she left Doug's office.

He had hoped to catch her before she left for Ryhan Corporation yesterday to talk with her and maybe clear the air between them. Outside of lunch the other day, and their brief encounter yesterday morning, he had hardly seen her.

It's for the best. You've got to try to forget her and what she's done. A part of him didn't believe what she had said that night, but a bigger part of him did. *How many times had she tried to push me away?*

He had seen her stop by the office one day, rushing through, not looking his way as if he didn't exist. It reminded him of sitting in his first meeting with her. He had found it so appealing to watch as she tried to tuck a curl behind her ear.

Unknowingly, Bruce kept him up-to-date on Tess. Jack would casually ask about how things at Ryhan Corporation were going. According to Bruce, she had a big fan club at Ryhan who hung on every word she said. Though they were hesitant to implement her suggestions.

He had heard of the first of the year clash between her and Doug, the heated debate behind closed doors with Doug nagging at her to do more and do it better. If he were in her shoes, Jack probably would have decked the man by now. Yet he knew that Tess would bite her tongue and continue to give it her all.

Picking up his towel, he wiped the sweat from his brow. Things were different here compared to how he had run things with his own company. They had been a smaller, tight-knit team who respected each other and their differences. Here, tension always seemed to thrive. The politics and policies were different. It was no longer fun to come to work.

Maybe it wasn't fun because he missed having lunch with one of the few employees he liked—the one who had made him feel comfortable. Tess had treated him like an average person, not as a person who was high-up on the corporate food chain.

He stopped pedaling the bicycle and went to the treadmill in the far corner. He punched several times at the buttons on the machine. Nothing happened. He tried again.

"It doesn't work," a female voice said.

Standing in front of him in a blue and red workout suit was Allie. "I broke it the other afternoon when I was in here." She stared at him intently.

"Did you tell anyone?" he asked.

"No. I was keeping it be a big secret." She jumped on the treadmill next to him. "*Of course* I told them at the front desk before I left, but Mike, over there, seemed to be more concerned with helping out a new-to-the-gym, hot-bodied member."

Jack switched to the treadmill on the other side of Allie. *What is she doing here this early in the morning?* He sometimes saw her coming in as he was leaving. But from what she just said, she must also be part of the late afternoon crowd who worked out before going home. Regardless, she was Tess's friend. She was the enemy who had put doubt in Tess's mind at the New Year's party.

He started the treadmill and began walking. He glanced over to see her running. He would pretend that she wasn't here so he wouldn't think about Tess any more—wouldn't think about how she laughed, how she scratched the back of her head when she was nervous, how she pouted her lips when she pretended to be upset, how she felt in his arms, how she tasted…but last of all, how he wanted her.

Allie startled him, standing next to him with her arms crossed. "I was the one who put her up to it. I thought it was a harmless bet. I mean, she hadn't been out on a date since she divorced that no-good cheater eight years ago. Not a single date."

She swatted the gym towel against her leg. "I told

her she was afraid, that she had forgotten how to act on a date, and that was the reason she avoided men. I also thought she was blind to men around her. I mean, except for you, all the others asked *her* out on the dates."

She stopped to kick at an invisible rock on the floor. "To tell you the truth, 'good ol' confident Tess' was scared of being hurt. She had been hurt once and didn't want to go through it again. She swore off all men and focused her energies on Claire and her work. The worst part of the stupid bet was that she ended up getting hurt again."

Jack didn't look at Allie. He didn't want to hear this.

However, she seemed to want to continue. "You know what the difference was between you and the others? She knew there would be only one date with them. With you, I think she was hoping for more, but I stopped her from that. Now I feel like crap about her decision yesterday."

She paused, "You know, she told Dana before the holidays that there was this guy at work whom she was attracted to but she had to behave herself because it couldn't work. She hated the company policy because she really liked him. When I saw you two at the party, I told her to end it before it started."

Allie started to walk away and then came back to stand in front of him. "One last thing before I forget. Tess hates to lose. Really hates it. Hates it so much she actually made herself sick when she realized she'd hurt you and, more importantly, lost you as a friend. Dana and I were there the next morning to see her pain. It was the first time I ever saw her cry. But now after what happened yesterday, I hope she realizes those were wasted tears."

She started to walk toward the locker room when something clicked in his head. "Allie!" he shouted, before she rounded the corner. He stepped from the treadmill and walked quickly toward the locker room.

She waited for him to come to her. "What?"

"*What* happened yesterday?"

"Like you don't know." She eyed him suspiciously, "Are you gonna stand there and tell me you know nothing about how Doug and the HR bitch reprimanded Tess about coming onto you and acting inappropriately, and wanting her to sign a statement of guilt?"

Bewildered, he said, "I have no idea what you are talking about."

Now it was Allie's turn to be surprised. She crossed her arms tightly. "You mean you haven't heard? We thought you'd be the first to know. Celebrating actually. We thought this was your way of getting back at her for what she did to you on New Year's."

"Heard what?" he asked impatiently.

"Tess handed in her resignation yesterday afternoon."

He was stunned. It couldn't be true, but the look on Allie's face told him it was so.

"No. She can't!" He stormed to the locker room for a shower.

This was not what he expected. No wonder she didn't answer her phone. He needed to get upstairs and start damage control immediately.

****

It was late when Jack turned off the light to his

office and locked the door. He stood outside contemplating where to stop to grab something to eat on the way home. He had eaten only half the lunch Sandra brought him just before he met with Judith to go over the events of the day before.

He had canceled his meeting with her yesterday to attend to other more important matters. He hadn't a clue, until his encounter with Allie this morning, that he had misjudged which of the two was most important.

The day was ending no better than it started. As he walked to the elevator he replayed the day's developments in his mind. He had been in and out of the shower in record time in his rush to get upstairs to check on the contract that was signed by Ryhan Corporation. It both reinforced his fears and gave him ammunition. Holding the contract in his hand he rushed into Doug's office, and asked, "Is there something you want to tell me?"

With too much confidence Doug answered, "Yes, Tess handed in her letter of resignation yesterday. She'll be out of here in two weeks, but I'm thinking of cutting her loose earlier. We don't need someone with her big ego in here. We need someone who can be more of a team player and who's willing to play by the rules."

Jack was ready to explode. "Doug, you really *don't get it*, do you? You should have treated her with more respect instead of looking for some way to force her out of here!"

"Why do you care so much?" Doug suddenly looked smug. "Or do you care because there is something—"

Jack slapped the contract on the desk, "I care

because we could possibly lose a valuable client. You didn't stop to think about that, did you? Look at the first paragraph of that contact. It is between Ryhan Corporation, *Tess Grayson,* and Tullamore. It's not between just Ryhan and us."

Jack picked up the contract and flipped to another page, before slamming in down in front of Doug, "Now look at the termination clause on page five. If Tess Grayson leaves us before the end of the two-year contract period, Ryhan has the option to follow her. I've got Brian Keller from legal looking this over to see what our options are. From his initial reaction, they aren't so good."

Shaken, Doug said, "Tess is over there at the Ryhan offices right now. I'm sure she's being very professional, but we don't know what she's told Ryhan. Bruce is keeping his ears open and will be glued to Tess's side all day."

"I've talked to Judith about what happened yesterday morning and…" Jack stopped before he exploded. Without saying more to Doug, he stomped out of the office.

Bruce called to say he was with Tess. She had told Ryhan she was leaving Tullamore, but that she didn't want to elaborate. For a brief moment, Jack breathed easier until he heard that Jeannie asked to speak to Tess alone and they went into a conference room for a half hour.

The news got worse. Bruce wasn't able to set up a meeting that day between Jack and Jeannie. Her earliest availability was next Tuesday morning and she wanted her director there. Jack needed to find out what Tess had said in that closed-door meeting.

It was Judith from HR who was able to get Tess to come in late in the day for a meeting. When she walked into his office with Judith, Tess looked different. Her hair was straight. During the meeting, Tess was very calm and professional, using all the right words and saying she'd never burn her bridges.

The conversation about her being an ice princess flashed in his mind. During the entire time, she showed no emotions. She side-stepped any questions or suggestions that her resignation was a result of the accusations made the day before. Jack wished he had been included in that meeting.

No matter how much he tried, he could not sway her mind about staying. He even suggested changing the reporting structure so she would not have to answer to Doug; she'd be his equal. This caused more than a few raised eye brows. She politely declined this offer with the coldness in her eyes directed at him.

Before standing to leave, in a flat voice she said she was still an employee of Tullamore and would continue her remaining time behaving as such.

Two hours later the elevator dinged and the doors opened in front of him. Jack was glad it was empty. Pushing the button for the lobby, he debated whether or not he should call Sharon for dinner. He immediately dismissed the idea. She wasn't spontaneous and would need time to prepare, even for dinner.

Seeing Sharon wasn't working for him. She was pretentious, and reminded him too much of Elizabeth. She wasn't the type who held her sides or slapped her leg when she laughed. She wasn't the type who, when touched, would rip his shirt off and push him toward her bedroom. Sharon would also not take the time to find out what he liked or disliked. She wasn't Tess.

When the elevator stopped on the eleventh floor, he sighed. The last thing he wanted was to ride down with anyone. When the doors opened, he was shocked to see Tess standing there with a box filled with her personal things.

She stepped back. "I'll grab the next one."

His heart was a traitor, ignoring the warning signals from his brain. As happened any time she was near, he ached for her, to be near her and talk with her.

He pushed the "open" button as the door began to slide shut. "Don't be that way," he said, gruffer than he intended. "Get in."

Her smile was forced as she stepped inside. She turned her back to him. She re-pushed the lobby button. He couldn't help staring at the back of her head which she held high. He thought back to New Year's Eve, to the back of her neck then and her semi-bare back. What he wouldn't give to go back and re-live those minutes again. Back when he thought she wanted him as much as he wanted her.

"Tess, I didn't know when Doug said he had to talk with you yesterday what it was going to be about us."

"I know. Allie told me how you reacted this morning."

"Any chance you've changed your mind in the last few hours?" he asked.

"Nope, my mind's made up." She remained facing the elevator doors with her back to him. "I'm taking tomorrow off. Please don't try to call me or otherwise persuade me."

"Big plans?" he asked.

"Claire doesn't have school tomorrow and she's

spending the night at her dad's tonight, so I've decided to take a mental health day and be completely lazy. If anyone from here tries to call, I won't answer."

The old feelings toward her were stirring though he tried unsuccessfully to suppress them. He couldn't think with her standing so close. He wished he could feel her lips on his.

Suddenly, she pushed the stop button. They were between the fourth and third floor when the elevator came to a stop.

"I'm really sorry, Jack. About everything that happened. I know I was mean and cruel to you on New Year's. And then yesterday I thought you'd thrown me under the bus. I thought I had friends here who were going to look out for me. I now realize that I need to look out for myself. I can't work like this."

She stopped rambling, and looked sadly into his eyes. "I wish...I wish I could go back...oh, never mind." She turned toward the button panel, changed her mind, and turned back to look at him. "I am sorry for what I said and did that night. You probably don't believe me, but I really am sorry for lying to you."

Before he could answer she turned back and pushed the lobby button again. Silence hung in the air like a heavy storm cloud. When the doors opened, she walked off the elevator, not waiting for him. The sound of her heels clicking across the marble floor echoed in the quiet lobby.

Catching up to her, he held the door.

"Thanks." She slipped by him.

They walked in silence through the parking garage. When he stopped at his car, she moved her box of personal effects to rest on her hip. "Have you eaten yet?"

"I have plans tonight," he lied.

She touched his shoulder. "I know you're upset thinking about Tullamore, but I hope one day you can forgive me and things can go back to the way they were. More than anything I want us to be friends again."

He looked at her face and then her hand. She quickly removed it from his shoulder.

"Have a good night, Jack"

He watched her walk away, her shoulders held high. She always rebounded after being knocked down. She walked like someone very sure of herself.

He was hungry, dinner with her sounded good, and he hated that he had lied to her. Being with her sounded even better. His heart told him not to let her go away like this. She had opened the door for him. He needed to walk through it. *It's now or never.*

"Tess," he yelled.

She stopped and turned; her face full of expectation. They stared at each other for what seemed like minutes. "Your hair. Straight. It doesn't suit you."

She said nothing. The look of disappointment on her face was clear. She shook her head and spun on her heal to get into the car.

The words came out wrong. He had just slammed the door in her face.

She had been the bigger person by saying she was sorry. Why couldn't he just accept her offer of friendship?

Because in his heart he wanted more, and knew he couldn't have it.

Chapter Thirty

Sipping her wine, Tess enjoyed the hot water evaporating all the tension knotted in her shoulders and the balls of her feet. She had so missed the luxury of sitting in a hot bath with no one interrupting her. She had turned off her cell phone so she could really enjoy her night of relaxation.

She hoped things were going well for Claire and Kevin. This was the first time in almost two months that he had spent time with his daughter. It had taken Claire finally telling her father that he hadn't called since their ski trip. She wanted the two of them to be close like they were before Leslie became a part of his life.

She closed her eyes and listened to the wind howl outside. February was blowing out with a vengeance. She decided that after her bath she'd crawl under the heavy comforter on her bed and finally read one of the books she had gotten for Christmas.

When the landline phone rang in her bedroom she covered her ears so not to hear the sharp trill. Whoever it was didn't leave a message. The phone rang again. She was not going to jump out of the tub to answer it. When the ringing stopped, she could once again hear the wind whipping around the house.

She lifted the washcloth to splash her face and thought about the men she had dated last year. She had behaved badly to each one, trying to find fault. The only one who didn't seem to have any was Jack—except that he worked with her.

She thought about Phil. Though he was a bit odd with his Elvis get-up, he seemed to be a good person inside. He was a little too eager to become committed. She laughed silently. *Maybe committed to a mental institution,* but he meant well and treated her right. The others just gave her the willies.

She stepped from the tub and dried herself off before slathering her body with pomegranate-scented lotion. Rubbing in the lotion, she reminded herself she was about to start a new life. A fresh start.

Beginning right this moment, she was going to pamper herself. She would not think about men, dating, or the fact that sometimes she did hate being alone. She would put all this behind her. She'd survive as she always had.

When the ringing started again, she wrapped her thick, cream-colored bathrobe around herself. She looked at the caller ID and wanted to scream. *Don't answer the phone!* She looked at the time on the clock. Tonight and tomorrow morning were to be about her. She needed to unwind and relax. Anything related to work was off limits. Her mind was numb with all that had happened in the last thirty-six hours.

Her hand picked up the phone. "Hello?" she said hesitantly. She closed her eyes tightly against whatever she was going to hear.

"I'm at your front door," Jack said quickly. "We need to talk."

"Give me a second," she answered, and hung up the phone.

"Jack?" was all she could muster when she opened the door. She blinked at him. He had changed from his work clothes into jeans, looking *too good*. Why had she answered the phone? She couldn't deal with him after his actions in the elevator and parking garage.

"Is everything okay?" she finally asked. "I thought you had plans tonight."

"We need to talk," he repeated. He stuffed his hands into his gray wool coat. "Can I come in?"

Opening the door wide, she nodded. As soon as he was inside, she shut the door to lean against it for support.

He took off both his gloves and coat, and carried them to the coat rack. He was wearing a sweater vest similar to the one he had on New Year's Eve. She wondered if he remembered how that look had turned her on that night, resulting in them landing half-naked in her bedroom.

She shook her head. She couldn't think about that. She was a thing of the past; both personally and professionally. He had Sharon now.

She didn't move from her spot. She realized she was naked underneath and pulled her robe closer around her.

"Did I come at a bad time," he asked rather stiffly.

"Oh, no. I was just taking a bath. My life is full of leisure now that I dropped that bomb on ya'll." She was trying to break the tension hanging in the air.

"I can come back tomorrow." He sounded uncomfortable.

She rolled her eyes. "Don't be silly, you're already here. Are you okay? You look a little stressed. Do you want something to drink?"

"Whatever you're having will be fine," he answered.

Thank goodness. She made a quick detour into her bathroom to pick up the empty wine glass from the counter. She looked wistfully at the empty tub; just moments earlier she had been lounging there, trying to forget about him and everything related to work.

She braced her arms on the counter and looked in the mirror to give herself a pep talk. *You can get through this, you can get through this.* She was lying. She couldn't get through this.

There were butterflies in her stomach, her mind was mush, and her legs were weak. To top it off, she looked a mess—no make-up, wet hair starting to curl from the humidity of the bath. Maybe she could close herself in the bathroom, he'd leave, and then she could slide her body between the sheets of her bed to forget his surprise visit.

Nope, that wasn't going to happen. He was here for a reason, and she had better pull herself together to hear what it was. She stared at herself in the mirror with her arms crossed. *Why is he here? What part of 'no' did he not understand?*

She wasn't going to rescind her resignation. What did she care about the millions of dollars Tullamore was destined to lose because Ryhan Corporation had signed a contract naming her as their consultant? Her one-sided company loyalty ended two days ago in Doug's office. Her mind was made up. She would stand her ground.

She turned from the mirror and walked back to the kitchen, where Jack was sitting at the bar stool reading the paper. He sat on the same stool, the same spot where they couldn't keep their hands off each other on New Year's Eve. It seemed ages ago, but the memory was still fresh in her mind. *Stop that! Stop reminding yourself. It's in the past, and should stay there.*

After pulling another wine glass from the cabinet and filling both, she slid the glass toward him. "Do you want to sit in the living room? It's more comfortable."

"Thank you," he said quietly, not looking at her. When he did lift his eyes, he commented, "I'm sorry about what I said about your hair. It came out wrong."

She stared into his tired hazel eyes. *Is he here to apologize about my hair?*

"Don't worry about it." She walked into the living room. "I knew what you meant."

"I just think you look better with curly hair. It's part of your personality." He stopped in front of the gas fireplace which she'd lit before her bath.

She sat on the couch across from the fireplace looking at his back.

"Thanks. I guess." She tucked a clump of her hair behind her ears. She folded her legs to her side making sure her robe adequately covered everything.

The CD changed from Bach to Vivaldi. Anyone looking through the window would assume this to be the perfect romantic setting. However the strain and tension present pushed any romance into the garbage.

Jack ran his fingers through his hair and sighed loudly.

She looked into the liquid in her glass. "Just like I told you earlier, I've made up my mind about leaving. I just hate that Doug was so determined to ruin me."

He set his glass on the fireplace mantel.

"I'm more concerned about why you were avoiding

me," he said quietly. "After I talked with Judith this morning, I called your cell, and even sent an email that we needed to talk about this. I finally had to have Judith run interference to get you into the office."

"I wasn't ready, Jack. I needed to think. Don't forget, for a while there, I thought you were part of the conspiracy against me. And then I had to get ready for the management committee meeting at Ryhan."

"What do they know?"

So this was why he was here. Business. "Nothing that would make Tullamore look bad, if that's why you're here." She swirled the wine in her glass. "They, of course, pushed, wondering why I was resigning. I had told them it was a personal matter, and that it was my decision to step away."

She couldn't tell them that besides Doug being a nut-case, more importantly, she was in love with Jack and couldn't think clearly when he was around.

"The contract with Ryhan contains a clause which names you as their Senior Consulting Executive. Should you go elsewhere, they will continue to employ your services."

"Yes, I know," she whispered. She took a sip of her wine before setting it on the table behind the couch. When she did this, her robe top opened up, revealing her breasts. She quickly shut it and tightened the belt.

Jack turned around and stared at her. It was the same look on his face as a few days earlier.

"I talked with Jeannie and the attorney at Ryhan about that this afternoon, before I came back to the office," she replied. "I know that's why you're here. To see if I'll reconsider. Well, I won't." She said this more harshly than she intended. She looked away.

How could he possibly understand what it had been like for her these last few months? At one point, she was on top of her game but had a manager who wanted nothing more than to see her fall. Well, she wasn't going to give anyone that satisfaction. She was just going to walk away.

Jeannie had talked to her about coming to work for Ryhan in their strategy unit. If Tess was interested, they would put together an offer. Tess had said she would need to think about it and would let them know by next Wednesday.

"Like I said in the parking garage, I just hope that one day when all this hubbub goes away, you and I can go back to just being friends."

Jack picked up his drink from the mantel and carried it to where she sat on the couch. Sitting down, he put his feet up on the ottoman to stare at the fire.

He was so close that all she had to do was reach out her hand to touch him. Run her fingers along the back of his neck.

"I can't 'just be friends' with you," he finally said.

It felt like someone pulled the rug from under her. Her stomach was in her throat. Her hand was trembling when she picked up her glass to gulp the last of the wine.

"Why?" she asked, quietly looking at her empty glass.

He narrowed his eyes at her. "You have to ask?"

Silently, she shook her head a few times. She knew the answer. She had rejected him and bruised his ego. He was only here because of the revenue she could take away from Tullamore. She had told him her mind was made up, so there was nothing more to say to each other but goodbye.

Suddenly she couldn't be near him. She stood up and walked to the fireplace. "I'm sorry you came all the way over here to try and change my mind, but it's not happening. I think you need to go."

He was right behind her, his gentle hands taking hers in his. His face was in the back of her hair. "That's not it," he said urgently. "I don't care about Tullamore or Ryhan right now. All I care about is *us*. Damn it, Tess, I want to be more than friends. I want to finish what we didn't that night. And I want to wake up in the morning next to you. Am I wrong to believe that you want the same?"

This was absolutely *not* what she had expected. Her knees felt weak as he pushed her hair to the side and kissed her neck.

She leaned her head to the side to let him continue. "What about Sharon?"

When he spun her around, she thought she was going to fall over. *Too much wine!* He braced his hands on her shoulders to steady her.

"There was never anything between Sharon and me, except an occasional dinner, with Bruce and Louisa. She may have wanted more, but I kept comparing her to you. She didn't make me feel alive like you do. She didn't laugh and smile like you. She didn't have—"

She put her finger on his lips. "I get the point," Tess whispered.

She kissed his lips until they opened and greeted her mouth. She ran her hands behind his neck and pushed her body into his. Her body was on fire. The tingling ran all the way to her curled-into-the-carpet toes.

She released her hands from behind his head and took hold of the bottom of his vest. She freed her mouth from his just long enough to pull the vest and shirt over his head. She ran her fingers through the hair on his chest before she took his hand in hers.

"Follow me," she whispered seductively. She led him into her bedroom, where she undid his belt and finished undressing him.

When he was standing naked in front of her, she undid her robe and walked into his arms, kissing him gently on his lips. Once his hands touched her, she was ready to pop out of her skin.

They fell onto the bed and made love. All the years pent up inside of her were released as they moved together. His hands moving along her body were incredible—strong and gentle at the same time. He seemed to know exactly where she wanted to be touched. She didn't want this to ever stop. Toward the end she moaned his name.

The sheets were a tangled mess. She threw her leg over his as she lay in his arms tracing circles on his chest. Surprisingly, she was not ashamed to be lying naked next to him.

She propped herself on her arm to get a better look at his face. He was staring at the ceiling. When he smiled, she felt her own face light up. She traced her finger over his lips.

"Does this mean we're friends again and we can go back to having lunch together?" she asked.

"Only if we can include breakfast and dinner in the mix."

She stopped tracing circles in his chest to smirk.

"Let me have my lawyer talk to yours."
****

The next morning Jack woke to the sound of a soft meow. On the other side of Tess's mass of curls were two black-and-gray kittens, staring at him. When he reached his hand out, they both scurried off the bed.

Tess was lying on her side with her face pressed into his chest. He wondered how she could possibly breathe. He didn't really care what time it was, but could tell it was late in the morning by the way the sun was spilling around the curtains.

They'd been up the most of the night, making love and discovering each other. There was no end to the passion she had.

Unlike being with Elizabeth, he had no problem getting it up with Tess. Now he realized he was fine; it was just the woman he had been with.

Now he was lying naked with the one who made him feel young and alive. She had laughed last night when he had told her he officially fell for her when she brought him that payback cup of coffee with the yellow sticky note attached.

She started to stir. Her right leg, which was sandwiched between his, stretched out. He ran his fingers through her hair.

A part of him worried she'd wake up, look at him and announce that they were going back to being just friends. After what he'd experienced last night, he couldn't handle that.

Her entire body stretched against his, and he was immediately aroused. She looked at him lazily and scooted her body up to be eye-to-eye.

"I thought you'd have tried to make your escape by

now." She lifted her hand to his cheek.

"Now why would I do that?" he asked.

"Second thoughts? Doubts?"

"Why? Are you having any?"

She ran her hand along the stubble on his face and down his neck. "No." She smiled. "Without sounding corny, I just experienced the best night of my life...with a man who made me feel like the center of everything." She started to move her free hand down his body while kissing him.

"Should I be worried about you pushing me away with talk of us only being friends?"

"Who are you kidding? In two weeks, I won't be working for you anymore, so the answer is a big fat no!"

She looked at him seriously. "You know, saying those words that night about killed me. The last thing I wanted to do was hurt you, and I know I did. I'm so sorry that I valued my job more than anything else. Now look where I am."

He rubbed her back, "I told you I'd look out for you and take care of you. I want you to be part of my life."

She was ready with a response when they heard the front door open with force and then slam hard. Tess quickly pulled the blankets up to cover their naked bodies

Claire shouted, "I am over them, Mom. I want a new father. The step-monster is driving me insane." She stopped at the bedroom door staring at them.

Sitting up, Tess said, "You're home early."

"I *hate* them." Claire dropped her bag on the floor to free up her hands to pick up one of the meowing kittens.

She seemed oblivious to the fact that Jack was in bed with her mother. She continued to stand in the doorway as she petted the cat. Claire finally looked at them. "Cool, I'm glad you two are back together. And since I am looking for a new dad—"

Tess interrupted, "Okay, Claire, take Addie upstairs and let me get dressed."

Claire picked up her bag and commented over her shoulder, "Well, it's okay with me if he stays here. He's an all right guy."

Tess fell back on the pillow. "Sorry about that," she said. "I didn't think she'd be home this early. So much for our lazy day in bed. If you want to run in terror, I'll understand."

"Nope." He leaned down to kiss her. "I think I'll stay, if it's okay with you. It's seems to be okay with Claire."

She smiled up at him. "As long as you want." She kissed him before jumping from the bed to close *and lock* the door.

Chapter Thirty-One

Flying from Chicago to Atlanta on a Friday afternoon was worse than rush hour traffic on a rainy Monday morning. Due to mechanical problems on the original plane, Jack's flight touched down in Atlanta almost three hours later than it was scheduled. To make matters worse, the parking attendant couldn't find his car at the park and ride.

The entire time, he kept trying to reach Tess with his cell phone. They were to go away to his house in the mountains for the weekend. Tonight was the night he was going to propose.

Claire had declared she was never spending another weekend with her father, so Tess's mom was going to stay at the house with her. Kevin never seemed to call to check on Claire now that his new wife was pregnant. This was why Claire had come home early that fateful day in a royal snit.

Jack called Bruce to see if Tess was at Ryhan, but was told she'd left early. Tess had taken the job at Ryhan in their strategic unit. She had kept her promise not to burn any bridges, so Tullamore was left with some consulting work.

He was beginning to worry at her non-responsiveness to his phone calls. She was never sick.

As soon as his car was brought around, Jack jumped inside and started driving north to her house.

After passing through the crawling downtown traffic, the cars in front of him crept along even slower. He knew, at this rate, there was no time to abduct her from whatever had come up and make the drive to his mountain house tonight.

He tried once more to reach her. There was still no answer. This wasn't sitting right with him. Something was definitely wrong. Why had she not left a message?

He leaned his head against the headrest. As he pulled into the driveway, though some of the lights were on, he knew no one was at home.

He pressed the garage door opener and saw that neither her car nor her mother's was there.

He drove to the street behind, where her brother lived. As soon as he rang the bell, Harry opened the door.

"Hey, Harry, I'm looking for Tess," he blurted out.

Harry slowly shook his head. "I thought she was going away with you this weekend," he answered. He was obviously in the dark on this.

Jack wasn't about to give up. "Is Dana here?"

Harry, obviously a man of few words, nodded his head. "Dana!" he called loudly.

When she appeared at the door, she did not seem overly surprised by his sudden appearance. Before Jack could ask, she answered, "She's not here. She said to tell you 'to go ahead as planned' and that you'd know what she meant."

Harry interjected, "Dana, what's going on?"

Dana shook her head and smiled, "Never mind, Harry. She said for you to go up as planned, Jack."

It suddenly dawned on him where she was.

"Where's Claire?" he asked.

"With mom and dad."

He drove up to the mountain house, wondering why she had gone up early. She must have wanted to make sure it was inhabitable for the weekend. That was good thinking—now they wouldn't have to spend time getting it ready when he had other things in mind.

On the hour drive up, he considered just how much his life had changed in these last months. The few nights he spent in his empty place in Buckhead were lonely ones. They were too quiet, now that he had infused himself into the Grayson household. Someone always seemed to be coming or going there.

Joel had visited a few times. At first, he and Claire had eyed each other suspiciously but now they seemed to get along. Ironically, Joel visited more now that Jack was practically living with Tess.

There had been the one uncomfortable incident when Joel made a comment about Jack helping Claire with her homework. He had never done that with his own son. Tess immediately picked up on it and was able to smooth things over in her typical fashion.

Jack now pulled into the driveway of the mountain-top home. Tess's vehicle sat outside the garage. Without even picking up his bags, he rushed inside, where he saw a candle-lit table for two had been set. He could see her through the back windows sipping a glass of wine on the deck.

She turned around to look at him, and he knew his decision was the right one. He walked onto the veranda and leaned down to kiss her. "You scared me by not answering your phone."

"Cell phone reception up here really sucks," she replied. "Why didn't you tell me you had someone come and freshen up the place? I took off early to get that out of the way."

He chuckled. "After Dana gave me your message, I figured that."

She motioned for him to sit on the cushioned love seat beside her. "You missed the sunset, but it's still pretty out here. So quiet."

He poured wine into the glass she had waiting for him. He leaned back in the chair, resting his arm on the back of the seat. "You make me feel alive."

"And you've turned me into a sex-fiend," she said, leaning into him.

He laughed at her unexpected remark.

After a few moments she said, "Dinner's cold."

He looked at the treetops silhouetted against the gray night sky. "That's okay." He was feeling nervous, wondering when the right time was to ask. He wanted it to be perfect.

She shivered, curled into a ball, and lay her head against his chest. *This is it,* he decided, reaching into his pocket.

"Tess, have you ever thought about us, and where we're going?"

He felt her body tense. She sat up straight and angled her body toward his.

"This had better not be a farewell speech coming. In case you haven't noticed, I've fallen head over heels in love with you. I can't spend the weekend with you knowing my heart would have to stop caring about you come Sunday night."

Jack was stunned. Tess had never verbalized her feelings before. She had shown him in her actions, but never said it. He had thought that was just her way.

Now he wondered if she had been scared to say it.

"I'm not leaving you," he whispered.

"Whew," she said, a little more calmly.

He slipped the ring he held in his hand onto her finger. "You see...I love you, and am not leaving you. Ever. I want to spend the rest of my life with you."

Had he accomplished the impossible? Was his curly-haired, sassy, talkative Tess actually speechless? She looked deeply into his eyes, not even glancing at what he had placed on her finger. "You want to spend the rest of your life with me?" she asked incredulously.

"I do."

She leaned in to kiss him like she'd never kissed him before. "Then my answer is *of course!*"

Chapter Thirty-Two

The air in Florida was always humid. The closer it got to summer, the worse it was. Maybe that was why Tullamore decided to move their annual sales conference to the middle of May instead of July.

Of course, the humidity was wreaking havoc on Tess's hair, as it always did. Today, it was so frizzy, it looked like she had put her finger in a light socket. As many times as she threatened to take a razor to her head and shave it all off, she was sternly reminded that was not an option.

When the moderator finished her introduction she calmly stood and walked to the stage, still not believing she was attending the conference this time as their guest keynote speaker. She was to talk about listening—really listening—to the client's needs.

The dessert plates were being cleared away as she walked up the steps. She would make this presentation short. After her presentation, for the first time ever, she was actually looking forward to what she used to refer to it as *The Night of Forced Fun.*

The lights on the stage were bright as she walked to the podium. She was nervous about her role for the night. *Please don't let me embarrass myself. Oh, why did I agree to do this? One slip and this will always be remembered as the night I made a fool of myself.*

She swallowed hard and took a deep breath. Her

heart was pounding. She looked out on the sea of faces.

"Hello," she said to the crowd of several hundred. "For those of you who don't know me, I'm Tess Maristone. For many years, I was with Tullamore in the Atlanta office."

As if it was not hot enough in Florida, they were increasing global warming by turning the spot light on her full blast. "Tullamore taught me more than I could imagine. I want to take this time to tell you what I learned that works and what doesn't work. Take these words of wisdom and do with them what you want. But listen hard to the words. I've seen what happens if these ten rules aren't followed. Sales aren't made. Clients are lost, and numbers aren't met."

She pushed a strand of hair off her forehead. "Number one. Always look your listener in the eye. Your eyes won't betray you and you will gain the trust of the client." She paused and looked into the audience.

She read from her bullet-pointed slides. Every few sentences she'd look to another member of the audience. There was Bruce who had taken Doug's place when he left the company. She made eye contact with her husband Jack, sitting at one of the front tables with the other vice-presidents.

She received a standing ovation at the end of her presentation.

"Thank you...thank you so much," *Oh lordy, am I starting to do my own Elvis imitation?* Briefly, she glanced over to Jack before turning back to the audience—Jack, whom she'd married two weeks earlier in a very small ceremony at which Phil-slash-Elvis had volunteered to sing.

Before she walked off the stage, she continued,

"Before turning tonight's event over to the Master of Ceremonies I had asked if I could kick off the 'really big show.'"

Tess moved to one corner of the stage and looked at a front table where Tom and a few of her other friends were sitting. "What makes each of you perfect for sales is your love of competition and wanting to be noticed. That is one of the reasons we have talent night. You can show everyone what you can do. I used to dread talent night. I mean, my best talent is shopping and spending money. But really, how can I get up on stage to show off that talent?"

She waited until the laughter died down. "But tonight, it's a different story. Tonight I have the pleasure of introducing the first act before the MC takes over. There is a kind of funny backstory to this first performance. As I stated earlier, salespeople love the thrill of competition."

She paused. "Well, at last year's conference our first performer made a bet with me. The loser had to get up on stage and sing a particular song at this year's talent show."

Someone from the audience called out, "What was the bet?"

"Well, I'm not telling you *that*." Tess could feel a big smile spread across her face. "But I can tell you this—it taught me a lot. Like being forty isn't a bad thing."

She was about to tell the audience, particularly the men, that women like a guy who doesn't care if you're wearing a thong or cotton panties, but after seeing Judith sitting in the front row she changed her mind.

"Fortunately, for everyone here tonight—because I

cannot sing two notes in the same key—I did win the bet. So I would like to introduce our first victim, oops, I mean, contestant, Allie McDonald..."

As she walked backwards and to the side of the platform, Tess swept her arm out to the side. She watched Allie strut on to the stage in tight leather pants, singing:

"If you want my body,
And you think I'm sexy..."

A word about the author...

Before moving to Northern Kentucky, Andrea lived in Atlanta, Georgia, for twenty years. While in Atlanta and traveling for her corporate sector career, she became inspired to write women's fiction. There were too many stories told amongst friends and strangers on planes to not put them on paper.

She is married and has two teenage children.

Thank you for purchasing
this publication of The Wild Rose Press, Inc.
If you enjoyed the story, we would appreciate your
letting others know by leaving a review.
For other wonderful stories,
please visit our on-line bookstore at
www.thewildrosepress.com.

For questions or more information
contact us at
info@thewildrosepress.com.

The Wild Rose Press, Inc.
www.thewildrosepress.com

To visit with authors of
The Wild Rose Press, Inc.
join our yahoo loop at
http://groups.yahoo.com/group/thewildrosepress/

Lightning Source UK Ltd.
Milton Keynes UK
UKHW021827030222
398153UK00009B/2190